THE PROPOSAL

He hesitated. "I know this must appear unusual to you—Dr. Schuber has explained that my family is regarded as unlucky, yes? It may not matter to you, but the Drachenfels are not without their honor, and I will do everything I can to ensure you are kept well, in a manner of your choosing. You will marry me?"

It was hardly a romantic proposal, but the fact that there was doubt in his voice, that he had not assumed that I would jump at the chance, at the money, won me over.

Praise For THE COUNT

"Young, fresh, compulsive, original and fun. . . .
A highly enjoyable romp."
—*The Bookseller* (Great Britain)

"A wonderful modern fairy story,
a romance which keeps you guessing."
—*Midweek News* (Great Britain)

THE
COUNT

✠

HELENA DELA

HarperPaperbacks
A Division of HarperCollins Publishers

HarperPaperbacks
A Division of HarperCollinsPublishers
10 East 53rd Street, New York, NY 10022-5299

This is a work of fiction. The characters, incidents, and
dialogues are products of the author's imagination and are not to be
construed as real. Any resemblance to actual events or
persons, living or dead, is entirely coincidental.

ISBN 0-06-109884-1

HarperCollins®, 📕®, and HarperPaperbacks™
are trademarks of HarperCollins *Publishers*, Inc.

Previous editions of this book were published in 1991
and 1999 by Judy Piatkus Ltd.

Cover illustration by Donna Gordon
Cover design by Saksa Art and Design

First paperback printing: March 2000

Printed in the United States of America

Visit HarperPaperbacks on the World Wide Web at
http://www.harpercollins.com

❖ 10 9 8 7 6 5 4 3 2 1

To My Parents

Acknowledgments

Thanks to:

Duine and Monica Campbell, in whose back bedroom at Home Farm I first had the idea. The friends who listened, encouraged and told me to get a move on: Yang May, Angie, Hermione, Sharon, Moo, Martin.

Julia Casterton, for allowing me to write frivolously.

Laura, for all her enthusiasm, kindness and unfailing good temper.

David, for making soothing noises when I tripped over a particularly malevolent troll.

Above all, to Janine and Jonathan, for all the friendship, dinners, films, gossip, practical criticism and the name of the perfect agent.

And of course to Elenore, Kate and all at Piatkus, for both faith and works.

Nun! Sie besammeln sich in weiten Raum
Des alten Rittersaals, er faßt sie kaum.
Auf breite Wande Teppiche spendiert,
Mit Rüstung Eck' und Nischen ausgeziert.
Hier braucht es, dacht ich, keine Zaubermorte;
Die Geister finden sich zum selbst zum Orte.

—Goethe, *Faust*, Part II (1832), Act I

(*Now they gather in the wide space of the old Knights'
Hall; it scarce contains them all. On the broad walls
hang tapestries; every corner, every niche is bedecked
with armor. Here, I think, there is no need for magic
words; the ghosts come of their own accord.*)

PROLOGUE

I DIDN'T KNOW I WAS SUPPOSED TO BE DEAD WITHIN a year of marrying Rudi. Rudi knew, of course; he and Nadine had planned it. But that was all in Paris, and I wasn't even there.

Mathilde told me all about it, and though I may have invented some of the detail, flesh on the bones of Mathilde's story, I know the words they spoke and the order they said them in, because Rudi told me too.

He was a straightforward man, once you broke through the surface. It was a handsome surface, big and blond with a deep patina, and I know this makes him sound like an expensive piece of furniture, but to begin with, that's all he was to me. His face was all straight lines, interrupted only by a pair of turquoise eyes, while age had drawn a couple of horizontal furrows on his brow that only added to his attractiveness; it took a long time for him to relax enough to let his face move into the curve of a smile.

When I first met him, he seemed as glossy and untouchable as the bumper on a brand-new Rolls, as if I might be hustled out on the showroom for even breathing near him; to be honest, I didn't try to come too close back then, but later I grew to see how isolated he'd been, how unused he was to the rough-and-tumble of family life, and therefore what a perfect target he'd made for someone like Nadine.

He would never have said so, of course; weakness wasn't in his line. All he ever said about Nadine was that she was *petite*. Funny how I can't say that word without spitting. I mean, *you* might like little women—you might even *be* one, but I'm not, all right?—and I just don't see the attraction.

Rudi always used to stay at Nadine's six-room apartment in the *XIVìme arrondissement,* rather than book into an hotel, whenever he was in Paris. The room service was more interesting, for a start. That September, though, Nadine was in a bad mood.

"I want to marry you, I want to, I want to," she stormed, wearing a track through the Aubusson as she paced up and down in front of him.

Rudi, languid on the spindly Louis XV sofa, sighed. "I think it would be most unwise, *mein Pudelchen.* We both know what would happen."

His "little poodle" stopped, her red curls quivering. "No, we don't! I only have your word that this stupid family curse exists—you, who never even see your family. You never take me to your castle, I never meet the rest of your family, and all everyone tells me is, "Oh, those von Drachenfels! There's a curse on them, you know." You're using it as an excuse not to marry me. I can't bear it! I don't want to see you any more!" She was off again, across the carpet to the balconied windows.

Rudi sat bolt upright. "*Mein Schatz,* be reasonable." He knew, even as he said the words, what a vain hope that was. "I can't take you to meet my relatives because I don't have any. The curse has seen to that. We von Drachenfels have always done everything properly, and when we have a curse, it works. There isn't a noble family in Europe who would let their daughter marry a von Drachenfels." He sank back onto the eau-de-nil cushions.

"You are joking."

"No, I'm not. It's exactly twenty generations since Anna-Maria, wife of the third Count, died in childbirth, cursing her husband for the affair he was having at the time. No one believed then that her curse would last, although she apparently studied magic, and her uncle was imprisoned for practicing alchemy. She ordered a copper-smith to engrave her dying words, to set the curse into metal, a piece of which survived the sixteenth-century fire and is now set over the fireplace in the main hall."

"How very charming. I expect you tell that to all the tourists. Presumably you keep quiet about all in the inconvenient exceptions, the women who lived to a ripe old age."

"That's a horrible thing—there aren't any. No Drachenfels wife has lived more than two days beyond the birth of her first child, and that child has always been a boy. For twenty generations. It is not a coincidence. *It is not*. How can it be?"

"You're serious, aren't you?"

"Yes, I am. My father, who in all respects was a most rational man, believed in it too. He told me how much he had loved my mother, never once thinking the curse could still work in the twentieth century. He was devas-tated when she died, and warned me, when I reached eighteen, of the full extent of my inheritance. The bank, the castle—and the curse."

"Surely there's some way round this? The power of suggestion can be strong, but an exorcism, perhaps?"

"It's been tried twice—in 1722 and again in 1809. It didn't work. Still they do. Do you want me to run through the names of the women in my family? I know them all, and the years of their death, always coinciding with the birth of the next heir. Twenty deaths, twenty births. I know them all, from Anna-Maria to my own mother."

"Well, it can't be hereditary, if they're all marrying into the family. Hmm. So what are you going to do?"

Rudi sighed. "I don't know. I spent some time in my twenties researching, trying to find some options. I could adopt; a number of German aristocrats without issue have sold their titles, their inheritance, by adopting wealthy middle-aged Americans in search of a title. I hardly need the money, but it would prevent our name from dying out. On the other hand, I don't think they would be getting a very good bargain. And it does against the grain to adopt a person who is my own age or older, and to see the castle go to someone with no link to it. I still feel a sense of duty to my family line."

"Well, in that case, marry me, *mon chérie*. I can't believe it can be as bad as you make out. I don't believe in curses."

"I do." His straight mouth twisted into something approaching despair. "I have a duty to my family line, but it does not extend to killing you."

Nadine turned from the window, her brown eyes suddenly calculating. "Haven't any of the men remarried?"

"I don't know. My father and his housekeeper were very happy together in Cap d'Antibes for many years before he died, but I don't think he ever entirely recovered from the death of my mother."

She clicked her tongue impatiently. *Idiot!* What I mean is, does the curse extend to all wives, or only to *first* wives?"

"Ah, I see where *mein Pudelchen* is going, with that smart little brain. The curse is on the mother of the heir of Schloss Drachenfels."

"So you could marry someone, have an heir, then I could marry you, and simply not have children?"

Here Rudi had to put his foot down. "What you are suggesting is immoral. I have a duty as a von Drachenfels to preserve the family name, *natürlich*—but not this way."

"Duty!" she cried, stamping her size 4 foot, almost breaking the heel off her Charles Jourdan stiletto. "How can you talk of duty, when you have love? Haven't I always given you everything? My time, my love, my self?" The tears were beginning to flow. "How can you talk of duty, with your cold heart? If you really loved me, you would find a way."

Rudi lifted both his hands in a stiff parody of a shrug. "What can I say? If I marry you, I must have a child, and then you will die. Some day, I will have to marry, and then I will face that responsibility, but not yet, not yet."

Nadine turned her bright tear-filled eyes on him. "Why not? Why marry someone now, produce an heir, then marry me, while we are both still young? I cannot grow old, and gray, and unattractive, waiting until you leave me, to marry someone else. I will not face the pity of my friends: "Poor Nadine! She spent so many years with that von Drachenfels, but he never married her." I *will* not. If you do not marry me within the next three years, I must find someone who will. In fact, why don't you go and pack now?"

"Be reasonable, Nadine. You cannot suggest that I marry another woman knowing that she will die?"

"That's exactly what I'm suggesting."

"What if she doesn't die? What if we are incredibly unlucky?"

"Then you can divorce her anyway, and marry me. Would it make much difference?"

"No, no." Rudi was silent, biting his lip as he tried to find fault. "Are you sure it's not the idea of being Countess that you want so much, rather than me?"

Nadine ignored the question because the phone had started to ring, and she snatched up the receiver. "Yes—

What do you mean, exceeded the limit?—No, call it in now.
I want all fucking fifty million on my desk by the morning.—
No, I don't give a bugger about the Slovak economy—We're
talking bottom line here. Do it or I sack the whole fucking lot
of you." The harsh planes of her jaw softened as she turned
back to Rudi. "Where were we, *mon ange*?"

"No one ever gets the better of you, do they, Nadine?"

"Not if they want to reach old age."

"So petite, yet so fierce."

"Yes, that's what the man at the rifle club keeps saying. And when my aikido instructor said I had to learn to
control my aggressive impulses, I sacked him."

He smiled indulgently, and pulled one of her curls
straight. She flicked his hand away.

"When are you going to do it, then?" she said.

"But where would I find a woman to marry?"

"Oh anywhere. There must be lots of poor women
who would adore to be married to a count for a year."

"A year?" Rudi was momentarily shocked.

"By the time she has become pregnant—say two to
three months—and had the baby—nine months—yes,
about a year."

"Always the banker, my dear."

"Yes, well, I don't own my own bank. I have to work
for my promotions."

Rudi ignored the spite behind this remark, still concen-
trating on the flaws in Nadine's plan. "Where would I find
anyone who has not heard of the Curse of the Drachenfels,
or if they had heard the story, would ignore it?"

Bon Dieu—I had never heard of it. I do not spend my life
reading cheap magazines. I leave that to you Germans."

"I don't think we have a monopoly on the sensationalist press." He kept his voice calm. "To return to the matter in hand, I think it would be ethical to inform any
woman I was to marry of the family misfortunes, so that
her decision may be well considered."

"And how long do you think it will take then, to find such a woman? Don't be a fool! She'll think you have mental problems, with all this curse business."

"Mental problems? I think you're right, I had better go and pack." He rose abruptly, and strode toward the bedroom.

Nadine was after him in an instant, arms around his waist, clinging. "Oh Rudi, Rudi my darling, I didn't mean it. Please stay. I love you so much, don't leave me."

He continued into the bedroom, then disentangled her, like seaweed from a rock. "I have to pack anyway. I am going to London tomorrow."

"London?" Nadine started to pout, then her face brightened. "You could find a girl to marry in London. They like titles in Britain, and are too calm, too phlegmatic, to worry about ancient scorceries."

"Even if they read sensationalist newspapers?" he inquired, a little sneer forming the edges of his mouth.

Nadine waved the thought away like a fly. "Find someone, I want you to find someone."

"Now?" he said, pulling her onto the bed with him. "This very minute? You're very single-minded, my dear."

"Perhaps tomorrow," she conceded. "You could find someone to marry tomorrow."

✠

1

London is where I come in. I was living in London, but only just. Only just living, rather than only just in London. I was in a near-squat in Islington; the one thing that stopped it from being an actual squat was that the owner was still living in it. The house was semi-derelict and subsiding, and Mrs. Watkins with it, but she continued to let out a series of collapsing rooms on the first and second floors to the poor and desperate. She never stirred from the ground floor, her weight and arthritis allowing her only the most limited range of movement; I think the house moved more than Mrs. Watkins did.

I wasn't living there because I found squalor picturesque, or took delight in eccentric characters, or because it was convenient for anything. It was a bleak, windswept fifteen-minute walk to the nearest tube or bus-stop, when I could afford to take public transport. Mostly I walked, in particular to the British Library and back, where my ill-paid job in book restoration was the only thing that kept me this side of the borders of insanity.

Perhaps the side I was on then, wasn't the same side. I look back now and wonder. The truth was that since Mark had died, I had been on my knees, mentally, physically, and above all, financially. I had been married to Mark for five years, four of them happy; the last, terrifying year as cancer took him deeper and deeper under, not at all so. In that last year, his furniture business slid away from under us; I was too concerned about Mark to fuss over rates and orders and repayments and things. The moment he died, the vultures swooped, forcing me to sell the flat and the car, every nice piece of furniture I had ever owned ... and eventually I ended up at Mrs. Watkins'.

It's not easy to look back on a happy marriage after it's been taken away from you. I can't even remember why we were so happy. We were living in a flat over a pair of garages in Wandsworth, and Mark had made his workshop in the garages; he took the back wall out and replaced it with glass bricks, so the whole space was light and airy, and during the day he would carve and sand and varnish. I used to hate it when he varnished, because the smell would filter up into our flat, but I loved it when he had a new consignment of wood in, and he would come upstairs smelling like a newly sharpened pencils, with sawdust on his shoes.

I used to take the train in to Waterloo during the week, and would come back each evening and shout, "Honey, I'm home!" as I came up the stairs. He would appear at the top of them and say, "Had a nice day at the office, dear?" and we would always laugh, then tell each other how our day had been. Sometimes, after dinner, he would go back down to the workshop, but he was always there when I came home, ready to join me in a drink and to make encouraging noises while I cooked. He did cook, occasionally, but he only knew how to make two things, lasagna and spaghetti bolognaise. Sometimes I was grate-

ful for his cooking, at other times I grew bored with
mince, and would rather do my own thing, or something
out of Delia.

We didn't eat out much, because all our spare cash
went into Mark's business, though I never minded
because we were building for our future, and none of our
friends were much better off. We knew a lot of people
locally; many of them had commissioned furniture from
Mark, so there was a steady flow of invitations to dinner,
to drinks, to garden parties in the summer; some of those
houses have massive gardens. We enjoyed them all. We
were young and in love and always laughing. I don't know
what we laughed about, trivial things that lose all their
shine later, like wet pebbles on the beach, so dull when
you take them out of your pocket at home.

Mark wasn't dull, though. He shone, with hair the
color of hazelnuts and eyes that sparked with mischief.
He seemed very calm, for the wood-carving demanded a
steady hand, but underneath his impassive air, little
brooks of high-spiritedness ran, and when he wasn't
working, or thinking about work, you could always see
trouble brewing, if you watched him closely enough.

I used to watch him all the time, when I didn't think
he'd notice, when he was watching television, or sitting
reading, curled up on the big stripey sofa we used to live
on in the evenings. I noticed the point when the mischief
started to dim, and his brown eyes became blank, and the
indigestion he'd had for so long started to come more fre-
quently, and I remember, clear as yesterday, the first night
he didn't want to eat at all, when I insisted he see a doctor
the next day. Pancreatitis, the doctor said, and sent him
off to St. George's for tests. It was too late by then.

Mark had been dead for over eighteen months, but I
still wanted to die. Without him, there wasn't any point to
anything. If I couldn't have my old life, my life with Mark,
I didn't want a life at all. People at work would ask me,

"How are you?" and I always replied "I want to die." I gave up seeing our old friends, or perhaps they gave up seeing me. I had to move away from our old neighborhood, and I no longer felt like going back.

I thought about suicide all the time, but it seemed too much effort, swallowing all those pills or jumping off things. If I'd lived out in the country I would have found a quiet stretch of railway track, and lain on it, fallen asleep, so that I would never have known when my last moment came. In London, the minimum tube fare had gone up so much that even to get near the line cost a fortune. Suicide seemed an extravagance I couldn't afford. People never leave you alone, either; I knew that if I'd tried to lie down on the line, any number of commuters would have pulled me off again, so that I didn't delay their train.

There must have been murderers out there who wanted to kill, with no way of finding those who wanted to be dead. If there had been some way of contacting them, a date-with-death line, I would have called them to set up a meeting. The current ways of death seemed too haphazard; it was all left up to chance. Had Chance come up, tapped me on the shoulder, said "Oi, you—long black tunnel, white light, off you go," I wouldn't have complained.

It was like having frostbite all over—feeling numb and in pain at the same time. Only while I worked could I forget, sometimes. The concentration focused into the end of a scalpel as I pared thin shavings of leather from the underside of the corners, to achieve a smooth fit when the leather was folded round the boards. The linen thread, to sew bundles of paper into neatly folded sections, to stitch on the striped headbands at the top of the spine. The delicate, millimeter-by-millimeter lifting of old endpapers from crumbling boards, the leather turned to amber dust. The sharp smell of chemicals used to treat fungus, the silky feel of acid-free tissue paper to protect the plates from foxing. The careful inspection of new acquisitions, the list of recommendations: wormholes filled, repair tape on the rip on page 52, leather dressed. Only here, in these minutiae, could I find any sense of order and reason. I had done this before I met Mark, and while I lived with Mark, and now without Mark.

Dr. Schuber, my boss, kept an eye out for me, and I think worried sometimes, in his own withdrawn sort of way. On days when I came in soaking wet, he would fetch me cups of tea, and insist that I sit on the one radiator in the department (too much heat dries the books) until I was drier. "Soggy staff make soggy books," he would mutter, but we all liked to think he genuinely carried about us, as well as the books.

He had gray hair and bushy gray eyebrows that kept trying to grow up into his hair, but his hair kept running away. Nev in Pamphlets had drawn several cartoons of the receding hairline, but I always chucked them in the bin. I liked Dr. Schuber far too much ever to laugh at him. It would have been an exaggeration to say we were friends, but I liked to think we could have been if we'd tried.

One day in late September, Dr. Schuber wanted to see me as soon as I arrived at work.

"I would like to have lunch with you. There is something I must discuss. Shall we say twelve-thirty?"

This was most unlike Dr. Schuber, who never went out to lunch, but I agreed. That morning, I did not need the slow scratch of the scalpel to distract me from my thoughts, for my thoughts were on something new, something not-Mark. The hours to lunchtime ran away, and I was startled when Dr. Schuber cleared his throat behind me, and said, "Are you ready?"

We went around the corner, to a café in Museum street, to have fried everything and chips.

The Good Doctor looked decidedly shifty, and I was well into my third forkful of oily blackened mushrooms before he tried to begin.

"I wanted to tell you . . . No, Graf von Drachenfels asked me to . . . I would not say this if . . ." He was becoming so entangled I felt obliged to cut across him.

"Who is this Graf? Am I supposed to have heard of him?"

This decided him. "I think I should start with work. There is a big problem."

"You're not happy with my work," I said dully, putting my fork down. This was not what I was expecting.

"No, no, it is far worse than that." He caught himself. "I mean, I am happy with your work, but—you must promise not to discuss this with anyone else at the Library?"

I promised.

"You know we have been delayed in moving to the new building at Euston? And that the cost has overrun exceedingly? In light of this, the Conservation Department in its current form will not exist. A new department will be formed in Cardiff, and all books for restoration will be driven to Wales to be worked upon."

"What are you going to do?"

"I will be taking early retirement," he sighed. "A new man in Cardiff has already been appointed Head—I was told last week. The general announcement will be made in two months' time, and you all will be invited to apply for the posts in Cardiff."

I knew what this meant. Fewer jobs, at even lower salaries. "Why are you telling me this?" I demanded miserably. "So I can cut my wrists now? You know I'll never find another job, not if the rest of the department are out on the streets as well."

Dr. Schuber looked even more unhappy. "No, no. It is because I think that more than any of the department you will find work, you are ten years younger than anyone else, but you have less support than the rest of us, and I wanted to prepare you for the blow. Is that wrong?"

I started to pull at the edge of the formica table. "No—thanks Dr. Schuber. I just ask myself, what's the point? What's the point of going on? I really don't see how my life could get any worse. I mean, are other people's lives this bad? Why do some people manage to have money and partners and everything runs smoothly?"

Dr. Schuber gave me a half-smile. "Yes, I've just had the same conversation with a very wealthy young man who can't find anyone to marry, and swears his life will be over if he doesn't. Rudi came to me two days ago, with the most preposterous request. He wants to get married, purely as a business arrangement, in order to produce a son and heir. All he wants is someone calm and unexcitable, who would be prepared to have a child, and in return, he would undertake to keep his wife in comfort, and not to interfere. I told him I knew of no one who would do such a thing, that anything I knew no young women except you."

"So what's wrong with him, then? Hideously ugly, nasty temperament, unsightly skin disease?"

"I don't think so. He seemed normal enough on Sunday. You should know that the von Drachenfels have an unfortunate reputation for, shall we say, *losing* their women. Rudi's father was much affected by the death of Rudi's mother, only days after he was born. His grandfather the same. I am a rationalist, I do not believe in curses, but the family has not been lucky.

"They say this of many rich families, to deflect envy, but in the case of the Drachenfels, there appears to be an element of truth in the legend. There are never any Drachenfels daughters, only sons, and the mother always seems to die during or soon after childbirth. I know this was common in medieval times, but it seems to have continued into this century. The Drachenfels heirs have always been only children, and this perhaps has affected Rudi's mind. He thinks that if he explains the situation and pays well, some young woman will marry him. I can't imagine why he thinks anyone rational would do this."

I trifled with a lace like piece of egg. "Is he very rich then?"

"You are not taking me seriously? You are too intelligent to be affected by wealth. Yes, the Bankhaus D G Dornreich, which the family owns, is extremely rich. It is a big *Privatbank*. His father used to buy books the Library could not afford."

"What you're telling me, if I've got this straight, is: (a) I won't have this job for much longer, and (b) this unknown Count would pay me well for marrying him. It all seems very simple."

"No, no, it is not," Dr. Schuber hissed. "Do you not hear? It is a mad idea, and for some reason his family have no luck with women. It is not clear why they die in childbirth—perhaps contaminated drinking water at the family castle"—

"Anthrax in the christening robes?" I interrupted.

"I do not know—I have always thought there must be a rational explanation," he fussed. "Still I would not do this. Your long-term survival might be in question."

"At the moment, my short-term survival is in question. This marriage thing is a sort of *Mission: Impossible*, then? Less than a fifty-fifty chance of making it?"

"Precisely." Dr. Schuber closed his eyes, I think with relief. "At last you understand me."

I went back to picking at my fried bread, now cold. "What makes you think that matters to me? Mark's dead, my mother's dead, my sister's in Newcastle, I live in a horrible dump and I'm about to lose my job. Tell me more about von Drachenfels."

He shook his head, then told me anyway. "Von und zu Drachenfels," he said, irony tightening his voice. "The 'zu' means the family is not only *from* Drachenfels, but still *is* there. A nineteenth-century affectation, but so few families still have their original land. Schloss Drachenfels, in the mountains south of Munich, on the Austrian border, has been in the family for over five hundred years, though I do not think it is lived in now."

"And how old is the Count?"

"He must be—well, perhaps close to forty now. His father died some fifteen years ago, and I have had no contact with the family since then."

"Wouldn't they mind if he married a commoner?" I was genuinely curious, though I had not, at that point, made up my mind to marry him.

"The von Drachenfels cannot afford to mind, or they would never marry. I believe his grandmother worked in a glove shop."

We both stared at our congealed plates for a while, before deciding to skip the bile-black coffee, and return to the Library. As we hovered optimistically, on the edge of the zebra crossing in front of the British Museum gates, taxis almost skimming our noses, I said to Dr. Schuber: "I might do it, you know. Will you tell him?"

Dr. Schuber almost fell into the gap in the traffic given to us by a friendly van-driver. I nodded to the man in thanks, and hurried across, holding Dr. Schuber's sleeve. Once through the gates, he stopped, and stared at me for a long moment.

"I do not wish to make you unhappy."

"I *am* unhappy," I said. "It won't make me any worse."

✠

Dr. Schuber invited me around for dinner the next day. This was not as unusual as it seemed, for he had a kind heart, and though his sociability was buried deep, it was there nonetheless; many of his staff had visited him at home, and it had always been a pleasure, not a duty, to go. When I turned up at his narrow sooty-bricked house in

Clerkenwell, I heard voices as I paused on his front doorstep, hand poised over the doorbell. Dr. Schuber's house had no hallway; the rooms were so narrow that the hall had been removed to widen the front room, with the result that the street door opened directly into the sitting room. I had no real intention of eavesdropping, but words seemed to float out through the letterbox. They spoke in German, I could tell that much, but the German I had done at school was too rusty for me to make out more than the occasional phrase. "After the move to Cardiff . . . She [or maybe they] will find it very difficult . . . not very happy with the idea," all in Dr. Schuber's voice. The other voice was light and persuasive, but I could make no sense of the words, so I relinquished my invisible hovering on the outskirts of the conversation and rang the tinny-sounding bell.

Dr. Schuber greeted me almost anxiously, I felt, but I soon realized why he was nervous when he introduced me to his other guest. "May I present Rudiger, Graf von Drachenfels?"

I took the warm outstretched hand carefully, but he was too polite to recoil from my ice-fingered grasp—I hated shaking hands in winter, because my hands never held any heat.

"Good evening," I said. "I'm afraid my knowledge of German etiquette is somewhat limited. Is there a German equivalent of 'my lord' or 'Your Grace,' or do I call you Graf von Drachenfels?"

He gave me a grave smile. "I very much hope you will call me Rudi. Manfred" (he gestured toward Dr. Schuber) "was a friend of my father's, and knew me as a small boy, long before I inherited the title. Please, call me Rudi."

I returned his smile, I hope graciously, but I was momentarily stunned, mostly by the fact that Dr. Schuber had a first name. I had worked for him for nine years, with no inkling of the "Manfred" behind his gray-haired formality. In part, though, I was surprised by the unexpected guest—his height, good looks, the expensive glow to his skin that told of frequent holidays and all the right vitamins. His golden hair, feathered like a duck's bottom, had a sheen that reflected the warm lamplight, intensified by the contrast with his matt dark blue suit and white shirt.

Being a blonde myself, albeit of a muddy, verging on the mouse sort, I don't normally go in for fair men, but I was prepared to make an exception in Rudi's case; that is, if I'd been prepared to do anything at all, other than stand there like a poker, until Der Schuber more or less had to drag me to the sofa and sit me down with a drink.

I don't now remember a great deal about that evening, but I do remember that I almost enjoyed myself. Since Mark's death, of course, all enjoyment was completely impossible, but that evening the grief released its hold for a while. Rudi had an effortless charm, not necessarily a quality you might associate with a German accent, but it was there, and he used it to its full extent. His height, too, meant I could unfold, and sprawl across the sofa, knowing he was too tall to be unnerved by my full five foot nine. The wine flowed freely, Rudi told amusing stories about his father, for whom Dr. Schuber had acquired books at London auctions ("Never in conflict with the Library's requirements, you understand"), and I just sat and listened, at ease in front of the warm imitation-log gas fire. We ate supper on our laps while watching some television program on economics, which we talked across, another concession to informality. It was a side of Dr. Schuber I had never seen, but his apparent ease and comfort with this stranger affected me, and I felt that I was in the company of relatives, distant enough for us not to fight, but close enough that we needed to make no efforts to impress.

We talked about all kinds of things, but what interested me most were Dr. Schuber's reminiscences of Rudi's

father, Alexander, with whom he had enjoyed a lengthy
friendship. Mostly Dr. Schuber remembered the auction
houses across Europe where they had met, the other col-
lectors they had rivaled, and the books that got away. He
realized, though, that neither Rudi nor I were sufficiently
well-versed in the lore of book-collecting to appreciate
some of his triumphs, so he turned instead to a battered
mahogany tallboy crammed into one corner of the room.

"Here's something that might interest you," he said,
pulling out a small framed picture, a woodcut or engraving. He walked over to Rudi, placing it carefully in his lap.

Rudi looked down, smiling, then his expression
faded. "Where did this come from?" he asked.

Dr. Schuber, settling himself back into his faded red
armchair, said, "Your father sent me the woodcut in the
early fifties. He took it to Cap de'Antibes with him, but
said it brought back bad memories. I myself have an interest in fifteenth- and sixteenth-century woodcuts, and
think it is a particularly fine example, though colored in
by a later hand."

Rudi said nothing, but stared unsettlingly into the distance.

"Of course, if it is a family heirloom—if you think it is
yours by right," our host said hastily, "perhaps your father
should not have . . . By all means, take it if you wish."

"No, no," said Rudi, recovering. "I never wish to see
this again. I don't want it. I—" He broke off again, and
stared at his lap, then looked away hurriedly, as if he had
found maggots in his dinner.

He leaned over. "May I?" I said, taking one edge of the
picture frame.

"Please," He almost threw the object into my hands. It
was a heavy black-lined engraving of a square-set castle
on a mountainside. I remember it still: at one side, a deep
chasm opens up, into which a young woman is falling,
headfirst, her white horse following. The woman has been

colored red, fading to orange in places, and despite her headlong fall, her skirts remain billowing about her ankles. On the edge of the abyss, a young man teeters, his brown horse about to lose its footing. His hat—a black tricorn—has fallen from his head, and is sailing into nothingness. He seems about to follow it.

My eye kept being drawn back to the woman in red, her hair wrapped in a red scarf. She seemed so bright; the rest of the scene was in such somber colors that the one vivid hue was out of place. Behind, the castle lurked. Was it my imagination, or did a small face look out from one of the towers?

I had no time to look more closely, for Dr. Schuber said, "That, as you can see, Ella, is Schloss von Drachenfels, the family castle. Alex was going to tell me more about the picture one day, and how the young gypsy girl met her end, but he never did. Rudi, do you know—?"

"No," he said abruptly. "My father and I never discussed it."

"Some coffee, perhaps?" said Dr. Schuber, changing the subject smoothly. He took the framed woodcut from me, replaced it in its drawer, and went out into the kitchen.

An uneasy pall seemed to hang over the room, Rudi's eyes darting anxiously to the tallboy and back. I started to murmur inane comments about instant coffee, and how unlike any other form of coffee it was, until Rudi brought his attention back to me, and away from the woodcut that had upset him.

At the end of the evening, Rudi insisted that he take me home.

"But it's not on your way," I protested, not wanting him to see the full squalor of Mrs. Watkins' establishment.

He ignored my protest in a gentlemanly way. "In a fast car, anywhere is on my way. Your coat?"

I gave up arguing. Of course I would rather be driven home in a heated car than have a long walk back, past every derelict and drop-out not yet drunk enough to be unconscious. I let him lead me out onto the pavement, where he handed me into a large black BMW, more like a hearse than an ordinary car.

I refused to direct him further than the end of my street, but as I put my left hand on the door to get it, he took my right hand and raised it to his lips. After kissing my hand, he laid it gently back across my lap and said, "I have very much enjoyed this evening. I hope we may meet again."

Surprised, I could only murmur, "Yes, that would be lovely," knowing how insincere the phrase was, yet wanting to sound convinced and positive. Embarrassed, I scrambled from the car, a flurry of arms and legs. Not what the Lucy Clayton School of Modeling would teach.

He smiled, and said good night as I bent to shut the car door, then drove off, black into black.

The next afternoon, Dr. Schuber came out of his office and said, "My dear, I have von Drachenfels on the phone. He would like to speak to you."

I stropped trying to force a rusty-screwed book-press shut, and went with him.

"Ella," came the warm voice from the receiver. It was a shock to hear my name. "I understand Manfred has outlined my proposal to you. Would you care to meet me at my hotel this evening?" I said yes. "Brown's Hotel, at shall we say six? I look forward to discussing the—ah—arrangements."

I decided on the extravagance of a tube ticket when I left work at five-thirty, so pushed my way through the scurrying crowds around to Russell Square in the December dark. I wanted to be in good time to discuss the—ah—arrangements.

2

When I arrived at Rudi's hotel, I was directed toward the bar, where he was already waiting, a heavy tumbler in hand as he rose from the brown leather armchair. A white-jacketed waiter materialized immediately, and I hesitated over ordering a gin, because I knew it made me moody, before choosing the social camouflage option. "Oh, I'll have what you're having. Whiskey, is it? Yes, with water, please. Bit chilly out, isn't it?"

I sat down quickly, before Rudi could note too carefully what I was wearing. I suddenly felt very old and shabby in my battered black skirt, shapeless black sweater, my thick black tights and flat shoes, so worn and flattened by walking everywhere to save money that they looked more like slippers. There is no easy way of tucking your feet under the chair you're sitting in, but nevertheless I tried, grateful for the dim lighting of the bar. Perhaps he wouldn't notice that I had tied my hair back with a rubber band I'd found in my desk. Or maybe he would think it charmingly eccentric.

I stopped caring quite so much when I realized his attention was entirely focused on his cuff links. They didn't seem to be doing their job properly, because he kept checking them, pinching at the end of his shirt cuffs, as if the silver links were about to fly apart, and the only way of keeping his cuffs closed was to hold them shut manually, one wrist clasped over the other. Even after my drink and a large bowl of cashnew nuts arrived, it took a long moment before he lost interest in his shirt and was able to look at me.

"Ah—I understand that Dr. Schuber has informed you of my wish to be married."

"Ye-es," I said encouragingly.

"And also that I wish to have a son, to inherit my title?"

"Mm-hmm."

"Can I take it that your presence here indicates that you would consider such a proposal?"

I nodded. I could see that he wasn't finding this easy. Nor was I.

"In return, I would make a suitable financial settlement upon you, in order that you might live in a befitting manner. I should prefer it if, initially, you accompanied me to Munch, where I have a house, so that I might take you to Schloss Drachenfels. The castle is in need of some restoration works, but it could make a good home. Later, you may live where you choose, but at first there would be much talk if we did not live close together."

"Oh, we couldn't have that, could we?" I murmured.

He hesitated. "I know this must appear unusual to you—Dr. Schuber has explained that my family is regarded as unlucky, yes? It may not matter to you, but the Drachenfels are not without their honor, and I will do everything I can to insure that you are kept well, in a manner of your choosing. You will marry me?"

It was hardly a romantic proposal, but the fact that

there was doubt in his voice, that he had not assumed that I would jump at the chance, at the money, won me over. Had he been self-assured and pompous, I might still have backed out, but his hesitancy convinced me that he by no means took me for granted.

"Yes, I will. Had you a date in mind?"

"Soon," he said hurriedly. "I would like to be married soon. In January, perhaps. You have family you wish to invite?"

"My sister, if she can get away. My father and his new wife—they may want to come. Otherwise, not really. I'd like a small low-key wedding, if that's possible."

"I too, would prefer it. I will ask the German Embassy for the correct procedure."

"I think it's quite simple if you want a registry office wedding. You just have to fill in some forms a couple of weeks beforehand."

He smiled at me, properly. "You are very practical, I see. Do not worry, I will make all the arrangements, if you will suggest a date that is convenient to you."

I didn't have a diary to flick through, so I rummaged through my head for a moment before saying, "Any time in January would be fine."

"Very good. I will arrange for the family ring to be adjusted for you." He took my left hand and turned it over, his face changing when he saw I still wore my wedding and engagement ring from Mark. "I remember now. You have been married. Would you wish to wear the Drachenfels engagement ring?"

I shrugged. I really had no idea. It would make no difference to Mark what I wore. "Yes, if you like."

He patted my hand and gave it back. "I will arrange it. Now, we must have an engagement dinner, and then I can send an announcement to the newspapers."

"I don't w-want to."

His face went gray. "I thought—"

"I can't go out to dinner—I don't have any smart clothes. It would just be embarrassing. Can't we just be engaged anyway?" I hated saying it, but felt better once I'd admitted that I wasn't dressed this way out of eccentricity, just poverty. Is it better to be poor or mad? I could admit to both, but decided to stick with poverty. "I haven't got much money recently."

He was so relieved he managed to kick his glass off the edge of the coffee table. Fortunately it bounced. "My dear, do not concern yourself with this. It can be arranged. It is Thursday today. If we have the dinner on Saturday evening, I will ensure that you are suitably dressed for it."

I was dubious. "You're going to take me shopping?"

"No, I will pay someone else to take you shopping." He laughed at my doubting expression. "Waiter, a bottle of champagne, please." He turned back to me. "Let us drink to our engagement, and then on Saturday we will discuss any final matters arising. I will call you tomorrow about buying dresses, if you have some time on Saturday to shop?"

I'd forgotten what shopping was, but I was in no hurry to relearn, and before I spent his money, there was one Big Issue to discuss—and I don't mean homeless people. "This son and heir thing. What if it takes a long time to . . . er? I'm nearly thirty, you know."

His cuff links had been reafflicted with their old trouble. "I had considered this. I will not insult you by insisting on a fertility test, but I should warn you that if you prove to be infertile, I may divorce you. You will not find me ungenerous. If the—bed aspects are disagreeable to you, there is the option of artificial insemination. But I would be pleased to try the more usual methods."

"Might as well give it a whirl," I said brightly. I did not recognize the woman who was speaking: it was not me, it was a sophisticated two-thousand-year-old woman who had seen it all. Far down in my frozen depths, something squeaked. A protest? Whatever it was, I was going to drown it in champagne.

We clinked glasses, neither of us quite daring to look the other in the eye. "To our engagement—and to Saturday."

✠

At ten o'clock on Saturday morning, I presented myself, as Rudi had phoned to instruct me, at one of the side entrances to Harrods, where Elisabeth, my "personal shopper," met me. Her gushing welcome was explained by her first words.

"Graf von Drachenfels sent £10,000 around by courier yesterday, and has asked you to charge anything in excess of that to his account. He has sent us a list of your requirements, and I've planned the day accordingly. Shall we start with Evening Wear?"

Shall we? Why not? I followed Elisabeth around Harrods like a newly hatched duckling, as she guided me through Evening Wear, Shoes, Lingerie, back downstairs to Make-up & Perfume, then off again to Designer Day Wear. I was flagging by this point, and protested, "I thought I was just here to buy an evening dress!"

"Oh no," she overrode me charmingly. "Graf von Drachenfels has asked us to replenish your wardrobe entirely. We can stop for lunch soon, though, and you can put your feet up in the beauty salon this afternoon."

At one o'clock, Elisabeth gathered up an armful of foreign *Vogues* from the book department, and parked me in a relatively quiet corner of the restaurant. I was immobile with fatigue, and would have eaten half a doormat, if served on a wide enough plate. I was lost in the bizarre shallows of an Italian *Vogue* when the relentless Elisabeth returned.

"Your clothes have all been sent to your room at Claridges. Now for your hair and nails!"

I nearly explained that I didn't have a room at Claridges, but then I thought that Rudi had probably had a busy time "arranging" things, so maybe I did have a room there. I kept quiet. I was beginning to hate Elisabeth. She was too nice, too well-groomed. I was tired and grouchy, and wanted to curl up with a good book somewhere quiet.

The giant hair salon was the last place on earth I expected to relax, but by the time I had had my head massaged, my hair snipped to a neat shoulder-length bob and my nails given a French manicure, I was feeling almost benevolent again. One facial and pedicure later, I could take on the world. Or even maybe a tube journey.

There was no need. A limousine (I think that's what it was—it was long and navy-blue and shiny, and the driver wore a peaked cap) took me to Claridges, where a room was apparently waiting for me. It was. And in the middle of the large double bed lay a note from Rudi.

My dear, it ran, *as we are dining here tonight, I have taken the liberty of booking you a room to rest in and change before dinner. I trust you have found something to wear. I will call for you at seven-thirty. Von Drachenfels.*

His surname sounded so formal. Was I being forward, thinking of him by his first name? But how considerate he was. I wondered if the hotel staff thought I was his mistress. I felt like a mistress—spoiled, a pampered lapdog. I began to disapprove of myself and the enjoyment I was deriving from all this conspicuous consumption. It's only money, I told myself, as I ran a deep hot bath, in which I gently steamed for almost an hour, flicking on the hot tap from time to time with a pink-nailed foot.

Then I rustled through all the carrier bags and tissue paper until I found my pale silver-blue Ben de Lisi silk evening dress, with its matching silver shoes and bag. Suddenly I was six foot tall and silver-blonde; the dress reflected from my hair in the strangest way, and the high-heeled shoes made me pull my back straight for balance. I had chosen the simplest dress I could find—I'm too big for frills—yet at once I looked both sophisticated and younger. Amazing what you can do with a bit of money, I thought cynically.

Rudi, however, expressed no such cynicism when he arrived, punctually, at seven-thirty. "My dear Ella, you look charming."

I simpered at him, then caught myself. "You are too kind," I said as soberly as I could. I was playing a part in some custom drama; I was no longer the real me, who would have turned and fled before the front entrance of Claridges.

The sense of unreality grew when I caught sight of myself as we passed a mirror. Rudi, with his golden hair and skin, and the dinner jacket, seemed gold and black blur, an expensive fountain pen moving fast across a page, and I was just a silver column, blue-white arms and dress and silvered hair. I was no longer me, only a color, an impression of a color.

We were shown into a discreet and candle lit corner of the restaurant, where Rudi ordered champagne—again? This was becoming boring. Half of me watched, unbelieving, while the other half of me made polite conversation, hesitated over the menu, thanked Rudi for the clothes. Somehow he sensed this, but held his tongue until the pudding arrived, when he said, "This must appear very artificial to you. I want you to look on this as a form of ritual only, almost a religious ritual. A solemn performance of a part."

He hadn't had that much to drink. I looked straight into his eyes, probably for the first time that evening. "Is this what this is to you?"

"Yes, in a way." His gaze was steady. "I am not in the habit of marrying people I have only met twice. Three times, including tonight."

His tone was gentle, but I felt tears brimming. "Neither am I. It's just that . . ." I started to feel for my bag, hoping I had remembered a handkerchief.

"I know, I know. We each offer the other an escape. I hope it is a fair exchange," he said gently, handing me both his handkerchief and a small green velvet box. I paid more attention to his hanky, initially, until I realized he was watching me. I opened the box, in which lay a large emerald and diamond ring, gleaming sullenly with reflected light.

"I had it flown over from Munich yesterday," he said, "but I have not had time to have it altered. It was my mother's, and my grandmother's."

It fitted perfectly. I showed him.

"I shall take it as a favorable omen. Shall we drink to our future happ—— to the success of our marriage?"

"To the success of our marriage!" I raised my glass. I could see that "our future happiness" would be over-optimistic. Yet for the first time since Mark died, I felt a vague shimmer of hope.

3

"You're shagging this bloke for the money, right?"
My sister Jenny was in full, and bluntest, form.

"I haven't slept with him yet—we're waiting until we get married." I couldn't believe how prim I sounded.

Jenny snorted. Maybe it had been a mistake to spend Christmas in Newcastle with her. I'd ducked spending last Christmas with anyone, so soon after Mark's death, my first Christmas without him, and I'd intended to do the same this year, but Jenny had been so insistent that I come and stay with her and Kevin, and the kids. My two little nephews had been pleased to see me, especially as I had a lot of parcels with their name on them. Rudi had gone back to Munich, leaving me a large check and a gold credit card, telling me to charge whatever I needed to his account, so I decided he could stand the odd purchase or two from Hamley's. I liked Kevin, as well; he was the nicest dentist I knew. Jenny, who still worked as a nurse, had met him in Casualty: a nervous patient had bitten his hand through to the bone, and he had needed four stitches. Despite this unromantic start, the two of them went on to be very happy together, for almost as long as Mark and I had been together. Everything about their marriage reminded me of how my own world had collapsed. Jenny was my younger sister; it wasn't fair that she should be so happy. I should never have come.

"Do you think he's gay, and he just wants you as a window-dressing?" Jenny persisted.

"No, I don't think so. Oh, maybe. No."

"Well, I should have an AIDS test before you marry him, and if you find you've got AIDS afterwards, you can sue him to buggery. So to speak."

I said nothing. I was too busy thinking back over my few meetings with Rudi, to see if anything I could remember gave any clues as to his preferences. He had appreciated that I needed a new dress: was that being gay, or just being sensitive? He'd been very well dressed, but perhaps that was because he was rich. I knew what Jenny meant. There had to be more to this whole story, more than Rudi or Dr. Schuber had told me. Or was I not listening properly when they told me? I had lost confidence in my ability to think rationally, to remember clearly, and Jenny obviously had very little confidence in me either.

"You know, I feel bad about not spending more time with you after Mark. It must have been very hard on you. You were very calm at the funeral. Far too calm."

"Far too calm for what? Too calm to throw myself onto the conveyor belt into the crematorium furnace with him?" I retorted, angry now. "What are you trying to say?"

Jenny made a heroic attempt at tact. "It's just that— well, sometimes, when people are grieving—they do things that they might not do otherwise."

"Such as marrying wealthy German Counts? So I'm unhinged. Let me be unhinged, OK?"

I refused to listen to any more of Jenny's doubts. She wasn't in my position, and I was older than her, and could do what the hell I liked. I'd deliberately kept quiet about the having-his-baby aspect, but I could hear her, through the paper-thin walls of their modern estate house, whispering to Kevin in the night, "Do you think she'll have children?"

Kevin, bless his little rubber gloves, was completely uninterested, and I just wishes Jens would shut up and leave me be. The trouble with Christmas is that you're trapped for days and days: the trains stop running and you have to stay where you are. I had to grit my teeth while Jens rambled on about happier days, and how I would be happy again one day. No, I wouldn't. Not ever.

✠

My father was far more positive about my remarriage, and when I phoned him, said of course he would come to London for the register office ceremony. My stepmother, who was very well-meaning, made all the appropriate noises, but I don't think it ever struck either of them as odd. As long as I didn't want to come and live with them, it didn't seem to matter what I did. The date had been set—January 17—and a table booked for tea at the Ritz afterward. Jenny arranged to leave the kids with Kevin's mother for the day, so we were all set for a game of Happy Families.

Reader, I married him. It was over in five minutes, and some simple black cabs took us to the Ritz. Amid the fronds of the Palm Court, against the clink of bone china teacups and the snap of patent-leather handbag clasps, a string quartet played, and all I could think was—*They must be female impersonators. The one with the cello looks just like Alistair Sim.* Rudi had heaped sandwiches on my plate, but I took no notice of anything except the strange musicians, until Jenny nudged me.

"Where's the loo? I want to fix my mascara. You can lend me yours. Come with me," she said, jerking my chair away.

I had to go with her. Once safely inside the mirrored mansion of the ladies' conveniences, she burst out: "God, he's gorgeous. You didn't tell me he was good-looking. And he's not gay either, he definitely tried to look at my tits. Good childbearing tits, these," she said, patting her exposed cleavage.

I absolutely did not need to hear any of this. "Yes, thank you, Jennifer. You'll catch your death, dressed like that. Would you like to borrow my mascara?"

"No thanks, I've got my own. Now look, why didn't he bring any of his family? Why did he just bring his friend from the bank?"

"He hasn't got any family, apparently, apart from an antique aunt in Wiesbaden. Or so he tells me."

"Well, it looks fishy, but *he* certainly looks all right. You can tell he's got a hairy chest, through that fine cotton shirt. I like men with hairy chests."

A dowager in purple tweed came out of the loo and goggled at us.

"Look, Jen, if you're cross with me because I didn't have a girls' night out before the wedding, I'm sorry, but here is not the place to have a hen party. Come out to Germany and stay with me, once I've settled in."

"Sure. Are you all right? You look a bit white."

"Yes, I'm fine. Absolutely fine. Can we go back now?"

Our wedding night was spent on the plane, an overnight flight to the Seychelles, sacked out in first-class seats, which still don't tip all the way back. It was a little bit awkward, being married to someone I had never even kissed properly, but Rudi managed to sleep the whole way. I lay awake, *War and Peace* propped up against my chest, a single beam of light above me slicing through the dark cabin. The flight was full, and somehow the snoring from the seat behind me emphasized my loneliness and wakefulness. I felt as though I was standing guard over Rudi, watching him as a mother watches a sick child, and once again I felt Egyptian-mummy old, sad and wise and ready to crumble into dust.

We landed into a tropical dawn, and Rudi woke up and laughed at *War and Peace*.

"Ditto," he said, reaching into the bag under his seat, and pulling out a copy of *Krieg und Frieden*. "You are how many pages ahead of me?"

I had to laugh too. We had both anticipated having a lot of reading time.

✠

I could do a big travelogue about the Seychelles here, and drone on about the white sand and the clear sea, and the marvelous Hotel X, but the truth is, I never left the marvelous Hotel X and its private beach. You all know what a beach looks like, don't you? All I will say is that the island we were on was the perfect setting for a perfect honeymoon, with its warm breezes and the hills covered in unknown trees. I tried asking the staff the names of some of the plants, but could not understand their heavily accented replies, so I can only tell you there were palm trees, and as there are 120 varieties of palm, I don't suppose you'll be much the wiser.

Our high-ceilinged room, where the fans revolved with a lazy *thwop-thwop*, led out onto a white verandah, which in turn led out into luxuriant gardens that hid the path to the beach. The white-jacketed staff were silent, and fluttered like startled birds whenever we tried to speak to them. I spent most of my days in a deck-chair, either on our veranda or on the beach. Rudi was mostly off somewhere, engaged in every water sport known to man, but I had no wish to spend two weeks falling off a wind-surfer. And I did have *War and Peace* to get through.

Did I sleep with him? I expect you're wondering. Yes, I did. Twice a day. It became a sort of ritual, like brushing your teeth or washing your face. Wake up, sex, wash, dress. Go to bed, undress, sex, sleep. Each time he would turn me over, like a cushion, so that I lay face down, and would briskly come to a climax, his chest bristling against my back. We never kissed, I never looked in his face. It was like being scrubbed down twice a day, efficiently but with no real involvement.

The funny thing is, I never minded. I think my sister might have been right, that I was still in some limbo of grief, where emotions fail to penetrate. When I look back now, I don't know how either of us did it. I can only plead insanity. Rudi never hurt me, he was always considerate, but our time together, particularly our evening meals, had all the quality of strangers meeting on a train; conversation flowed, but nothing of real significance was ever said. I found out a great deal about investment banking, and Munch, a little about Schloss von Drachenfels, and almost nothing about his friends or family. At the end of two weeks, I had slept with a man almost thirty times without knowing more about him than I might have learned at a cocktail party.

Perhaps my chief memory of our honeymoon was a feeling of lightness. A physical sense of lightness, of having shed the January layers of winter clothing, to live barefoot, in a swimming costume and T-shirt until dusk, as well as a moral lightness, with no sense of responsibility or duty, or even caring about anything. I was slim enough to be unconcerned at the sight of myself in a bikini; the combination of walking everywhere in London, and not eating, had gnawed any surplus weight from my bones. People think that food cheers you up, that a doughnut cures all ills, but this only works for trivial complaints. When real disaster strikes, food chokes you. I might as well have been eating cat litter for the last eighteen months. Now, I could appreciate the result, and the light tan I acquired, and the effect of two weeks' swimming in a warm coral sea, had made me look almost human again, not the gray-faced zombie who had sleepwalked onto the plane at Heathrow.

It was almost a surprise when Rudi said, "We must pack, we fly back tomorrow."

"Back" this time meant not London, except for a couple of hours at Heathrow, but Munich. My pathetic belongings had already been crated up in London and sent to the castle, to await my arrival. Rudi had planned for me to spend a couple of nights at his house in Munich, and to meet some friends of his, and then—the House of Horrors, Headlong Hall, Castle Dracula, the Castle of Otranto and all the other names I had privately dreamed up . . . was to be mine—manic laugh—*all mine*.

4
___

Munich was gray in February, as gray as London, and the stark modernity of Rudi's flat, with its hard-edged austere furniture, did nothing to cheer me. I thought less about Mark, now, but I did once think that Mark would not have liked Rudi's furniture. I wasn't comparing them, I couldn't, Mark had loved wood in flowing rounded shapes, and all the furniture he had made glowed with life. Rudi had filled his place with iron and steel, everything black, gray or neutral. There was no warmth or color.

I don't know why I'm withering on about Rudi's furniture; all I wanted that winter was to see Schloss Drachenfels, my future home. But first I had to kick my heels at Munich for a few days, while my new husband checked in with his bank and caught up with some of his paperwork, and had me officially registered as something-or-other, so I could have a nice shiny ID card with my photo, under which it said *Ella, Gräfin von und zu Drachenfels. Gräfin*—it sounds like *gray fin*—made me think of sharks, a thin gray spike above the water, the deadly mass silent beneath. Apparently if they stop swimming, sharks drown. I would have to keep swimming, now I was a registered shark.

Only the women get to be sharks, the men all stay mathematical—*graphs,* or Counts; in any European language, they are people who count. What do they count? Their money, I suppose, or land. Each Count had a County. The old names survived, the old medieval customs were still there, under the surface.

Anyway, my medieval survival and I drove south from Munich on an unseasonably warm day toward the end of February. We soon turned off the autobahn that led to Austria, the Eastern Reich, and headed up into the mountains, around bend after bend. We stopped in a lay-by to put on snow-chains, each wheel being jacked up in turn, and light-weight aluminum chains jingled into place. They rattled terribly on the slush-filled road when we set off again, but soon we were on less-frequented roads, where the snow-plows rarely traveled, and only the thickly compacted strips with tire-marks showed where the road lay underneath. I lost all sense of direction. The road was hedged in by pine-trees, and rare glimpses into the white valleys beneath revealed little; the occasional wood-shuttered house, narrow twists of road, signposts to invisible villages.

"We are driving up under the Drachenfels now," Rudi announced. "The rock is so called because it resembles a sleeping dragon, but one can only see this from the opposite side of the valley. I will show you later in the year, when the mountain roads to that side are open again."

I tried to curl my neck sideways to look up the side of the mountain, but I could see nothing.

"We will reach the gatehouse soon, but the castle is well-hidden. You will see nothing before we reach it. I must warn you that the house has not been lived in since I was a boy. My father did not care for it, you see. The structure is in good repair, and is regularly surveyed, but the interior has had no repairs for almost forty years." He waved a casual hand. It unnerved me, when he was driving on such twisted roads.

"I engaged a housekeeper via an agency in Munich—a Frau Feldstein. I hope she will prove satisfactory, but you must of course arrange matters as you see fit. Georg and Elsa have lived at the gatehouse for almost fifteen years now, and will be able to help you if you need them to. But why should you? Everything will be fine."

He was beginning to gabble now. He was obviously nervous, worried that I wouldn't want to stay in some ruined pile, and would plead to come and clutter up his clinically neat, sterile house in Munich. Well, I would rather stay up some mountain, thanks, play little Hedi in the hills than spend my life in Munich, with everyone in their loden coats looking like walking heaps of moss. I would hide out up here, and in the spring I would buy some leather shorts and an alpenstock, and a feather for my hat, and I could go a-wandering, my knapsack on my back. I was just beginning to consider the possibility of yodeling lessons, when Rudi slowed the car.

"The gatehouse," he said helpfully, for if there had ever been any gates, they were long since gone, and the gray stone and concrete building at the side of the road resembled nothing so much as a pillbox, one of those concrete coastal fortifications built to hide a man with a Bren gun. My sister and I had played in one once, on holiday. It was full of rabbit droppings, but it was out of the salty blast my parents had thought so good for us.

"It doesn't look very old," I said dubiously.

"Ah, the interior is medieval, but we have had to strengthen the exterior against landslides and avalanches. The house is in a vulnerable position here."

We both climbed out of the car, and I looked up at the almost sheer mountainside behind the gatehouse, so steep that little snow had settled, and the bare rock had shaken itself free from the earth.

Rudi pointed upward. "You see those cracks in the rock? Each year, water falls in them then freezes, forcing the cracks further apart. Every few years, lumps of rocks break off, and roll down the mountain, past this spot. Look down there, at that strip between the trees."

I dutifully looked down, to the other side of the gate-house, where the ground sloped away more gradually into a pine belt. A swathe of open lane, with battered tree-stumps poking through the deep snow, perhaps fifty yards across, had been cut down through the trees.

"That is the path the rocks took ten years ago. Georg still finds tiles from his old roof hundreds of meters away. He will tell you how terrible the avalanche was that year."

Georg had come out now, followed by Elsa, both in big rubber boots and silver-buttoned hand-knitted cardi-gans, both black-haired and red-cheeked—in their forties, I guessed. They greeted Rudi with enthusiasm, but me with more caution. I smiled and hung back. I would no doubt see them again.

Elsa pressed us to come in for *"Kaffee und Kuchen,"* but Rudi was anxious to get on; he promised that he would come down the next day to enjoy her home-baked cake. I just nodded in agreement, but as we left, I heard Elsa say softly, as an aside to Georg, *"Die Arme."*

The arms? What was wrong with my arms? I was so busy puzzling this out that I almost didn't see the castle. I only noticed we'd stopped because I could hear Rudi drumming his fingers on the leather steering-wheel, which mean the engine had been switched off. I looked up, and out, and realized I was in a cobbled courtyard, brown-gray stone walls on three sides. The large blocks of stone rose in mathematical layers above me. Rudi was waiting for me to get out, so I obliged. There was only a thin layer of snow over the cobbles; the protecting walls had kept the courtyard clear, and yet my boots appeared to have no grip. I could feel each rounded lump beneath my feet, like walking on babies' heads, as we made our way to a heavy wooden side door, with huge iron hinges and lock. I stood, shivering on the low step, while Rudi took out from inside his jacket a key the size of a bread-knife.

"I thought we would come in the back way. It is easier," he said.

I wondered what size the front-door key must be, if the back-door one required Rudi to use both hands to turn it, and a broad shoulder to shove the door open. I remembered the Hans Christian Andersen story, where a man has to pass a dog with eyes the size of saucers, then dinner plates, then windmills . . . what happened to the man in the end? It might not have been immediately relevant, but the thought of doors and keys growing ever bigger had sparked off a wondering trail of thought, and the old childhood story niggled at me, so that I quite forgot the puzzle of Elsa's words. Instead, I followed Rudi into Schloss Drachenfels.

The iron hinges squealed like a sore-throated banshee as Rudi stepped into the dark stone passageway. I had expected him to strike a match, at the very least, if not to pluck a flaming brand from its brazier on the wall, so I was slightly disappointed when I heard the plastic click of an electric light-switch.

"Oh. You have electricity," I said, unafraid to state the obvious.

"Yes, but only in the central part of the castle. The east wing has not been connected. It is not possible to have more until they build a—what do you call those small concrete buildings with machinery in for electricity?"

"Substations?"

"Yes, a substation. It is very difficult, so far up the mountain. But if you are to live here, I can arrange it."

We continued along bare passages, Rudi flicking
lights on and off behind us, pushing various heavy paneled doors, all closed, until he opened another door, one
of a pair of double doors, which led up a short flight of
steps into a vast marble-floored hall.

I gaped openly. Twin staircases, curved, with orna-
mental wrought-iron banisters, led to an upper story, and
between the two staircases was an enormous fireplace,
large enough to roast two oxen, a jumble of fire-irons on
the hearth. Set into the chimney-breast was an inscription
in Gothic lettering, made of some kind of metal—copper,
perhaps, to judge from the greenish color. The whole area,
for it was too large to be called a room, was the oddest
blend of the medieval and the classical, the white marble
busts on pillars face to face with gray steel suits of armor,
and eighteenth-century painted scenes of Italy sur-
mounted by crossed pikes. The war like and the cultured,
Mars and Apollo, aspects of the hall clashed, and it was
hard to say if there was a winner.

I went to the fireplace, standing there a moment to
look back at the huge carved and paneled entrance doors,
and the high windows that let light down into the room
while giving no view out, but I was drawn to the inscription, touching the metal which appeared to have been
stamped into the stone. I traced my fingers across, as if it
were Braille, the metal cold to my ungloved hand. Rudi
watched, his face motionless.

> "Sorge immer segnet
> Bis die Helle regnet,"

I spelled out. "What does it mean?"
Rudi hesitated before answering. "Roughly, it means,
'Sorrow will always sway until the light rules.' It is
believed to have been set there by the wife of an ancestor
of mine, who died in 1462. The wife, that is. She was

apparently the originator of the Drachenfels curse. Let us continue our tour."

"But why did she curse the family?" I persisted.

Rudi looked unhappy. "Something to do with infidelity. Her husband had been unfaithful while she was expecting their first child. It does not cast my ancestor in a particularly good light. He was in love with a gypsy girl, but married someone more suitable to bear him a son and heir. The wife found out, and swore she would be revenged on her faithless husband. Unfortunately, she died in childbirth, and it is reported that her dying words were a curse upon her husband and his lover, that they might have as little chance for happiness as they allowed her." He would say no more, I could tell from the way he pressed his lips together, so I let him be, and followed him into the next room.

Here the furniture was shrouded in white sheeting, and in the room beyond. The ancient wallpaper had faded to yellow shadows on parchment-colored walls, the heavy brocade curtains thick with dust as I touched them. Tarnished gilt mirrors hung over the fireplaces and opposite the windows of the first room—the Mirrored Salon, Rudi called it. Lit with a thousand candles, the heat and light reflecting off the mirrors, the room must have sparkled once, but time and dust had done their worst, and my face, gray and distorted in the old glass, which had flowed out of its original lines in some previous century, looked like a ghost. The next room, the Music Salon, was almost as bad, a worm-eaten baroque harpsichord leaning lopsidedly where one leg was giving way, a harp with broken strings in another corner, half-covered with a dust-sheet.

"These rooms have been little used this century," my husband murmured. "The private apartments are on the next floor."

"Let's go up then," I said quickly. These decaying rooms had wrapped me in a widening sheet of gloom.

Our footsteps echoed through the rooms as we returned to the hall. There we took the left-hand staircase, and turned left at the top. "To the right, the Long Gallery leads to the east wing, and the east tower. The west wing is where my father had his apartments."

Rudi pushed aside a long red and blue tapestry, which I had assumed was covering a blank wall, and walked into a narrow corridor, where he clicked on another light. Suddenly there was thick carpeting underfoot, the plastered walls had had a recent coat of white paint, and when I followed Rudi into a brightly furnished light room, with a fire in the grate, the 1920s-style furniture all clean and polished, my spirits began to rise. A jug of fresh yellow early daffodils stood on a table by the window, and I crossed to look out. Down below, the white mountainside fell away, sharply at first, then leveling into a gradual slope, the road we had traveled lost quickly among the trees. There was no sign of the gatehouse, or of any other human habitation. We may have been less than a hundred miles from Munich, but it felt a thousand miles from anywhere. In the spring, when the snows were melted, the white landscape might offer friendliness, but just then, I was happy to leave the windows to their crimson velvet curtains, and to return to the fire.

Rudi picked another log out of the log-basket and dropped it onto the embers. He rubbed his hands briskly, saying, "Ah, I see Frau Feldstein has done her work."

Rudi had told me about the housekeeper he had hired to set some rooms in order for me. She had been in residence since January, but even so, I was impressed with the good condition of the Master's Apartments, as he called them. There were four bedrooms, each with its own dressing room and bathroom, plus a sitting room and a study, as well as a small dining room and a sort of pantry, with just a fridge, a sink and an electric kettle perched incongruously on the broad white windowsill. The cooking was all done in the main kitchen, back down that corridor where we had first entered the castle. I was in no hurry to go back down to inspect the domestic offices.

There was a tight staircase at the end of the passage that led up to the next floor of the Master's Apartments. Where I found a schoolroom (with a blackboard), a playroom, another bathroom, and some cluttered lumber rooms, but everything looked clean, and I was glad to see there was an electric light and cold taps in the bathrooms. I had envisioned myself as châtelaine of some ancient ruin, candelabra in hand as I glided down the stairs in a long dress, but when I grew practical, and contemplated baths in a tin tub in front of the fire, or emptying chamber pots daily, I grew thankful for the inventions of the twentieth century. My life in Islington had been primitive enough; I was not ready for more privations.

Rudi had thought of everything, however, and pulled out a mobile phone from his coat pocket.

"The bell system in this house never worked when I was a child, so I have equipped Frau Feldstein with a portable telephone. I shall tell her we are ready for tea."

From somewhere in the depths, he summoned Frau Feldstein, and within a few minutes came a slow tread and the clank of a tea tray. There was a tap on the door, and Rudi opened it with a flourish. "*Grüsse*, Frau Feldstein. As you can see, we have arrived."

His cheery greeting fell on stony ground. Frau F. was the most boot-faced old bat I had ever seen, and I had been to a school where gargoyle features were a prerequisite for staff employment. She was tall and thin, with a very square face that seemed too big for her body, her bony jaw and cheekbones stretching her lips tight over the sallow skin. She had very deep-set dark eyes, but her hair had a peculiarly flat look to it, as though badly dyed. The plain black dress gave no clue as to her age or personality, and she wore no jewelry except a plain gold band on one large and knobbly hand. As she put the tray down, I could see she was also wearing a black apron, with a mobile phone in the pocket, but I resisted the attempt to adapt Mae West's famous line: "Is that a phone in your pocket or are you just pleased to see me?" Something told me that Frau Feldstein was unlikely to have a sense of humor.

Placing the tray quietly on the coffee table, with a muttered, "*Bitte schön*," the housekeeper backed out of the room. I glanced sideways at Rudi, who seemed a little nonplussed. When he met my gaze, he said defensively, "She came with the highest possible recommendations."

"Love-lee," I said.

He sighed. "Drink your tea, dear."

"Yes, dear. One arsenic or two?"

He had to laugh then. For the first time, we seemed to have something in common. We were both trapped in a decaying castle with a mad old ghoul, or maybe a retired KGB Colonel on the run—a close relative of Rosa Kleb of SMERSH—or a badly aged member of the Baader-Meinhof gang. It was the first time I had ever seen one of Rudi's "arrangements" go wrong, and I was almost ready to enjoy it.

"Didn't you interview her?"

"No, I left it all to the agency. I was very busy, you know."

"Hmmm." I drank my tea. "Where does she sleep? Next door?"

"No, the servants' quarters are in the east tower. There is only one room with electricity, but the plumbing is excellent."

"How enlightened of you."

"We would never have any staff if there were no bathrooms."

"Enlightened self-interest—I see."

We bickered a little and teased each other until the tea

ran out, then Rudi insisted on showing me the rest of the
house before it grew too dark. We fetched our cases from
the car first, so Rudi could find his torch. He had obviously been a Boy Scout once; his car contained kits for
every eventuality.

Once we had left our cases in the warm, modernish
apartment, we set off down the endless gloomy wastes of
the Long Gallery, then through the portrait gallery, which
Rudi hurried me past. "Tomorrow, tomorrow," he said. It
was too dark now to see the pictures clearly, and Rudi
would not allow me to linger; he held the torch, and if I
was not to be abandoned, lightless, with the walls closing
in, then I had to keep up with him. In the dusk I saw the
state bedchambers, Rudi's great-grandfather's museum of
stuffed animals, and the east tower, where Frau F. was
installed and where the rest of the staff would live. At present
the Bride of Frankenstein had the tower to herself, and an
unlit oil-lamp stood on a table by the tower entranceway,
ready for her return from the kitchens.

The stone steps that spiraled away into darkness connected directly with the kitchens, Rudi said, but I was lost
now. I felt like a new girl at school all over again, where
everyone knew their place except me; a kinder-than-the-
rest older pupil was showing me where things were, but
there was too much, and I was no better off. I nearly
despaired, as we stood in front of that unlit tower, nearly
broke down and begged Rudi to take me back to Munich,
but I was a big girl now.

I let Rudi lead me through more bedchambers, the
hangings almost in rags now, the windows smaller in this
part of the castle. Another corridor, leading to the north
tower. There were only three towers in all. The south
tower was never built, because the castle was laid out in
the shape of a pentagon, open at the bottom, and towers
were only constructed on the three angles that faced the
road from the valley. Just then Rudi stopped so abruptly

in front of a Gothic-arched oak door that I bumped into his back, and had to apologize.

He ignored me, saying, "Now this may interest you, Ella. This is where my father kept his book collection; he moved the old library here. He was a great collector, as Manfred Schuber must have told you, and after he died, all the books he kept at Cap d'Antibes came here. However, the oldest, most precious of his books were always sent here, for he said the sea air ruined them. There is a special key—wait."

There was a wall-clock hanging in the passage, silent now, with the words *Tempus Clavis Est* lettered in italic across its ivory face. The pendulum was contained in a glass case, which Rudi opened. He took out a key, which I would have thought to be an ordinary clock-winding key, had Rudi not fitted it into the door ahead of us.

"Cunning," I murmured, and Rudi smiled with pride.

"The same key winds the clock. My father had the clock and the key made at the same time, by two brothers, one of whom was a locksmith, the other a watchmaker. No one would look for the key on a clock-case, my father reasoned. He was a clever man. I wish I had known him better."

We went through a hallway, then another door. The room we entered stunned me. Not only was it filled with bookshelves, at least twelve feet high, but every inch of the floor, every inch of the tables, was covered in cardboard boxes of books, leaving only a narrow aisle leading through to the back of the room.

Rudi shrugged as I looked at him. "The next two floors of the library are clearer, but all the new books were left in here. They need sorting."

I opened the nearest box, quite casually, to find what even I knew to be a rare sixteenth-century work in its original binding, that started to crumble at the edges as I lifted it. I put it back carefully. I should have been wearing gloves—who knew what damage my sweat could have done to the leather? I opened the next box, and a musty smell of damp came up from it. I could see the box was only cardboard, and had been set on top of a bare stone floor. Damp, condensation. What had been done to these books?

I grabbed the torch from Rudi, making no pretense at politeness. "Give it here."

I shone the torch into another box, this one on a table. Inside, loose pages of unbound manuscript lay, curled at the edges, but as yet untouched by mice. What was this writing? Looking at the dates, it looked like some kind of diary, in a flowing but illegible hand. Latin, I thought. The next box had a Sotheby's receipt on the top, and the total, especially taking into account the date of 1952, made me shudder.

"Rudi," I said, shining the torch on his face accusingly, "nobody's touched this stuff in decades. It'll be bloody ruined."

He scarcely blinked. "I was hoping you would know what to do with them. It might keep you busy."

I was furious. These books had been left to rot, a fortune's worth, perhaps beyond saying. But I had to give it a try. These books needed me.

"It could keep me busy for the rest of my life," I retorted. He didn't answer me, though; he appeared to be looking at something over my shoulder. He took the torch from me, almost roughly, and shone it against the far wall. I thought I heard a sound behind us, and whirled around. Then Rudi dropped the torch and the batteries fell out.

5

I think my anger must have upset Rudi, because by the time we'd found the batteries and reassembled the torch, he was quivering, and said he's had enough exploring for one day. I held my tongue. There had been no need for me to snarl at him; he obviously didn't know the care old books required. The whole castle had been neglected for decades—why should the books have fared any better? Wordlessly, we paced back through the dark corridors, the dusty rooms.

Once again the light and warmth and cheer of the Master's Apartments, hidden behind the tapestry, struck me as some mystic's vision of paradise after years spent toiling through the empty wastes. Rudi made straight for the drinks tray and poured himself a large whiskey, which he sank in one gulp. I watched him curiously as he poured himself another, but said nothing as he drowned his second glass. It seemed to pull him around, and he was able to smile and say, "Sorry. Would you like a drink?"

"Yes, please. A small gin and tonic, if you have such a thing."

"Of course. Would you like ice? It's in the fridge."

"No, that's all right. I can always hold my glass out of the window if it gets too warm."

He handed me my drink, and poured himself a third whiskey. I hadn't remembered him drinking this much on our honeymoon.

"Rudi, is anything wrong?"

I'd never seen such an unconvincing smile. "No, no, why should anything be wrong?"

"Because you've just had three whiskies in three minutes, that's why. Look, I expect this is very difficult for you, coming back after all these years with me in tow—the place must hold so many memories for you. Why don't I go off to my room for a while? I've brought some good books, and you can call me when it's time for dinner."

"No, no," he said, and clutched at my shoulder as he spoke. "It is as you say, just memories. I used to sleep on the floor above her, and when I was playing, I used to imagine these women would come, and . . . oh, it was just foolish childhood imaginings."

"Tell me," I invited, settling back into my armchair. He came and sat on the sofa opposite, and began to stare into the fire.

"I do not quite remember these women, but they were very old. One of them wore a black dress. And it was strange, but when we stood in the library just now, I felt someone was watching that might have been her. But it is not possible, for that was just a childish fancy."

"I didn't see anything. You don't think it was Frau Feldstein passing, and you just caught a glimpse of her out of the corner of one eye?"

"No. It was nothing." He waved a hand, flicking away imaginary cobwebs.

I tried to change the subject. "Well, I must go and unpack, anyway, as I'm staying here. You're back off to Munich in the morning then?"

"Yes, the bank needs me. I will have the car I've ordered for you delivered as soon as possible. Georg will take you if you need to go anywhere. I will write down for you all the phone numbers, and leave you this telephone." He tapped his jacket pocket.

I just nodded. He could have ordered me a Sherman tank, for all I knew or cared. The trouble with Rudi was he arranged everything for me, so I had lost any connection to my own life, lost all sense of cause and effect. My life just happened to me, with no input from myself, and somehow I had no gratitude. I had longed for my burdens to be lifted, back in London, longed for some respite from the daily struggle for existence, thinking ease would come only with death, but now that I had been "rescued," I felt like a glove puppet—well and truly stuffed, with someone else's hand up my bottom.

In reality, I should have welcomed the emotion, thrown it a little party, for it was my first genuine feeling since Mark's death. Right then, though, I could not see the anger, both over the books and Rudi's well-meaning organizing, as a positive sign, and went off to unpack, in a disgruntled, furniture-kicking sort of way.

The heavy nineteenth-century oak bed, with its matching wardrobe and chests of drawers, gave my bedroom a solid, *mittel-Europea* look. The only concession to femininity, if hardly to frivolity, were the weighty pink brocade curtains and bedspread; the curtains would certainly have killed anyone they fell on. I heaved my case up onto the high bed, and unsnapped the locks. My clothes were quickly divided into four piles: underwear, shirts, sweaters, and jeans. Only the shirts needed hanging. The wardrobe door-handles gave me an unpleasant start: the last time I had seen anything similar, it was on a coffin. The creak of the polished wood, too, jarred me, belonging to that octave of fingernails on blackboards and hunting foxes, a little yelping scream. Must get some oil, I thought.

Everything else was thrown into drawers in the usual pattern: bras and knickers to the left, socks to the right, then nightdresses and T-shirts, and sweaters at the bottom. What would happen if I put socks in the bottom drawer? The chest of drawers was too solid to fall over, I was young enough to bend right down on a daily basis. I was beginning to rebel against the established order.

My other case, the one with dresses and skirts in, I ignored. *Not Wanted On Voyage.* Those were my city clothes, my smart clothes for downtown Munich. Up here, I could wear anything I liked. A brief vision of myself as châtelaine, in a floor-length velvet dress with pointy-hemmed sleeves, a chain around my waist, with keys and scissors and medieval metalwork clinking as I moved, floated through my mind, but I dismissed the thought to the parallel universe from where it came. This room was too cold to linger in. The fireplace, a sparse gray stone affair, contained a neat assemblage of logs and kindling, but the fire was unlit. I had no idea what time fires were usually lit in bedrooms—but it was after dark, and I was beginning to be able to see my breath indoors.

There were matches on the mantelpiece, so I lit the fire carefully, uncertain of the technique. The fire had been well-laid, though, for the twiggy kindling soon crackled up to heat the logs as I watched, half-anxious, half-admiring. I did not hear the door opening behind me, heard nothing in fact, until Rudi said in my ear, "*Wundurbar.* I shall unpack also."

I looked around, startled, "Oh! Where are you sleeping?"

"In here, I think." He flourished his case. "It is safer. I mean, I would be happier." He looked in the top drawer of one of the chests, saw it was now mine, and moved to the next one. His overnight case was dumped on top, and he began hurling tightly rolled balls of socks into a drawer. Why do men wear bright red socks, I wondered.

"You've got a lot of socks for one night," I commented.

"I am leaving some extra clothes, so that if I come at a weekend, I will have clothes here."

"Oh, all right. Will you come here often?"

"Mm, that depends."

"On what?"

He looked almost embarrassed. "It depends on whether you . . . if we manage . . . when you know. . . ."

I waited, brows furrowed with concentration.

"If you become *pregnant,*" he finally managed to say.

"Oh, I see. You mean you won't need to come here if I'm expecting."

He felt for his cufflinks, then realized his shirt had buttoned cuffs. He couldn't quite look me in the eye.

"You will tell me if you know, won't you?" he said quietly.

"Of course I will," I shrugged. "I just hadn't given it much thought, that's all. Anyway, what's for dinner?"

He seized the change of subject, and proceeded to worry it to death. "Now then, I could telephone Frau Feldstein and ask her, or I could order it for seven-thirty, or would that be too early? Or too late? It depends on . . ." I let him ramble, and watched the fire take hold. Eventually, Rudi came to a conclusion and telephoned Frau F., who told him dimmer would be served in the small dining room at a quarter to eight, but hors d'oeuvres could be produced immediately.

I loved the way in which Rudi pronounced *hors d'ouvres,* and wondered if this was German for "two bags of crisps." It was unknown to me. Frau F., as smoothly as a cable car, slid into the sitting room a few minutes later with a tray of interesting snacks, little pastries and things rolled around other things, unidentifiably delicious.

Dinner, too, was magnificent, and despite the dark

and gloomy journey from downstairs, hot. Contrary to her fearsome appearance, Frau F. obviously had hidden talents, and once she left us with dessert and coffee, Rudi and I were able to talk freely again, after the stilted silence of the meal.

"Rudi, I meant to ask you earlier, what's the German word for arms?"

"*Die Ärme*—why?"

"Oh—not *Arme?*"

"No, *Ärme*, with an umlaut."

"Then what does "Arme" mean, without an umlaut?"

"Poor, as in miserable, unlucky. Or no money. Why do you want to know?"

"Just something I heard somewhere," I muttered. "Silly of me to mix the words up."

"Perhaps you have considered German lessons?"

"Yes, that would be a good idea." I knew he meant to be helpful.

"Elsa, at the gatehouse, has a sister who teaches in the village. I have not met her, but I can ask Elsa if she thinks it would be suitable."

I nodded, but my attention had been caught by something else he had said. "Village? Which village? I didn't see one on the way."

"No, Oberkirchen is hidden by a fold in the mountains, but it is around four kilometers from here. It is called Oberkirchen because its church has the highest altitude of any in this region. The nearest church after this is at Unterkirchen, five hundred meters lower down."

It was obviously a source of local pride, so I nodded appreciatively.

"There is little in Oberkirchen apart from the church and a couple of shops. I have arranged for food to be delivered to the gatehouse, and have left Frau Feldstein to order as she sees fit. She will show you the books of account on a monthly basis."

"What, you mean I have to check everything, like some feudal lady of the manor? And count sheets and things?"

Rudi gave a little snort of indulgent laughter. "My dear, it is not so bad. I do not expect the housekeeper to cheat you, but it is customary for the lady of the house to show an interest in these things."

"All right, all right. What else do I have to do?"

He thought about this for a moment. "Nothing. You may want to make changes. Just speak to me, and I can arrange them. The container with your things from London has arrived. Anything else you need, I can send from Munich. But I must ask you—please telephone first if you wish to come to Munich. I am often away on business."

That was fine by me. I had no particular desire to see Munich again, and I could tell he didn't want me dropping by unannounced. None of my business, really.

I very nearly said, "So what or whom am I not supposed to see?" but some unexpected fit of tact came over me, and I let the man be. Even though he *was* my husband, I still had a healthy respect for him, and despite my earlier annoyance, I was growing quite . . . fond, perhaps of Rudi—or at least well-inclined toward him. He was being extremely kind, so I strove to entertain him as we returned to the sitting room.

"Fancy a game of Snap?"

Rudi had never heard of it, but by the time I'd lost most of my cards to him, I could tell he was getting the hang of it. We played cards till the fire burned low, and then went to bed.

Bed in cold climates is a protracted ritual, involving hot-water bottles (Frau F. had left strange aluminum thermos-flask shaped objects, which Rudi assured me were intended for feet, for the warming of, and he boiled a kettle to demonstrate the cunning technology employed), and steaming hot baths, and furry slippers, and scurrying like mice into the now-warm bedroom. Still lobster-pink from the path, I flinched as my feet hit the metal bottle in the bed.

"Bed-socks," said Rudi firmly, and leapt out in his blue flannel pajamas to fetch me a pair of his woolly knee-length socks. It was the first time I had ever seen him in pajamas, and he looked sweetly boyish. I was glad of the socks, too, and after we put the lights out, the room now lit only by a dim fire-glow, I whispered, "Thanks, Rudi. Sleep well."

A heavy arm reached out under the bulky eiderdown, and lay across my ribs, as he shuffled a little closer.

"*Schlaf gut*," he murmured, and fell asleep.

6

When I awoke, I had no idea what time it was. The pink curtains were too thick to let in much light, so I tottered over to them, and after a few ineffectual tugs realized there was a cord to pull. Jerkily the curtains moved a couple of feet apart, and white light, snow reflecting sunshine, ran into every corner of the room. I padded back to bed, now able to read my wristwatch. Eight-thirty.

Rudi stirred and mumbled. I lay next to him, wondering whether to get up and risk the cold, or to stay warm in bed. Rudi turned to face me, his murmuring louder. "No—*no,* I tell you," he said audibly. Then his hand was on my throat. "I cannot. *Can-not.* We must stop now. No, Na—" He broke off as I drew a gasping breath, my hands desperately trying to drag the weight of his hand from around my neck. At once his grip slackened. He subsided into an incoherent muttering, and as I wriggled free, he sat bolt upright, as if thrown there. "Where am I?"

"In bed, strangling your wife," I said crossly. "Go back to sleep."

He said something I couldn't hear, then lay down, pulling me close to him again. I rested my head on his chest, hearing his heartbeat, galloping at first, subside to a slow steady rhythm. He stroked the back of my neck with one hand, then bent his head toward me, this time gently moving my face up to meet his. He kissed me, a warm, relaxed, Sunday-morning kiss, as if we had all the time in the world to get this one kiss right. I felt the warmth rise in me, and responded.

"Shall we? To be quite sure?" he said in my ear.

I shrugged one shoulder, the one I wasn't lying on. "Do what you like. It's your castle."

He let me go then. "No, my dear, this is your domain," he told me quietly. "I leave this castle to your keeping."

"Sorry, I didn't mean to sound—you know. Do what you want."

"I think I want some breakfast," he said, running the knuckles of one hand softly down the side of my face. "Shall I summon the Breakfast Dragon?"

I agreed, and he telephoned Frau Feldstein. It was cheating, somehow, to phone; I wanted a tasseled bell-pull, that tolled in some deep recess of the castle with a sonorous clangor. The word reminded me of an ancient television program about the Clangers, who lived on the dark side of the moon, and who would whistle their way along to the Soup Dragon for soup. The Soup Dragon had a booming, bottom-of-a-drain voice. I smiled as I remembered the jerky movements of the little puppets, then noticed that Rudi was fully dressed and watching me, a faint glow of golden stubble catching the sunlight from the window. Where had the time gone?

I dressed, while Rudi went off to shave, then we both had a slow breakfast, intermittently attended by the Gorgon-featured Frau F., whose gaze I dared not meet. Afterward, Rudi took me on the promised tour, retour and detour, around the rest of the Schloss, starting with the

portrait gallery. The earliest paintings, nearest the staircase, were so crackled and darkened that I could barely
distinguish between the sexes, and the heavy black frames
cast dark shadows over the faces. There was only a hand-
ful of these, however, and we soon reached the Lutheran,
Elizabethan-type portraits, which Rudi said were from the
Thirty Years' War. All the subjects were in black with
white ruffs, and little jewelry, but generally with a skull
somewhere beside them—*a momento mori*. There were
more of these, several yards' worth of gloomy black,
before the bright eruption of eighteenth-century color.

"Why are so many of these black and white portraits?" I asked.

"A high mortality rate." A dour answer.

As we reached the more recent paintings, he began to
talk me through some of them. His great-great-grand-
mother, Prussian to the core, her hard blue eyes belying
the pretty face, beside his great-great-grandfather Otto
with his favorite dog, a deer-hound. Names of strange
European provinces, like some dimly remembered history
lesson. Memories of Mecklenburg, Pomerania, Franconia,
Hessen, flowed over me. I was beginning to suffer from
gallery fatigue (four paintings and I'm pooped), so paid
very little attention to Rudi's monologue, until we reached
the portraits of his parents. His father had many of Rudi's
features, but I was surprised at the portrait of his
mother—not her actual appearance, although she greatly
resembled the young Ingrid Bergman—but the flat, lifeless quality of the picture, the oil-paint equivalent of a
police mug-shot. Tactlessly, I mentioned this to Rudi.

"Hmm. Yes. It was painted from a photograph after
her death. There was not time for one before." He looked
down at me. "Yes, I must arrange for your portrait to be
painted, to be on the safe side."

"To go next to yours?" There was a painting of Rudi,
aged not more than about twenty, in an oval gilt frame. He

was wearing a white shirt, his blond hair a little too long and floppy, his cheekbones razor-edged underneath his skin. He looked so young, so confident, so unafraid. *Unafraid.* The word reverberated against a sounding-board in my mind. That was why I had felt uneasy—I had sensed Rudi's fear, or reluctance at least, to walk down this gallery. He was not at ease here among his own ances-tors. I wanted to know more.

"Rudi, the family curse. . . . The woman who started it—is there a picture?"

"Anna-Maria. No. That was destroyed when part of the castle burned down in 1537."

"Do you believe in the family curse?"

"Yes, I do. Without wanting to. I have always pre-ferred to believe there is a rational explanation for every-thing. Take Anna-Maria's husband, Dietmar, and his gypsy girlfriend. Their horses must have bolted. And yet the stories persist, for generation after generation. None of this is logical, but. . . . My father was a great logician, you know, and has the original works of most of the great philosophers of the Enlightenment. We have a first edi-tion of the *Critique of Pure Reason*," he informed me.

"Fascinating," I murmured. "You have a family inter-est in rationality, then?"

I do not understand why so many people cling to irra-tional ideas. Instead of fairy stories, my father used to read me Schopenhauer at bedtime when I was a boy."

"Bet you went straight off to sleep."

"It was very interesting to me," he said stiffly.

I stopped teasing him. "But there is no logical expla-nation why so many women in your family have died young, is there?"

Rudi bit his lip. "I have considered the blood factors most carefully—if, for example, the rhesus positive blood of the mother meets the rhesus negative blood of the child, in the past, the outcome was not always good. But our blood groups are compatible—you told me you were O positive."

I had forgotten, but Rudi had been keen to know my blood group when we first met. "Yes, I thought it very ghoulish of you to ask." It was impossible not to tease Rudi. He was so well-behaved, sober and upright, more like a waxwork sometimes, that I could not resist the occasional prod.

He ignored, me and said, "It is not good to think too much of these things. The hypnotic power of suggestion, perhaps combined with isolation, may have affected these women." He waved his hand down the somber rogues' gallery.

"At least I'm not saurian."

"Sorry?"

"Cold-blooded. If I were, I'd have gone into a coma by now. Rudi, I'm freezing my ar—— ——I'm a bit cold."

"Shall we leave my only relatives, then, and go and visit Georg and Elsa at the gatehouse?"

Again I sensed his unease, his reaching toward the staircase, a door, any exit at all. "Sure," I said, and followed him to the Master's Apartments for our coats.

✠

Georg and Elsa were a five-minute scrunch down the hill, the car in first gear as the snow-chains scrabbled for purchase. The brilliant sunshine was melting the top layer of snow, and a glistening sheet of water rested on the white surface. Georg and Elsa's bunkerlike house was surrounded by piled-up mounds of snow and chippings of ice, but the path to their door was well-salted, and no sooner had our feet met its gritty surface than Georg came out to welcome us with a hearty, "*Grüss Gott.*"

We scraped our feet on the steel doormat, a rigid Venetian blind construction, then entered their stone-flagged hallway. Almost immediately the door to the living room opened, and I was overwhelmed by a sweet scent, which I discovered to be hyacinths. Every windowsill was clustered with them, some in pots, some in the traditional glass bulb vases, where the bulb is grown in water, rather than soil, and drifting in the water, visible through the cut glass, float a hundred white rootlets, a fragile counterpoint to the solid scaly mass of the bulb above. The thick flexible stalks held flowers of every color, opening bells of blue and yellow and red and white, and then orange. I had never seen an orange hyacinth, and I was so surprised that I failed to spot Elsa, standing to one side of the room. Only after Rudi had greeted her, then come to nudge me subtly toward her, did I realize how rude I must have seemed.

"*Entschuldigen*," I apologized, "*aber die Blumen—die Hyazinthen. . . .*" I gestured toward them, to show how awestruck I had been.

Elsa smiled; those flowers were her winter's work, she said. Surely not just the flowers, for every surface of the cozy room showed signs of labor, of craftmanship, from the lacy mats under every ornament and the lace tablecloths on the two side tables, to the carved wooden boxes along the ancient mantelpiece; from the hand-hooked red and orange hearth rug to the lumpy clay ashtrays, all seemed to indicate hours of toil, of cottage industry.

In halting German, I admired the bright orange woven cushion, strident against the yellow sofa, and Elsa's smile grew broader. She had learned to weave last winter, she said. She would show me her loom—but first, coffee. And what cup of coffee is complete without a slice of cake? If the magic arts are still practiced in the more out-of-the-way parts of Central Europe, then cake-making is one of them. The people who could imagine a whole house made of gingerbread are a people who know their cakes. There is an invisible line vertically down the center of Europe, and along this line, the best cakes are to be found. East and west of this line, you may find good plain cooking, simple unadorned cakes, or fancy but dull-tasting ones, but to experience the art, and angels dancing on your tongue, you must find that line starts somewhere in Scandinavia, continues on down through Germany and into Austria; I have tracked it no further, but who is to say if the meridian does not still hold its power in Italy? However, there are hundreds of people who have never given cakes much thought, and upon whom cream and chocolate and marzipan with a hint of kirsch have no effect. They are missing out.

None of this is to say that Georg and Elsa were the typical *bürgerlich* type, with Elsa as the happy *Hausfrau*. They were more of the hippie persuasion, despite Georg's now short hair. There were photos of them in flowered shirts, with love-beads, and the record on top of the stereo had an alarmingly lurid color, lettered in the squishy doughnut writing I had on my schoolbag when I was eight or nine, words like LOVE. Georg and Elsa were roughly Rudi's age, had been teenagers in the sixties, but hippiedom lingered in pockets of northern Europe like some ancient heresy, long after Britain had turned to black clothing and anarchy in the UK. Georg and Elsa had been students together at Marburg, and had done a variety of odd jobs before settling high in these hills to caretake Schloss Drachenfels.

Slowly I began to feel at ease with their accents, as they and Rudi talked, but I was still glad that Elsa said, when Rudi mentioned German lessons, "Oh, you will understand Beate much better. She speaks a good German."

I let Rudi arrange weekly lessons for me; all I had to do was turn up at the gatehouse on Friday mornings, when Beate would come up from Unterkirchen.

It was all so easy, and I could have stayed in that bright warm room all day, the white snow-light filtering through the greenery at the windows. Rudi, though, was impatient after half an hour or so.

"I have to return to Munich," was all he said. I returned with him to the castle, then watched him pack his bags. His face was closed as he left, no traces of emotion lingered, so I said nothing except, "Goodbye," but I followed his car out of the courtyard, and watched him as he drove away down the mountainside, not just until he was lost to view, but until I could no longer hear anything except the slow drip of melting snow running from the castle walls.

7

Rudi drove back to Munich at a pace that would have seemed furious to anyone else. He enjoyed the challenge of keeping a large heavy car on narrow, snow-filled roads, then, after the fast release of snow-chains, the smooth expanse of Autobahn. The concentration required kept him from thinking. He didn't want to think. He wanted to stay on the motorway to Hamburg and beyond, to keep driving until his eyes closed.

The car knew its own way home though, and well before he was ready, it was nosing its way into the underground garage beneath his flat. He turned off the engine and sat in the dim light for several long minutes, unwilling to move, before gathering himself together enough to leave the car, to take his bags from the boot and return to his empty flat.

He was handling things very badly, had handled them badly from the start, and was making things worse. He didn't want to behave badly; moreover, he never liked to make a mistake. He had been uneasy about the entire marriage plan, marriage to a stranger, and he had been right to feel that way, though not for the reasons he had anticipated.

It had all seemed so simple, almost as if predestined. A woman who had put his scruples to rest had appeared before he had even started looking. He'd been in London, and had intended to telephone a few dating agencies, then look up one or two old friends, but a chance poster for a book sale had caught his eye, and he'd remembered for the first time in years his father's old friend, Manfred Schuber. It was his first night in London, so he'd decided to put off the matrimony project for a day or two, and had invited Dr. Schuber out to dinner that night.

Dr. Schuber had come, though insisting he be allowed to reciprocate Rudi's hospitality, and the two men had shared a long, relaxed meal at La Tante Claire, the steady flow of wine easing into the conversation Dr. Schuber's worries about his staff, in particular the youngest, a widow still grieving for her dead husband.

"She talks about death all the time," he said sadly, shaking his head so that his glasses wobbled. "She insisted that she herself wants to die, to the point where I worry that she will kill herself. Not now, she is too depressed, but when she starts to recover a little. Then she will have the energy to find the means. But perhaps, the shock of the move will push her—I do not know what I should do."

"What move is this, Manfred?" Rudi asked.

"I shouldn't be telling you this, but the official announcement is soon. Our department is moving to Wales, and I fear most of the staff will not be able to move with their jobs."

"Cheaper office space, lower staff costs? I know, I know. It's happening everywhere. It looks good on the balance sheet."

"They never think of the people, though, do they?"

Dr. Schuber slammed an angry fist on the table. "The lives they damage, the trouble. . . . I'm the one who has to break the news to my family. My staff are all the family I have."

Rudi nodded. "I know. I'm sorry. I'm sorry I never got in touch. After my father. . . ." He gulped down the rest of his glass, and gestured to the waiter for another bottle.

Dr. Schuber looked at him, a tear in the corner of one blood shot eye. "Your father got me out. I owe him a lot. He was a good man, despite the army uniform. He helped me all the way to Switzerland. He sent me money."

"I think he wished he could have helped more. He tried to stay out of the war as much as he could, my Aunt Adalheid said. He hid at Drachenfels. He was a scholar, not a soldier. He had no interest in patrolling the Austrian borders. If he had a sense of duty, it was to Drachenfels, not to the Reich."

"I know." Dr. Schuber patted the tablecloth with a heavy hand. "You remind me of him. But you—you do not go to Drachenfels now? You have never married? No children?"

"Not yet. But I need to be married, to have an heir. I can't put it off any longer. If I don't get married soon, my chance of happiness is gone. That's why I'm in London. I was going to ring a few dating agencies. Listen, Manfred, I know it's a long shot, but this woman on your staff, the one you worry about—will you introduce me?"

"Whatever for?"

"I need to be married. It doesn't matter to whom, it's not as if I need to marry for money. It might solve a problem for you, too."

"Rudi, you're demented."

"Yes, I know. Introduce me anyway."

And he had. The good old man had arranged dinner at his house, a funny narrow old house in an industrial part of London, for later that week. The widow, the girl Ella, would have been attractive if she had not seemed so colorless, the gray-white of an English fog, and about as substantial. He wondered, afterward, if she had heard a word he had said. She had been calm, and pleasant, and presentable, but curiously blank. The first was the most important, though. He couldn't cope with another Nadine in his life.

She had been quite open about wanting to die, had made some grim little jest about ringing up the local murderers, to say, "Can I book myself in for next Thursday? Beheading, please, a lot off the top, not too much off the sides." He had laughed, but it had been an uncomfortable laughter, her death-wish too plainly visible. It was as if she was trailing the Grim Reaper, trying to catch up. He found it uncanny. Not normal in a girl of her age. Woman. She was almost thirty.

He had asked her to marry him, after warning her about the family history. Had he told her properly, though—really made her understand? He'd questioned Dr. Schuber, who had said, "Yes, I told her, too, but I am not sure if she believed me." That was the trouble. People never liked to believe in bad luck, though they were happy to believe their lottery numbers would come up. He could lay all the proof out, the family tree, oddly truncated as it was, so few side branches, so few siblings. He could point to birth and death dates, more than five hundred years' worth. Few families in the *Almanac de Gotha* had been so carefully recorded. And yet, add in the first hint of the nonrational, and everyone assumed you were mad—inbred, over-fanciful. He was not, he was a serious man, and it irked him when others refused to take him seriously.

The tabloid press did, of course. The miseries of the rich and famous were what they lived for. Nothing like a good gloat. Why was it that he could be taken seriously by the people he despised most, while those whose trust he valued refused to believe a word?

He wanted Ella to take him seriously. He paced through his flat, impatiently, before deciding to make coffee. He put water on to boil, igniting the gas on his catering-standard steel range with an angry flick. The coffee was in the freezer. Then, with affection, he pulled the battered old blue tin coffeepot out of the back of the kitchen cupboard, where he had hidden it behind the rice. He had a new chrome-plated pot, but the old blue one had been there from his student days, the bottom all blackened from leaving it on the hob to keep hot, the spout dented from the time he had hit Augustin with it. It had poured better ever since, Augustin's thick little French skull having finally come in useful for something.

He heaped several black plastic scoops of coffee into the pot, doused them with near-boiling water, holding his face over the judge to breathe in the dark fumes. God, he needed this. He needed something.

When had he first become so agitated? It must have been at Georg and Elsa's, as they sat there, having the kind of Sunday afternoon that married couples are supposed to have, coffee with friends, inconsequential chat about hyacinths, and handicrafts, and will the wood supply last the winter? He missed it, but he'd never had that, so how could he miss it? He led a busy, metropolitan, international lifestyle, full of important people who ran multinational concerns. Why should he miss some gatehouse in Bavaria?

He looked again at his old coffeepot, all he had left of his student days, apart from a black gown, folded and put away, and a few certificates. The gatehouse wasn't any old gatehouse in Bavaria. It was the gatehouse to Schloss Drachenfels, the gateway to his home. A castle that gave him the shudders. He had always felt there was something in the very fabric of the building, lurking just out of sight. As a child, he remembered whirling around, trying to catch the watchers in the shadows, but they were too quick for him. He knew, though, that there *was* something there, something the others could not see. Ella, it seemed, had noticed nothing.

She was there, now, in his family home, the castle he had left when he was nine, to go away to school. His father had moved to the South of France, and Rudi had never stayed at Drachenfels again. He had always, in recent years, come up for a quick look, then stayed the night in Georg and Elsa's spare room, sharing the space with the looms, quilting frames, drying clay, whatever Elsa's project of the moment happened to be. The couple always seemed so happy together, and he had always felt a little as if he intruded, but today, with Ella there, he had no longer felt that way. Everything had felt—right. Right? How could it? What was right about his marriage, compared to theirs?

He wasn't even sure if Ella liked him very much. He'd kissed her that morning, in bed, the kind of kiss to show her he meant business, but then when he'd suggested they go further, she'd shrugged, and said, "If you like." Not at all interested. To be fair, he hadn't given her any grounds to think it would be a thrilling experience. Not after that honeymoon.

He buried his face in his hands as he remembered the routine, monotonous—well, sex was all it was. He'd thought, somehow, he'd be staying faithful to Nadine if he didn't enjoy himself too much, or allow Ella to get too close to him. She hadn't even tried. After a couple of days, he'd found himself wanting to do more, to feel her respond to him, to have her call out his name. There was no point; she was only temporary. He wouldn't see her again once she was pregnant; he'd promised himself that. This was purely a business arrangement. He was only sleeping with her until she was pregnant. He had to remember that.

To help himself remember, or forget, he'd windsurfed each day until he was sick of the lurid plastic sails, dived the maximum time his system could stand, then snorkeled himself silly, till he could bear the sound of his own breathing no longer. And each evening he came back, and she was there, calm, serene and indifferent to him. He was fitter after that holiday than he'd ever been. Whenever he went away with Nadine, the Caribbean usually, he could never leave her side for more than fifteen minutes; always she wanted suntan lotion rubbing in, drinks, entertainment, magazines fetching, and if he was away for too long, she would be flirting with the pool attendant, the tennis coach or anyone else she could lay her expensively manicured fingers on. Holidays with Nadine were hard work.

It was impossible to compare them. Nadine was the woman with whom he had shared so many moments of passion, *un amour fou;* she was the sorceress who had enslaved him. He caught and held those last words in her mind. Yes, she had enslaved him, caused him to do things no man in his right mind should ever have done. He had gone to London for her sake, to find—Ella.

Thinking about the two of them, the morning's dream began to trickle back to him. He had been holding Ella, on the edge of a mountain, and Nadine, and a little woman in green, each had hold of one of Ella's feet; they were both below him, floating in the air, and they were tugging, trying to drag Ella's feet from the path, while he was pulling her back, holding her close to him, the two other women leered up at him, Nadine's face contorted into a sneer as she hissed like a cat, and called out: "Let her go. Push her. Push her down to me. Push her *do-own*," so he pulled Ella even closer—until she protested, and woke him up, because it was only a dream, and they were both still in bed together. He held her, more loosely, then pulled her closer. He had been awake then, he was sure of it. He wanted to remember that she kissed him back.

Nothing she had ever done before or since had given him any indication that she had the remotest spark of feeling for him. He'd wanted a business arrangement, and that was what he'd got. She had tactfully refrained from mentioning her dead husband, and he of course had said nothing about Nadine. Should he tell her about Nadine? There was no good reason to, but. . . . His conscience struggled with the ethics of the situation. It had felt wrong, sleeping with Ella on honeymoon, but now it felt wrong to return to Nadine's arms.

He would explain to Nadine that in order to avoid scandal, for everyone's sake, it would be best if they didn't see each other for a while. It would be putting Ella in an unfair position, not that he was about to tell Nadine that. Nadine would understand the importance of appearances. No one must think there was anything untoward about this marriage; to return to Nadine, and to Paris, so soon would only expose both of them to contempt. He would explain it all to Nadine.

8

I had a hard time finding my way back through the labyrinth of dark passages that led from the side door to the main hall and, uncertain where the light switches were, I had to grope around each time the passages twisted in a new direction, but I dared not walk through them in pitch darkness, for fear of cobwebby fingers across my face or sudden plunges into concealed dungeons, or worse still—Frau Feldstein. Now it was just the two of us, alone in a rambling castle of which I still knew very little.

A torch, I decided, would be the first item on the list of things I needed, but maybe I could find a candlestick or lantern somewhere to use for the time being. Rudi had said to telephone him for anything I wanted, and he would arrange for things to be sent and delivered to the gatehouse. I would try and save up my lists, to make them weekly ones rather than daily, but I could already tell that the first list would be a long one. The thought of lists occupied my mind happily since I had found the Master's

Apartments, and I sat in an armchair in front of the fire, a spiral-bound notebook in one hand, dividing pages up into spurious categories such as *Household, Book Needs* and *Me*. Oddly enough, there was very little in the *Me* column; it seemed I had almost everything I needed. Several packing-cases, containing the few things I had wanted to bring from London, awaited my attention in the second-best bedroom, the Green Room.

Not that it was particularly green, but one wall was almost entirely filled by a woodland scene—a Victorian oil-painting that was so vivid that the whole room seemed merely to be a frame for the painting. It had a wonderful life of its own, so that anyone sleeping in the room would be hard put to keep their eyes closed; even the faintest hint of light, and they would be compelled to stare into the viridian depths. It took me a long time to examine my packing-cases, with the painting looking over my shoulder all the time. Or something *in* the painting, perhaps. I felt I was being watched, or watched over—I was not sure which. There was nothing threatening in this, but always the feeling that something was there, something just out of sight.

The feeling left me as I carried armfuls of my belongings into the crimson sitting room and propped the rows of cheerful paperbacks into the empty bookcase. The sitting room was empty; no watchers here. My books, my old friends, which I had so nearly left behind in London, in my rush to start a new life—how glad I was I had brought them. They would fill the evening hours, and I would reread my old favorites, and during the day I would work through the castle library, to try and find out what it contained, to see where buried treasure lay.

Before I knew where the time had gone, it was evening, and Frau Feldstein telephoned to ask what time I would require supper. I found it so strange, the sudden *pirp* of the telephone, from someone a few rooms away. I intended to find out where Frau Feldstein's den was, in the lower reaches of the castle, so we could agree on some kind of routine. Ideally I wanted to see as little of her as possible. In the meantime, we had agreed that supper would be served at eight.

She appeared, silently and promptly, at the door to the sitting room as the little ebony mantel-clock struck eight, carrying a tray with two silver domes, under each of which lay a plate with my main course and pudding respectively, the appropriate cutlery laid by each plate, and a starched damask napkin, enclosed by a silver napkin ring, across the top of the tray.

"Shall I set the table in the dining room?" she asked expressionlessly.

"Oh no, I'd much rather eat here, in front of the fire. Thank you."

"Very well." She turned to go.

"Er—one moment, Frau Feldstein. I wouldn't wish to put you to any inconvenience. Perhaps we could arrange some kind of routine, set mealtimes and so on, so that we can both work around a timetable."

"As the Countess wishes. Shall we discuss this when I bring the coffee?"

"Yes, that would be a good idea. And do bring a cup for yourself, so that we can sit and discuss things comfortably." I was determined to make the woman like me, to become less stonelike.

She was unmoved. "Very good," she said, and withdrew.

The food was excellent again, and I don't think any of it came out of packets. I ate slowly, however, suddenly unhungry. A faint prickle of unease reached me before I was halfway through my apple pudding. I tried to dismiss the pangs, and by the time Frau Feldstein returned with the white porcelain coffeepot and the cups, I had almost succeeded.

"Please sit down," I said to her.

She sat carefully, on the edge of an armchair, still corset-rigid, as if slumping or relaxing were unknown concepts. I poured the coffee, determined to keep the upper hand.

"Now, I intend to make my own breakfast," I said firmly, "so that I can get up when I please without disturbing you. Lunch—shall we say one o'clock?"

Frau Feldstein agreed wordlessly to everything I said. Exasperated by her lack of reaction, I said, "Or perhaps you have your own way of running things?"

She looked down at her lap. "It is as the Countess wishes. I am only the housekeeper."

It was an answer I had not expected. She was much older than I, so harsh-featured, that this submissiveness disconcerted me. Suddenly the tables had been turned. I was the cruel mistress and she the uncomplaining victim. I'd discovered what "the servant problem" was: what on earth did one do with them? I was used to making my own dinner, and loading my own clothes into the washing machine, and while I was happy to let someone else do the washing-up, the dusting, and the cleaning, I would have liked to choose the person who performed these tasks, the only other living soul in this remote chilly stone castle.

"Perhaps it is very quiet for you here?" I suggested gently. "You must be used to more lively places."

"Oh no," said the housekeeper. "The Count made it quite clear to me that I would be housekeeper to only the one lady in an empty castle. But I had expected an *older* lady."

So that you could influence me into changing my will, then push my wheelchair a little too hard near the top of the stairs? Or tell everyone how confused I was, then feed me a dozen of my own heart tablets crushed into my food, so that everyone thought I was so muddled I'd taken an overdose? Come to think of it, I had felt rather sick during supper. My smile became extremely rigid, and I tried to relax my facial muscles.

"I am so sorry if the Count misled you on that score. I will be here for quite some time, so if there are any problems, do let me know. Was there anything else?"

Frau Feldstein shook her head sullenly and rose to go, stacking the coffee-tray on top of the supper-tray. She glowered at me as I opened the door for her. Maybe real Countesses didn't help at all. Or maybe I should have been firmer with her, just jolly well told her what's what, and one peep out of her and I'd . . . I'd what? I didn't know, but I had a horrible feeling I was going to have to keep an eye on her.

✠

I also had a horrible feeling that someone was keeping an eye on *me,* over the next few days. I never saw anybody, but I had that sensation when all the hairs on your spine prickle slightly, that someone was near me. Often I turned, looked around, pulled doors open suddenly, in case someone was lurking behind them. I paid little heed to the strange creakings that come and go in old buildings, because they bore no relation to the strange tingle down my spine, which often came when the timbers were at their quietest. At first, I suspected Frau F. of using secret passages, hidden in the castle walls, to spy on me, suspected her of slipping noiselessly around the place, always keeping me in her sight, for some nefarious purpose of her own.

It was several days before I exposed the fallacy of this argument to myself, while in the library tower. As part of my paranoia, I had examined the entrance to the tower quite carefully, followed the staircase all the way around and taken measurements with string (the only satisfactory way of dealing with spiral staircases), and I was reasonably satisfied that there was no space unaccounted for, at least no space wide enough to accommodate a human being. There may have been the old rat-run under the floorboards, but the tower was the one place I was sure had no secret panels, trapdoors or hidden entrances out of which Frau F. could suddenly pop.

How could I be so sure? Because of the windows. None of them were deep-set, there was never more than six inches of stone protruding inward from the glass. The glass was so old it was beginning to reveal the liquid it had once been; the flow-lines and whorls distorted the landscape outside. One day the window might turn to sand. I had heard of that happening with old, rare glass— a sudden knock to the cabinet in which it was stored, a loud clap of thunder, and then there was only a little heap of dust, sand, and silica, devitrified. Funny how the molecules remembered they used to be separate, not part of this new glass thing they had joined.

I spent a great deal of time staring out of the tower windows. Having established that there could be no concealed passages, and having a key to lock myself in with, I passed my days in the north tower. It had electricity, of a ropy 1930s sort, which had to be turned on at a mains box with a square handle that you pulled up to turn the power on. Under a pile of books I had found an electric bar-heater, and once it had been on for a couple of hours, I could keep my gloves off for long enough to do some useful work.

The tower went up four floors. The top one was empty, I didn't know why; the roof was sound. I decided to move everything that was standing on the floor or in boxes on the "ground" floor of the tower (which was at first-floor level of the rest of the castle) up to the top floor, where I could catalogue the books myself, or at least make lists of titles, and search for the main catalogue, if there was one.

It took almost a week before I discovered that indeed there was a catalogue, hidden in an ordinary-looking mahogany cabinet on the first floor. When I opened the door, it revealed the familiar rows of little wooden drawers full of cards, each card having the name of the book written in beautifully calligraphed letters above the details. It appeared to have been constructed in the last century, for the black ink had browned with age, yet the handwriting was still clear to me. There were updatings, in two or three different, more recent hands, but each card bore a complicated series of letters that seemed to refer to the book's location in the library. I could see no shelf-marks on the bookcases themselves, but I felt sure that the system had a logic of its own.

Above the card index were two shelves, bearing two ancient black-bound ledgers. With difficulty, I eased the first of these off its shelf, sneezing as a cloud of dust rose up. The ledger was entitled simply *Libri Novi* which I managed to translate as *New Books*. New several centuries ago. I hefted the book over to the heavy-footed oak table, and began to turn the thick sagging pages. The titles were wonderful, but all in Latin: *Liber artis auriferae, quem Chemiam vocant*. The book of making gold, which they call chemistry. Or alchemy. There was a hobby for rainy afternoons. I could have my own laboratory. But knowing my luck, I'd probably burn down half the castle, as apparently Theobald the Ugly had in 1537. Still, where would Frankenstein have been if he had been poor, and had had no castle with an indoor lab? Trying to make a monster out of bits of wood and string on the kitchen table, that's where.

Anyway, I struggled for days with the catalogue, comparing it to the books on the shelves, but I could make no sense of their order. Sometimes books on the same subjects were lumped together, and sometimes they weren't. At one point I found a large collection of medieval medical textbooks, with the most grisly illustrations I had ever seen. The primitiveness, the simplicity of the drawings seemed more shocking than full color photographs; the drawings of dissections looked the product of wanton barbarity rather than scientific research. The compulsion to read on, to see *all* the pictures, was strong, but I managed to close the pages and hold them fast shut, one hand on the binding to keep the images from escaping out into the room, stop the ghastly severed limbs from hopping out. Keeping my elbow on the book of horrors, I picked up a much smaller, inoffensive black-bound volume: *De Venenis*. Of Poisons.

Here the illustrations, though few, were charming: flowers, leaves, the occasional insect. I understood very little, and most of the plants were unknown to me, apart from the yew berries and laburnum pods. Yet, despite the innocuousness of the little volume, a creeping tide of nausea slid over me as I sat at the oak table, my feet on the bar beneath it, the dusty books spread about. The sense of internal unease grew, and my feet began to feel distant, unrelated to me. I dropped the book, and lay facedown on the table, clutching my cold forehead, feeling tiny fragments of book-dust stick to my cheek.

I'd seen *Name of the Rose*, in which there was a book with poisoned ink, where anyone licking their fingers as they turned a page would die a swift-poisoned death. I hadn't thought to wear gloves. And where better to place a poison than in a book called *On Poisons?* I lay very still, the nausea rising and falling, for a long while, before I decided I would have to try and make myself sick.

Trying didn't come into it. I was halfway across the room when I knew, with an unstoppable certainty, that I had to throw up. I rushed to the window, wrenched it open, and was noisily sick down the outside of the tower. I hoped it would rain soon, or snow again. Afterward, I was trembling, but felt a bit better. I needed a cup of tea.

Back in the pantry of the Master's Apartments, as I waited for the kettle to boil, I thought over what I'd eaten that day. Poisoned porridge oats? Off milk? I'd made breakfast myself, and I'd been eating the same thing for weeks. Lunch? Frau Feldstein could have put anything into it, and I'd have lapped it up and asked for seconds. Why would she want to poison me? I tried to talk myself out of this line of thought. For heaven's sake, it was probably just something that had disagreed with me. Maybe the meat in the stew I'd had for lunch was a little past its best. Maybe it was chopped-up sewer rat or one of the neighbors. I hadn't seen Elsa since that day with Rudi, though Georg had been up to the castle with deliveries, and I had been down to the gatehouse for a lesson with Beate, Elsa's sister. Did I have other neighbors? Probably not, now. I'd had meat stew quite a lot recently.

I spat into the sink several times, trying to clear the bitter taste, and when the kettle finally boiled (what they say about watched pots is entirely true), I put two teabags into my cup. I needed tea squared, super-tea. Nothing acts faster than tannin.

One cup of dyna-mud later, I felt human again, but when Frau Feldstein brought me my supper-tray, I glared at her suspiciously. "What are you having for supper?" I asked bluntly. "Are you having the same thing?"

She nodded.

"Well, it seems silly, you bringing a tray all the way up here. I could come down tomorrow and eat in the kitchen. I think it would save you a lot of trouble." And I can keep an eye on you, and insist we swap meals at the last moment, like they always do in films, so the wrong person drinks from the poisoned chalice. It's funny, I had wanted to die before, but the moment I felt someone was trying to kill me, I was ready to try every trick in the book to keep myself alive.

"It is as the Countess wills," she said flatly, and turned

on her heels, her footsteps echoing down the corridor.

It took me eight attempts to find which gloomy vault contained the kitchen the next day, but I persevered, and I watched Frau Feldstein serve up the food, and I could have sworn there was nothing to choose between my lunch-plate and hers. There was no bitter aftertaste or strange gritty bits in the onion pie with potatoes; everything seemed normal. And yet, that afternoon, back in front of the two glowing molten-metal red electric bars, there came once again the stirrings of nausea, the slow gorge rising. This time, there was no hesitation, and I headed back to the Master's Apartments and its bathroom, my shuffling feet taking up an urgent rhythm as I drew close.

Slamming the door back on its hinges, I dropped to my knees on the cold black-tiled floor, and rested my elbow on the toilet seat. An infinite number of tortured seconds passed, until the worst seemed to be over.

As I straightened up from my ignominious slouch over the toilet bowl, my eye fell on the dusty blue box behind the cistern. It wasn't poison. It was worse than that.

9

I was pregnant. My grandmother, who largely brought me up, had told me, "Morning sickness? Rubbish! I was fine in the mornings. It was the evenings were bad. I could scarce stand up to make your father's tea. Terrible, terrible. I'd be bent over the kitchen sink all evening." Maybe evening sickness was hereditary.

I remembered, as I looked at the nascent cobweb on the pale blue cardboard box, that I hadn't had a period in seven weeks. It wasn't just stress and upheaval that had stopped them; it was hormonal disturbance on a massive scale. I tried to put my finger in the waistband of my jeans, and realized that they felt tight, crushingly tight. Even when I relaxed, there was little room in those trousers. Oh my God, maternity clothes.

I decided to phone Rudi, after I'd had a cup of wake-the-dead tea, but just as I was about to dunk the second teabag in my cup, I stopped myself, folded the second teabag back on top of all the other little white pillows in their cardboard trunk. I was pregnant now. Who knew what effect strong tea could have? Then I thought, Sod it, and pulled out the recently spared bag to go to its watery grave. Funny, though, how you go from, "Hell, I'm pregnant" to "My baby" in under five minutes. Wonder if Rudi would be amused?

I reached him after a dozen warbles of the phone. "Rudi, does Munich have a branch of Mothercare?"

"What's Mothercare?" he asked.

"It's a place where you go to buy maternity clothes, baby things, that sort of stuff."

"Is this a present for someone?"

"No, it's for me."

There was a long pause. "What do you need?"

"All kinds of things. I'm pregnant!" I said brightly. "And Rudi, I keep throwing up, and I feel terrible and my jeans are too tight. . . ." And suddenly I was sobbing down the phone at him.

He was superb. He clucked and made shushing noises and told me how pleased he was, and how I would be absolutely fine, and he would drive over on Friday night, and it was already Thursday, so no need to panic, everything would be one hundred percent fine. Eventually, I stopped crying, mopped off the phone a bit, and let him get back to work.

I was shaken up by how much I suddenly needed him, wanted him to be with me. To distract myself, I phoned my sister, who was working nights, but she forgave me for interrupting her sleep when she found out why I was calling.

"That's fantastic!" she squealed. "I'm really pleased. The boys will have a cousin! Tell me, do you start to throw up about five every evening?"

I groaned. "Now she tells me. Did you?"

"Yes, like clockwork, until I was three months gone. How many weeks are you?"

I thought about this. "Four or five weeks, maybe, I

don't know." I paused. "You mean I could be throwing up for another couple of *months?*"

"Yes," she said with glee. "Isn't it terrible! Remember Gran?"

We both chorused, "Terrible, terrible." Then I said, "Will you come and stay with me when I have the baby?"

"You bet. But don't count your ova before they've hatched. Not every baby stays the course."

"Yeah, yeah." Her bluntness had no effect on me. "Now, what do I do, the next few weeks?"

"Hie thee to a surgery, for starters." Jenny took me through a few important details, such as giant-sized bras, while I listened, comforted by the mundane details, the things to do.

☩

It was that week, while I was busy with lists, and vague plans, thoughts about baby names, cots, and a million trivia, that I received a letter from Dr. Schuber. I had expected a congratulatory, or at least neutral missive, perhaps with news of my former colleagues. The bleak, almost blunt little note was out of key with my mood, and I did my best to put it from my mind, but I left it in the pantry, and every time I made a cup of tea, I read his words again.

> *My dear Ella,*
>
> *I expect by now you are settled in Schloss van Drachenfels. I fear I may have done you a grave disservice by introducing you to Rudi. I would ask you not to mention this letter to him, but wish you to reconsider whether he has your best interests at heart.*
>
> *There is the opportunity of a part-time conservator's job at the Fitzwilliam Museum, Cambridge, which I can arrange to have held open for the next few weeks. If you have any cause to doubt the wisdom of your*

recent actions, please return to England. I would not
say this if I did not feel concern for you, together with
regret at the part that I have played in this. You can
write, or telephone me at any time.
Assuring you of my friendship at all times,
Yours,
Manfred Schuber.

Bit late, Dr. Shuber, I thought. I'm expecting. And
besides, I was fine. I had no regrets about marrying Rudi.
When I thought back to how horrible my room in London
was, why would I ever want to return to that sort of life?

✠

I was almost feverish by the time Rudi arrived, I wanted
him so much. I had been down to the portrait gallery
twice already, to look at his youthful picture and to talk to
it; it was the nearest thing I had to the real Rudi. In my
more rational moments, I knew I was being irrational. I
had barely spoken to Rudi in weeks, had only ever spent a
couple of weeks with the man, and suddenly he was the
most important thing in my life.

I kept thinking back to that night we had spent
together in the castle, and in particular his kiss, that morning, in bed together, half asleep. A thousand trivial impressions came to mind, ones I hadn't even realized I'd stored.
Was it pregnancy sending my balance off-beam? One
minute I was heaving, the next paranoid, then elated and
exultant. It had to be hormones. That one kiss couldn't
have changed anything much. Couldn't have made me
long to see him again with the intensity of an oxyacetylene
welding flame.

I said nothing to Frau F., other than that the Count
would be coming for the weekend, and that I would resume
eating in the Master's Apartments while he was there.

My pregnancy was too precious to share with anyone

other than Rudi, and I longed for the sound of his car winding up the road. It was long after dark before he came, by which time I was exhausted with nausea and nerves. I waited upstairs when I heard the car arrive. Within moments he hurried in, looking peculiarly nervous.

"My dear, how *are* you?"

"OK, apart from being sick all the time," I sulked.

"*Gott in Himmel. Gott in Himmel.* We did it." He shook his head in disbelief.

"Well, isn't that what you wanted?"

"Yes, of course." He took my hand and patted it. "I just had no idea—so quick, my dear." He sat down on the arm of the sofa, and leaned over me. "You must see a good doctor—I will arrange a specialist in Munich, and the hospital—they will be the best."

"I don't want to go to Munich." I was still grumpy, but he took it all very well. He humored me, patted my hand a few more times, and made me a cup of tea, until I stopped grousing, and ruffled his almost spiky blond hair. We both laughed, he threw another log on the fire, and I was happy and at peace.

✠

The peace lasted all day Saturday and over half of Sunday, until I went to fetch a book from the library to show Rudi, the sweet little book on poisons that had caught my eye earlier in the week.

I hurried back through the dim passages, the chill library unappealing after the heat of the sitting room, and Rudi. I was about to push aside the tapestry at the entrance to the Apartments, when I heard a voice. Rudi's voice, speaking *sotto voce,* which intrigued me.

I paused by the curtain, one hand almost touching the fabric.

"No, I tell you, never phone me when I'm, here," he

said. "Yes, I'm fairly sure, now go away. Ssh. Yes, I still love my little poodle. Bye." And a snap as he turned the phone off.

I waited by the door, several long moments, then marched a few steps in place before pulling the curtain aside to enter the corridor of the Master's Apartments. Rudi stood at the far end by the window, telephone still in his hand.

"Oh, there you are," I said.

He looked at the phone. "Just about to call for tea. You would like some afternoon tea?"

Too slick, too fast. "No, don't want any. I expect I'll throw up soon. I generally do, about this time."

He looked at me then, sharply, but I wasn't joking. I could feel my lower lip begin to curl over and turn downward. Who was Rudi's "little poodle?" His secretary? I turned and headed for the bathroom, unwilling to let him see the rage and jealousy on my face. He could attribute my expression to nausea if he chose, but if I said one word, one tiny betraying word, he would know I had overheard. I no longer had the strength to struggle with myself, to control my emotions, so disappearing was my only defense. I slammed the bolt across the bathroom door and sank onto the floor, digging my fists into my eyes until I was sure the tears had been pushed back as far down the ducts as they would go. Then I squeezed my mouth with my hands a few times, until it had relearned how to smile, and stopped trembling. I might not have looked very convincing, but I was damned if I was going to spend the whole night in the loo.

I came out to find Rudi engrossed in a book, so I slunk into an armchair. Without looking up, he said, "Everything all right?"

"Mm," I mumbled. I didn't want to speak to him. I began to play with the braiding on a cushion, following the twists with one finger, over, under, over, under. We ignored each other in tense silence, until Rudi decided to ring for tea anyway, and I felt the first groundswell of evening sickness rise.

My obvious suffering brought out the kindly streak in him, and he was gentle toward me. Nevertheless the mood of the evening was marred now, without either of us mentioning it, and I was relieved when the time came for him to return to Munich. I saw him off with the briefest of murmurs, and when he kissed me goodbye, I stood immobile, responseless. He touched me on the elbow and let me go; I crawled back upward through the darkness, feeling as bleak and unloved as the castle itself.

I lay on the sofa for a long time, like a medieval knight on a tomb. If a knight had a dog beneath his feet, it meant he had died at home. I needed a dog beneath my feet, before I turned to marble. Something warm, something alive. The need for life and activity grew to a point where I had to turn the television on just for the noise.

The reception was good, this high up the mountain. There was an old Jerry Lewis/Dean Martin film, which normally I'd never have watched, but I was too depressed to change channels. The whole thing had been dubbed into German, so the details passed me by, and I was inventing the dialogue as I watched, so I can't claim to have been fully tuned in.

The room was dark, the curtains drawn, with only the flicker of the TV to illuminate my surroundings. I sat on one end of the sofa, a mohair rug over my knees, my feet curled up under me as I half-lay across the armrest on my right side. Despite the fire, my left side seemed to be growing colder and colder. For a long time I remained unaware of this, but then a slow prickle of unease told me the cold was unusual. I turned around to look at the rest of the room, but there was nothing there.

Then, as I concentrated on the screen I became certain that there was something in the room with me. I could see nothing, feel nothing, except an unusual sense of cold—but it was winter in the mountains, after all. Yet the sensation persisted, like the non-sound of electricity when the television is on but the sound is turned off. A high-frequency hum, technically inaudible but still detectable. As I watched Jerry Lewis cackle over some terrible gag, I slid my eyes slowly to the side, and began to see something—a shape.

I turned my face, but the image vanished. Puzzled, I returned my gaze to the TV screen. Once more, I gave a sideways glance, looking from the very corners of my eyes. This time I was more careful, and as I looked, my face turned forward, the image began to coalesce into more definite outlines. A young woman in a long forest-green dress. Younger than me, no more than twenty. A little shorter than me, darker hair swept back into a bun, a sharply pointed chin. The image began to clarify, like a photograph in a developing tank, until I could see her quite clearly, while still seeing the sofa through her.

If you've ever come across one of the "Magic Eye" books, where three-dimensional images are made up out of rows of dots, concealed within a seemingly random pattern, which resolve, as you look, into extraordinary clear pictures, you'll know how it was. For a long time you can see nothing. Then you discover there's a knack, to look without looking, to see beyond, to trick your brain into seeing a different level of images.

By watching television, and only allowing the corners of my eyes to do the looking, I was able to see something not in the usual field of vision. At first, I dared say nothing, unsure of the image's origin.

Then I said, still looking forward, "I can see you, you know. You're wearing a green dress."

The thing smiled. "Yes, it was always my favorite." She spoke in German, a clear, old-fashioned speech, distant yet audible.

"Who are you?" Slowly I turned my head, willing the image not to change. The edges flickered, but I kept my vision steady.

"Mathilde, Countess von Drachenfels. You are a Drachenfels too—you bear the blood."

"I—the blood?"

"If you did not have the blood, you could not see me. You are not a Drachenfels born? That cannot be."

"No, no, I'm not, I'm just married to. . . ."

She stretched out a thin hand toward me. "You bear the blood—the next heir. You can see me now, but I have seen you for a long time."

Nobody warns you about this in books on pregnancy. It's not just hormones; you start seeing the shades of your husband's ancestors.

"What—what do you want?"

Her smile returned, sadder this time. "A little heat, a little light, just for a little while. There is so little else. I will see more of you later."

Slowly she began to fade, like ink under ink-remover, then she was gone. I twisted my head from side to side in an effort to keep her, keep her clear, but there was nothing I could do. Like an ember fallen on the hearth, the light and color went out of her and I was alone again.

10

I went to bed early that evening, shaking my head at myself. I was spending so much time on my own, I was beginning to hallucinate, inventing imaginary playmates for myself. Quite usual in children, but at my age? And yet—how could I have invented that voice, that accent? A Dowager-Duchess pompous accent, yet spoken entirely naturally by a young woman, her words odd but clear—and she knew I was pregnant. I had told only Rudi, and even if Frau Feldstein had been eavesdropping, how could she have conjured up Mathilde, and the cold she brought with her, like an icy current in the sea that you swim into by accident.

Over and over I said to myself, "What the hell was *that*?" until I fell into a listless sleep.

✠

The next morning was bright and sunny, and in the broad sight of breakfast I managed to convince myself that the apparition of the previous night had been a dream, that I had nodded off on the sofa, confused dreams with reality, been over-tired. Now, the late-winter sunshine reflecting in the silver coffeepot revived me, and cast off the doubts of a dark evening. I buttered some more toast, and finished the paperback I had been reading the day before, trying not to lodge toast crumbs in the middle between the pages, not precisely the spine, but close enough, so that when you closed the book there was a faint crushing from the center. It's the reason why you shouldn't read at the table; it's not so much bad manners, but it wrecks your books. I was on my own, I could read all I liked, but I made sure it was only the latest detective stories that received buttery fingerprints on their margins.

From outside came faint nest-building twitters, the early sounds of spring; they tempted me from the library. I put on my thick sheepskin coat and gloves, looped a red Angora scarf around my neck, and stamped along the dark corridors on the ground floor, out to the courtyard where I had first entered the castle. I had noticed, the previous evening, while seeing Rudi off, a stone archway that seemed to lead off into a tangle of greenery—or brownery, at this time of year, the bare stems of shrubs wet and barren, frost-bitten, black dead leaves at their feet, rotting beneath the snow. I swayed a little as my feet slid from the icy path, and moved onto the grass, which crunched with frost. In the courtyard, the snow was still packed tight between the cobbles, but as I emerged through the ensnarled shrubs onto the hillside, the sun was beginning to melt the snow. It was hardly a pleasure garden, the ground fell away so steeply, but there had been a planned layout once upon a time; hedges flanked the path which led to a veritable Sleeping Beauty thicket near the bottom of this side of the hill, a high stone wall beyond.

The snow had drifted, leaving only a light covering at the top of the slope, but as I started to descend, my feet sank deeper and deeper beneath the crust until I abandoned the journey, the bottom of my trouser legs heavy with encrusted snow. There was no heat in the weak sun, and I had to keep moving, so I trailed around the neglected bushes, trying to identify them, but only the evergreen laurel and the euphorbias were recognizable, souvenirs of the suburban London I had left behind. The rest, all dead twigs, as if some poisoner had emptied his latest concoction at the roots, were beyond my horticultural grasp. The tangle of interlocking, overgrown shrubs began to depress me with their deadness, and started to take on a strangling malevolence. Dead—and they wanted to take me with them to the Underworld. Time to go in.

I kicked my boots against the castle wall until the wet clumps of snow flew from me, then ducked back into the doorway, the heavy oak protesting as I slammed the door into place. I let the labyrinth lead me, back to the north tower, the library, where I lit the fire, and waited until it was going before hanging my sheepskin from the high back of an ornately carved, but deeply uncomfortable chair.

My favorite chair was a blue velvet Victorian one, buttoned, overstuffed, on squeaky castors, and with a curved back that wrapped itself around me as if made to measure. My one regret was that it didn't swivel.

Having come to grips with the method of cataloguing, I still have a few boxes of books to unpack and catalogue, my handwriting appearing peculiarly English compared to all the hands that had gone before. My mind kept wandering from the dusty heaps of books I had laid on the table, wandering back to the dark-green ghost of yesterday. Another Countess. Were there more of them, or did the two of us share a lonely possession of this grim castle?

I had to know more, know that she *had* existed, was not some conjuring trick of my own mind, but a genuine contact with the Otherworld. There were family archives on the next floor up, boxes of deeds, collections of household bills, letters. I hadn't had time to look at them properly, they had seemed less important than the bound volumes in front of me. Impatiently, I threw my pen down and seizing an oil-light, bounded up the winding stone stairs to the next floor, the fuel in the lamp sloshing dangerously. Here the light was grayer, dimmer, for I had not cleaned the windows, and the dirt of half a century clouded the panes.

A family tree, not updated recently, ending with Rudi's grandfather, hung on the wall above the mahogany drawers which contained all the family's papers. Hurriedly I traced a finger over the various branches and twigs of the family. There were two Mathildes, but one was *1840–1860* and the other was—1402–1420. My Green Lady had to be the more recent Mathilde. The dress was right. And I would never have understood medieval German. Or did ghosts learn to update their language, to communicate in a more modern idiom? And if they *did* learn, how? Easier to believe that only the more recently departed bothered to come back—after a few centuries the language barrier would be too great.

Mathilde, Mathilde, Mathilde. I gave up trying to see if anything had been cataloged, and let my fingers pull out drawers at random. I found that serendipity, success by randomness, happened as much as success by painstaking labor. Mark always used to say, joking, instead of "good luck," "may the random factors align." For me, they often had.

Not thinking, sorting, ordering, I let my fingers feel through the drawers, until they reached of their own accord into the back of the bottom drawer, and tugged. Wedged in, between the back of the drawer and the neat folios of agricultural rents, was a black morocco-leather volume, small and flat, with spidery writing across the flyleaf: *Mathilde von Escheng. Not to be read without her permission.*

I slammed the drawer shut, and held the book close to the lamp. Feeling awkward, I said aloud, "I'm going to read this."

There was no reply, no sudden dimming of the lamp, no gust of cold wind to knock the book from my hand, so I took it back downstairs, to the fireside and the blue velvet chair, the threadbare footstool and the slow hiss of the lamp-flame. It was almost midday, but I had a little while to make a start before lunchtime.

Mathilde von Esching, it turned out, was eighteen and living near Lübeck, and spent her days in a girlish round of sketching and afternoon tea-parties, needlework and concerts, so I skipped the closely written pages until I found the word "Drachenfels":

✠

We put up a skating-party after luncheon, and took the carriage out to where the river floods the marshes. The ice was new but hard, and my skates flew across it as if they were dancing by themselves. My sisters and I had the ice and the fields and the sky to ourselves, skating almost until sunset; we were turning to go home when a dark figure came from nowhere, skimming across the ice. The man in the black cloak skated right up to us. His carriage horse was lame, he said, and his coachmen would have to walk the horse back. Were we returning to the center of Lübeck, he asked, and might he accompany us there? The governess was very shocked, but when he introduced himself as Albrecht, Graf von Drachenfels, she relented a little, and though she was cold toward him, she consented to his taking a seat in our carriage. We left him close to his hotel, for which he was effusive in his gratitude. We had exchanged no words during the carriage ride, other than commonplace sentiments regarding the weather, and the pleasant situation of Lübeck, but his thanks as he descended were most charming and gentlemanly. . . .

Von Drachenfels called today, to pay his respects to my parents. He came with Herr von Paasche, an old acquaintance of Papa's. They sat in Papa's study for over an hour before coming out to be presented to the ladies. I was in the drawing room, sketching Mama's pug puppy, the most comical little dog you ever saw. We were all laughing at it when von Drachenfels entered the room; I looked up and felt my heart quicken. I knew that to my own eyes, I looked very well in my red wool dress, but I hoped that he would find me so. He smiled at me most gravely, and admired my sketch. The gentleman stayed for tea, and talked with Mama for a long time. I wonder what he does in Lübeck . . . ?

Albrecht came again today, with some music, a new song I had never heard before. He turned the pages while I attempted to play, and he hummed the tune for me, over and over, until I had the trick of it. He is so unlike the young men I have ever met before; he knows everything that will delight me. He is the most excellent companion. . . .

It has been almost three months since Albrecht first approached us over the ice. How much longer will he stay? I do not think I can bear it if he returns south, to his family seat. He has told me he must go soon, his father is anxious for his return. Naturally his duty lies with his family. But oh! How I wish it lay with me. . . .

Papa was very somber all evening, and said he must speak with me privately after breakfast tomorrow. I wonder what the matter can be? Mama seemed flustered, but retired early, with one of her sick headaches. I do hope she will be improved by morning. . . .

I am astounded. Albrecht has asked Papa if he would consent to our marriage. Albrecht had not breathed one word of this to *me*. Naturally, it is proper to ask a parent's permission if one might pay one's respects, but I had no idea that our daily encounters had grown, in his breast, to assume the same significance they held for me, to echo the sentiments within my own breast—that my heart was answered. Strange, I had always thought I would feel that answering call thrilling through my veins, without need for words. yet with Albrecht, until the word came, via Papa, *Papa* if you please, I had no such presentiment. How unexpected life is. Of course I shall accept, but Mama is much shocked. He is seventeen years older than I, and Mama feels it cannot be quite an equal match. Both in birth and fortune he outranks me, and the disparity in our ages can only add to the differences between us, but true love conquers all. I know it will.

✠

I put the diary aside at this point, staring unblinking at the dusty surface of the desk. Poor Mathilde! So convinced that her life had taken a turn for the better. I didn't want to read on, to find out where things went horribly wrong. I could guess. But I wanted this love story, like all love stories, to end happily, the woman with the man she loved, and no question of whether their love was strong enough for the life in store for them. Had I kept a diary of my own, the tale would have been bleak from the start. At least Mathilde had had moments of happiness with her own von Drachenfels. I felt a little weepy and shaken after the last few pages of the journal, since they made Mathilde all the more real, all the less dismissible.

She came to me again that evening, as I sat in front of the television, her dark-green dress shimmering slowly into view. As I became aware of her presence, I reached for the remote, and pressed the mute button, stilling the noise of the program.

"Hello. I found your journal," I said.

"Yes, I wanted you to. Thank you."

"Why? Why did you want me to? What difference would it make?"

"I hoped—if you understood me—we could be friends."

I stared at her, but the intense gaze made her flicker too much on my retinas. Only if I turned my eyes away did her image remain steady.

"Friends? Yes, I'd like that. But—"

"I know, I know, we're worlds apart. But out here, I've been so bored, so lonely. There are others with me, and yet. . . ." Her hesitation mirrored my own.

"Yes, of course I'd like to be friends." Instinctively I reached toward her hand.

"No, don't do that. We can't touch, it—it does something to your skin, it's not comfortable."

I withdrew my hand. "If you say so."

"No one touches a ghost without feeling ill. If the two worlds collide, it pulls all the energy out of both."

"You know that you're a ghost?" I whispered.

"Yes, just as you know that you're not."

"So, tell me about being a ghost."

"I'd like to, but we are about to be interrupted. I will come again, and stay longer. One thing I know, ghosts and the living cannot be together for too long—it is harmful. To the living mostly. I must go."

She faded before I could stop her. As I sat gazing at the spot where she had been, there was a tap at the door.

"Frau Feldstein here, Countess. Forgive me for disturbing you, but a telegram came. I thought you might want to see it straight away."

"A telegram? Yes, of course. Thank you so much. You did the right thing. Thank you."

She handed it to me and left, without showing any sign of curiosity, without hovering. I ripped open the thick envelope and pulled out the printed sheet.

Come to Wiesbaden at once. Your Aunt Adalheid.

11

Wiesbaden. At vons. But I didn't *have* an Aunt Adalheid! I phoned Rudi to check though, the very next morning.

"Oh, that's my mother's sister Adalheid," he said airily. "Yes, by all means go and stay. She has an imperious manner. Don't worry about her telegram, it's her way of issuing an invitation. I think you should go. George will drive you."

I put the phone down, ready to scream. No one ever *asked* me if I wanted to go. People just assumed I was a parcel, to be posted to the next address. On the one hand, I needed the break, needed to be away from the castle and its strange occupants. On the other hand, oh what the hell, why argue with myself? The events of the last day or two had left me uncertain, no longer convinced my own perceptions could be trusted.

I rang Georg at the gatehouse and said, "I seem to need to go to Wiesbaden, to Rudi's Aunt Adalheid. When would be convenient?"

"We can leave this afternoon, Countess."

I sighed. I wasn't at ease with the title rather than my name. "Have you met Aunt Adalheid before? What's she like?"

Georg muttered something about *Junkermentalität,* which I think is German for "upper-class bastards."

"Thanks, Georg. Sorry to put you out like this."

"No, no." He sounded surprised. "You're most undemanding."

Thanks, Georg. "OK, I'll be ready after lunch."

✠

The navy-blue BMW was on top form, and so was Georg, all the way to Wiesbaden, and it was a long drive. I realized I hadn't told him or Elsa of my pregnancy, and he was gratifyingly pleased by the news. He was keen to come up to the castle to fix up a room for the nursery, but he understood when I said that I wanted to wait until I was past the three-month danger point. If my pregnancy continued after that, I'd probably stay pregnant, and then I could make plans for pastel-colored wallpaper and a cot.

As we chatted, down the winding mountain roads and up the Autobahn, I realized how little I knew Georg and Elsa, for all they lived only a few hundred yards away. I had lived those bleak winter months in almost total isolation, barely even making contact with Frau Feldstein. No wonder I was beginning to see things. Stupidly, it was all self-inflicted. There *were* people around, I could have taken regular German lessons with Elsa's sister instead of skipping them. Too late for regrets. My German was about to have to face a test on its own.

We came off the motorway through and around the hillsides, vineyards and past the river. Then came the usual industrial fringes of any town, all the unsightly labor and machinery banished to the edge of civilization. Then we drove past the gray industrial units into the center, from badlands to heartland. Everything in Wiesbaden was clean, well-spaced. No poor and huddled masses yearning to be free.

I couldn't put my finger on the difference between Wiesbaden and any British town until I realized there was nothing scruffy anywhere. Not just the absence of litter, but no posters glued up anyhow, half-soaked off by the rain, half-pasted over by another, later poster. No peeling plaster, leaning bus-stops or decaying buildings. Nothing ramshackle or ill-maintained. Where did Germans go for scruffiness? Berlin, I supposed, which is why everyone thought it so exciting, but even there, they inherited their scruffiness from the East. Give them another five years, it'll all be rebuilt or scrubbed down.

✠

We drove through Wiesbaden in twilight, at that moment when lights are switched on indoors but before the curtains have all been drawn, the blinds lowered and the shutters closed. Off the main streets, every house revealed a tableau of other lives: the old lady pulling dead leaves off the begonia on her windowsill, the child with the marmalade cat squashed uncomfortable to his chest, the couple clearing jigsaw pieces from their dining table, the lit but empty room that someone had just left.

Then the high hedges, the metal gates, with larger houses behind. Older houses, set apart, reserved.

Georg rang the bell at one of these, then put my case on the doorstep. I thought for one moment that he would turn and leave me there on the step, like an orphan, and I was going to clutch his sleeve, but he stayed.

After several moments, the door opened slowly, to show a black-clad young woman being elbowed out of the way by a tall, elegant white-haired lady who exuded refinement as saints are said to exude sanctity.

"Ah, Ella. Come in. Have your man bring your bag."

She turned, and I cast a helpless look at Georg. He winked at me, picked up my case, and followed me into the marble-floored hall.

Aunt Adalheid gave Georg instructions. "Up the stairs, first room on the right, for the bags. The kitchen is through that door there. The cook will see that you are fed."

I mumbled my thanks to Georg, but he was gone, and I was being led into the drawing room, all pink sofas and rose-patterned cushions. There was a lavish display of china, both plates and figurines, on shelves and bureaus and tiny tables, culminating in a massive figure of a Harlequin, in motley lozenges-patterned costume but with the curled cap of Mr. Punch, the purple tip of his cap bending down to meet a porcelain white chin that curled upward. At the same eye-level as the figure on a plinth was a lemon-crested cockatoo hanging wonkily from a mahogany perch.

Aunt Adalheid saw my glance. "Oh, Kiki falls off every time I open the door," she said, as she cuffed the cockatoo upright again. The bird had been a victim of gross taxidermal incompetence, its feathers bowing out at strange angles where it had been overzealously stuffed, its little black glass eyes set askew, and visible dirty fingerprints on the splayed tail-feathers.

"I know, I know, she's in a bit of a stage, but I couldn't face being without her all over again. I've had Kiki for a long time."

I smiled apologetically. "Did you have the bird—um—alive?"

"Yes, I've always had birds. Much better than husbands. They talk more, make less mess, and are much cheaper to feed. Plus you can keep them even after they're dead. Now sit down and tell me how you are."

I didn't resent the sharp change of subject. Aunt Adalheid was used to having her own way, but without it seeming like bullying. It was more a disregard for inessentials, as she saw life. Husbands probably fell into the category of inessentials. She rearranged her flowing navy jacket around her lap, while patting her trouser pockets, until she had found her cigarette lighter. She leaned over a wide table and clicked open a silver cigarette box, then waved it at me.

"Cigarette?"

I shook my head.

"You don't live forever, you know. Terrible thing to say, but there it is. Young people just don't seem to understand it. Never mind. How *are* you, in that gruesome castle?"

I hesitated before saying, "Fine, fine. It's a trifle cold at this time of year, but I expect it'll seem better in the summer."

Aunt Adalheid exhaled noisily, like a little dragon. "Rubbish, it's grisly all the time. Drove my sister mad. She kept muttering about ghosts. I never listened, of course. I was wrong there. I want to know now. Expect you'll need a Scotch first, I daresay, before you start telling stories."

She pulled up a footstool, lifted the needlepoint lid and hoisted out a bottle of Glenfiddich. I was fascinated, waiting for her to tear the top off with her teeth. Boringly, she handed the bottle to me, and went to fetch glasses from the rosewood bureau. Soon I was settled with a large heavy-bottomed glass full of whiskey. Her glass was only half full.

Disconcertingly, she noticed my glance again, her eyes far sharper than those of her dead avian friend. "I only pretend to drink a lot when I have company, so I can say rude things and be excused. You're family now, so I can say what I think. The question is, can you? You look to me as though you'll need at least a full glass before you tell me anything at all, except to give me a weather report on Schloss Drachenfels. I want more."

I looked at her, startled, and she laughed. "Now that
I'm old I can behave atrociously, but I still need an excuse
sometimes. Right, tell me everything young lady, starting
with my nephew. The boy never tells me anything."

I gave her a condensed account of my relationship
with Rudi to date, and a rather more detailed description
of the castle, my suspicions of poor Frau Feldstein, and
then, haltingly, my two encounters with Mathilde. At
some point Aunt Adalheid must have refilled my glass,
because when I finished speaking, it was still full, but I
was groggy with the effect of drink. "I suppose you think
I'm making it up," I muttered to the armrest of my chair.

"Too much time on your own? Seeing things? Incipi-
ent schizophrenia? Yes, that's what I thought with Anne-
Marie, my sister. She was the eldest, she always knew
best, so when it seemed she'd lost her marbles, I thought:
Serves her right. She tried to tell me, though. So did Rudi.
He had to go away to school very young, because of "the
lady in the smoke." He won't remember now, but when he
was three or four, he used to tell me about her. She frightened him very much. The lady in the smoke wore a green
dress, too. I should have listened then."

I shrugged. "What difference does it make? The castle's full of weird things. I'm pregnant with Rudi's child,
and now I'll probably go the way your sister did." I was
very tired.

Adalheid leaned forward and grasped my wrist. "No,
that's defeatist talk. There are rational explanations for
these things. You need life and young people and entertainment, that's all. Isolation brings no good to anyone.
Generations of isolated, lonely people have been unhappy
at Drachenfels. All you need is people. And a purpose."

Her piercing blue eyes gazed deep into mine, which
wavered, unable to hold her fixed stare. I had definitely
had too much whiskey. "Purpose?" I said. I could feel
myself wanting to give way, surrender to her belief that

she could save me. Then I shook my head. "What happens, happens."

She smiled—a sad, indulgent smile. "What happens is that you enjoy Wiesbaden. I've invited some young people to stay in a couple of days, once you are settled. Tomorrow I will show you around."

✠

The next morning, sunny breezes played over Wiesbaden as we took the air. Aunt Adalheid had inspected the clothes I had brought with me, and had dismissed them all as unsuitable—"They WILL NOT DO for Wiesbaden." She then lent me a large mint-green cashmere coat, which almost trailed along the ground. What with my increasing rotundity, I wandered around like an unripe pea as Aunt Adalheid greeted her various acquaintances with a lofty wave of the hand. Our tour of inspection ended in a cake-festooned *Konditorei*, where Aunt Adalheid *always* went on Tuesdays, to meet her cronies. She handed me over to them with sighs of exhaustion.

"I've had to walk all over the *whole* town," she boomed, as a frilly-aproned waitress hurried up. "I can't possibly go shopping as well. Frederike, *you* love shopping. Please do something with my niece. At once . . . oh yes, chocolate please, and Gugelhopf. My niece will have the same."

Frederike, a plump, benevolent-looking woman in her late sixties, smiled and patted my wrist. "Pink, my dear, you'll look adorable in pink. I know the very shop."

Both Aunt Adalheid and the third woman hooted. "Don't let her make you look like a poodle," Adalheid said bluntly. "Frederike has excellent taste—I even let her decorate my drawing room—but if it doesn't suit you, you must say so."

I smiled placatingly at all the women. "Yes—umm—whatever. Umm—it's just that—there's no need, really. I'll grow out of things fast."

"My niece is expecting, you know," Aunt Adalheid announced as a public broadcast.

Frederike beamed. "Then we'll have to go off to Frankfurt, so we can buy baby clothes as well. Oh, how lovely! Isn't it lovely?" she asked a pair of navy-suited elderly women who had taken the adjoining table.

They nodded and waved. They all seemed to know each other. I had fallen in with a gang of hardened cocoa-drinkers, who were making mysterious deals all around me. I understood nothing, but started to get that FBI-agent-in-peril feeling, "I'm in over my head, for God's sake get me out of here," or "Send back-up now." Within the space of two metal-handled glasses of hot chocolate, I had had my past and future rearranged to suit Aunt Adalheid's purposes. I was now the beloved and very close wife of her handsome nephew, with aspirations in the castle-refurbishment line. By lunchtime I had met "everyone who's important in Wiesbaden—the rest just work, you know."

Aunt Adalheid's view of society might have seemed idiosyncratic, but there was no doubt she was treated with respect wherever she went. Even her long-standing acquaintances showed a certain deference, but then her blunt manner, her instant scorn of woolly comments, encouraged caution.

⚜

Frederike was far easier to be with, but she shared with Aunt Adalheid a love of whiskey. Her chauffeur-driven white Mercedes was barely around the corner from Aunt A.'s before she had a bottle out from under her seat. A set of pewter beakers, with leather coverings, quickly followed from her handbag. "Here." She splashed a beaker of whiskey toward me before I had time to protest that I would be carsick, or that I was pregnant, and what about fetal alcohol syndrome . . . ?

However, no excuse for avoiding a drink carried any weight with Aunt Adalheid's set. I gritted my teeth, then ungritted them and drank. God knows what we'd end up buying—purple mohair hot-pants, probably. In maternity sizes. Still, it was Rudi's credit card. What the hell.

That was Frederike's motto, too, though she would have phrased it more genteelly. We ripped through a dozen shops, bought armfuls of pink clothes ("pink goes with everything, dear), flung them at the chauffeur, then tore back along the roads at eye-covering speeds while Frederike tried to recite Heine's greatest poems from memory, as if to prove that the afternoon hadn't been entirely one of crass materialism. I was beginning to regret the passivity of the morning. It had got me in with a bad crowd.

12

I was permitted a day of peace before Aunt Adalheid sprang into action once again.

"Of course, you haven't met any of Rudi's friends. He told me you were keen to set the castle in some kind of order, and I quite understand that you wouldn't want to entertain until the place is fit. So you must let me invite some people while you are here. Obviously the house is not so large, but there is room for a few of Rudi's friends and colleagues. I've invited some of the ones you must meet. And Easter's the ideal time—most people will have finished skiing, but won't yet be away for the summer. I managed to catch the Courchevals before they go to Provence. The Bölfingers are only in Heidelberg, too. Yes, I must make some phone calls to confirm."

I sat in the pink armchair while Aunt Adalheid continued her monologue, and watched while she performed it again in front of the housekeeper, the Courchevals and Bölfingers, the first in person, the latter two by means of modern telecommunication. She never paused long enough for me to detect any signs of agreement or dissent in her audience. She had made a plan, and all the universe had to do was fall in place around her. I was amused by her certainty, her sense of command. Had I been younger, the urge to say "No shan't" would have been strong within me, but now her force, like a waterfall, exhilarated me, her strength carried me in its wake, and a small element of it rubbed off onto me. My role seemed clear. I was the feeble niece who had to be jollied along, organized, taken out of herself. It was a role I fitted perfectly, and I was happy to let Adalheid play the all-wise, all-knowing aunt.

What pleased me most was that she had arranged for Rudi to come and stay for a couple of nights. I felt I had no right to say, "Rudi, I want to see you, please come," and would have despised myself for begging. Adalheid merely picked up the phone, and after bickering with Rudi's secretary ("I don't give a hoot about board meetings, I want to speak to him NOW"), said the German equivalent of, "Rudi, you blistering little pimple, shift your festering carcass over to Weisbaden for the weekend or else." I smiled to myself as I imagined Rudi's face, in his board meeting in Munich, listening to Aunt Adalheid steaming ahead.

The phone call to Rudi was the last of the sequence. All I'd had to do was sit on pink plumped-up cushions for an hour while tectonic plates, the earth's crust, shifted around me.

"I'm quite exhausted," said Aunt Adalheid in vigorous tones. "I think we deserve a little pick-me-up. Now, what do we have here?" She rummaged in the mahogany bureau, then filled a couple of brandy glasses almost to the brim with a clear liquid. "One of these, and we'll be our old selves in no time."

I took the glass gingerly. It seemed as though it should be bubbling from its test tube. "What is it?"

"Slivovitz. It's good for you."

I drank some. Dear God, please never let me drink

something that's bad for me. Every germ, every bacteria, every microorganism that ever contemplated taking up residence within me, was blasted into the stratosphere, exploded in some thermonuclear war of the alimentary canal. The tears rolling down my cheeks almost turned to steam as they hit the red-hot surface of my face.

"Are you feeling a bit low? Better have some more slivovitz."

I managed to gurgle no, dabbing at my eyes with a moth-eaten two-day-old tissue I'd found stuffed in the pocket of my jeans. I'd shredded it round the edges, trying to pull it out, because my jeans no longer fitted; my vanished waistline meant the zip no longer did its work, but was hidden, I hoped, by my baggy new jumper. I was a wreck, a pregnant gasping wreck. Never mind the baby being damaged by drink, it was about to kill *me* before it ever reached the baby, what was still an abstract non-real thing I somehow carried inside me. Now that the morning sickness seemed to be over, the reality of the pregnancy had faded again. I felt I was a fatter version of me, but still me. Not changed, the way I first felt when I knew. My size was going to force me into the clothes I had bought in Frankfurt with Adalheid's friend Frederike. Well, I'd match the sitting room, if nothing else.

✠

On Friday, the house hummed with preparations for the long weekend. I tried to help, but was shooed back into my room by assorted members of the household. My attempt to arrange flowers had been met with derisive scorn, so I gave up and went to sulk on my bed, with a lurid-jacketed detective story. Doors opened and closed, footsteps came and went, glasses clinked, silverware clanked, bedspreads flapped.

I sprawled across the white lace bedcovers, a woman under siege, with a sense that the enemy were coming,

best draw the wagons into a circle, or stockpile the stock-
ade or whatever one did in emergencies. Rolled bandages
or cleaned weapons. I should have held on to my *Girl
Guide Handbook*. There might have been a useful chapter
on stoicism. *Be Prepared,* the book said on the front. I
don't remember anything else about it.

Lunch was sandwiches, and at teatime I changed into
a pale blue woolen shirt-waister, or no-waister, more of a
dress that buttoned up the front and attempted to go in at
the waist. My hair was long now, pale and shining. I had
pale blue suede shoes on too, and skipped down the stairs
like Hansel and Gretel about to go out into the woods.
And we all know what happened to *them*.

☧

The Courchevals were the first to arrive, Sylvie and
Augustin. Every time Sylvie pronounced her husband's
name, she ended it with a little cry of distress—August-
ahhng. She was small, with waist-length dark hair, and
surprisingly child like for a woman of forty, with bright
pink lips and cheeks to match, the kind of colors I
painted on my dolls when I was six. Her cerise shirt did
horrible things for her burgundy suit. I wanted to like her,
really I did, but my color sense was too pained to greet
her with true enthusiasm.

August-*argh* I wasn't sure about. He was small, and
dark, and balding in an odd pattern, as if someone had
driven a tractor over his head, his remaining clumps of
hair spread in zigzags across a brown dome. He was tired
and said very little. A hard week at the bank, I supposed.
Aunt Adalheid had warned me that most of Rudi's friends
were in banking. He had on an immaculately-cut gray suit
and very shiny black shoes. Beside his wife he seemed so
understated as to be invisible, his muted greeting lost
beneath Sylvie's exclamations, her "oohs," her chatter
about the flight.

They spoke in French, Aunt Adalheid speaking a fluent and very formal French that I could understand perfectly, a funereal newsreader's voice. Slowly I began to realize from the questioning that Augustin had piloted his own plane from Paris. His exhaustion was due to the strain of having air-traffic control in one ear and Sylvie in the other.

"The skies are so busy at this time on a Friday," he explained wearily, in much the same tone as I used to say, "The North Circular was jammed solid,"—a resigned irritation. We want to go where we want to go, without let or hindrance, and though we know we can't, we want to all the same.

I asked Augustin when the best times to travel were, and he managed to rouse himself enough to discuss routes and cunning ways to avoid busy patches, but his heart wasn't in it. His eyes kept straying to his watch.

Aunt Adalheid understood perfectly, and rang for the maid to remove the tea-things. "You will want to relax before dinner, naturally," she said firmly. "If you require a drink beforehand, I have arranged for a selection to be in your room on a tray, but the maid can bring you whatever else you may need."

That was it, Augustin was off. Sylvie, giggling and flapping both hands in little "bye-ee" gestures, followed him at a more discreet pace.

Involuntarily, I said, "Hooh!" with relief, and Aunt Adalheid gave me one of her driest grins.

"Be nice to them—Augustin is one of Rudi's oldest friends. They were at INSTEAD together, when they were doing MBAs."

"So do you like them?" I asked.

"You tell me."

I glared at her. "I asked first."

"You need a drink as much as I do, dear."

"No, I don't. I haven't recovered from that plum stuff you gave me at lunchtime."

"Funny how temperamental pregnant women get. My sister was just the same. Convinced everyone was out to poison her."

"Was she?" I was struck by this. I had been so sure, weeks ago, of the same thing. "Do you know, that's funny, because I—"

Aunt Adalheid wasn't listening. "Must have a minute thimbleful before the Bölingers—oh, *Gott in Himmel.*"

The doorbell had just rung, an old-fashioned billowing peal. Not one of those modern electric buzzers, that say *bleaaat.* Footsteps across the marble-tiled hall, and the maid's face.

"Madame, Herr—"

"I know, I know." She rose and sailed out into the hall. "Heinrich, Rotraut! So pleased. Come in, come in. Meet my new niece, Ella."

Introductions again, a mention of the Courchevals' arrival, but no attempt to offer tea: Aunt Adalheid was too busy instructing the maid in how she wanted the Martinis. Covertly, the Bölfingers and I looked each other over, in case we were called upon to recognize each other again. Heinrich was a big, bluff man of over six foot, with an outdoors, red-brown complexion and brown hair, receding a little above the ears. Rotraut, too, was tall, with shoulder-length chestnut hair, glossy, swept off her face with a brown mock-crocodile skin hairband. Both wore dark green suits, and for this reason I christened them Tweedledum and Tweedledee. Neither was fat, they were simply solid, in a well-fed Teutonic Bürgerlich fashion. Families that had not been malnourished in generations. Dumplings at least twice a week. Not built for speed, but built to last.

They nodded at me from time to time, but I began to feel like the old crone at the fireside, the charity case, the one you've let in for a few moments to warm her aged bones and feed her a bowl of soup, before you fling her back outside, to return to her lowly hovel. Had I had dentures, I would probably have taken them out, and started muttering to myself, just for the attention.

I winked at the stuffed parrot. No one noticed. My martini grew warm in my hand. I sat the glass down behind my chair, so that Aunt Adalheid wouldn't realize I wasn't drinking it. The conversation turned to extraordinary goings-on at the Bundesbank, the nature of which I never quite grasped. Rotraut tried to ask me what I thought of the Euro as a currency, but my vocabulary wasn't up to it. In any language. I asked her if she had children.

"Yes, but we have someone to look after them." It was clear that this was not a valid topic for discussion. Talking about domestic arrangements in mixed company? My dear, it simply isn't done. I didn't know what *was* done, unfortunately. It wasn't that the Bölfingers were rude, simply that they met every comment of mine with amused blankness. I gave up again.

Just as I was debating the desirability of pretending to hunt for lice and then eating them, there was more bell-pealing, Aunt Adalheid sat to attention.

"That will be Rudi."

I sat upright too, ready to leap to my feet when my husband came in. I heard him bypass the maid in the hall. "No need, Christa, I'm expected," and I looked eagerly toward the door. There were two sets of footsteps, and two blond men came simultaneously into the drawing room.

Aunt Adalheid was startled, and leapt up. Rudi clicked his heels and bowed slightly to her, then to me, smiling, then to the Bölfingers. "May I present Lord Buntingford? I've asked him to join us for dinner."

"Er, Bunty, please," came a deprecating voice. "Had a bit of a bump with the Ferrari. Hope it's not too inconvenient. . . ." His face faded away.

Cor, lumme, strike me pink, where did they find 'im? I nearly bobbed a curtsy and said, "Charmed, I'm sure," a mock Cockney to his stage aristocrat.

The languid figure in sand-colored chinos and a red and white striped shirt was the same height as Rudi, but thinner, a skinniness that stopped marginally short of gaunt. In the ensuing hand-shaking orgy of German social occasions, I could feel every last carpal and metacarpal in Bunty's bony fingers, a hot crushing grip. I was frightened Rudi was going to shake my hand, or pretend he'd never met me before, but he put one arm loosely around my shoulder, then patted my stomach.

"Still there, is it?"

"Yup, far as I know. I'm fine too. Hello, Rudi."

For a moment we grinned at each other, oblivious to the roomful of people. Then he moved his arm, and was again the perfect German aristocrat. Polite chatter was then performed. Bunty was frog-marched to my side by Aunt Adalheid, who had discovered his German was a tad ropey.

"You can speak English to my niece," she told him in German.

Bunty seemed unsure about this, but once I asked him about his name, was happy to talk.

"Well, you could call me James, but only my mother does that, and you don't look a bit like her."

"Thank you. I think. Though I'm sure she's charming."

"Wouldn't be quite so sure if you'd ever met her. Villages tremble as she passes. I still do."

"You don't look the fear and trembling type to me."

"God, I tell you, crashing racing cars is nothing compared to lunch with my mother. I was toughened up at an early age, which is why I can take the wheel with a steady hand now."

"Oh, do you race cars?"

"No, I just design the engines, but I like to test my

own. That's what happened with the Ferrari. Experimental new widget. Little blighter burst into flames outside Mannheim. Luckily for me, Rudi came down the autobahn, saw me standing by the wreckage, and pulled over. I've had a garage tow the bits away, and it's back to the drawing board tomorrow."

"Oh dear, is it a complete write-off?"

He laughed. "No, just a bit blackened around the edges. I always have a couple of fire-extinguishers in the car, I seem to need them."

"Remind me never to accept a lift."

"Never lost a passenger yet. Well, actually, I have. Women keep getting out at the side of the road and saying they'd rather walk home, thanks. Can't understand it."

I had been ready to despise Bunty, but the way he set himself up, played the blithering idiot, deflected any envy or traditional mistrust of the ruling classes, depending on which way you wanted to look at it. It was a well-honed act; I searched in vain for signs of intelligence or low confidence. Awfully bad manners to display signs of either, I knew, but it didn't mean they weren't there. Made a nice change from people claiming that not only were they wonderful, but that their children were alarmingly bright because, like circus horses, they could stamp their feet up to five if asked the right question.

"So how do you know Rudi?"

"His bank sponsors a team I've done engines for— we've met at a few tracks, and Big Pricks sorts of events."

"Big—sorry?"

"Grand Prix, you know. Just a little joke."

"Oh, a joke, ah ha ha."

"I'll flag the next few as they come up, just so you know."

"Thank you, that would be most helpful."

We started needling each other, until our burst of laughter fell into suddenly silent air. Aunt A. and Rudi had stopped talking to the Bölfingers, and all four were staring at us.

"I think it's time to change for dinner," said Aunt Adalheid glacially.

"Oh," I said, and nodded to James aka Bunty, then to the Bölfingers. "Must go heave myself into a bigger tent."

Bunty looked at Rudi. "Afraid I didn't have a DJ with me."

"I have a spare," Rudi replied curtly. "Come with me."

I left, leaving Aunt A. to sort out the Bölfingers, and plodded up to my room. I'd forgotten to ask what time dinner was, but knowing Aunt Adalheid she'd have a giant gong somewhere, probably with a bronzed loin-cloth-wearing gong-beater . . . Which film company, I mused, had started its films with a shivering bronze beaten gong, a million little coin-shaped dents quivering with the vibration before the music started?

All my new evening things were pink. I think I'd let Frederike do too much of my buying. I tried a long-sleeved, but low-cut, pink velvet dress. I think my bosom must have grown in the couple of days since I bought the dress, for it seemed much tighter than I remembered. I felt like an opera singer, in one of those corseted cos-tumes. Every time I breathed in, my bosom definitely heaved. Maybe it would impress Rudi. I decided to keep it on. A quick touch of mascara, and I was done. Then I sat in a chair, hands poised on knees, ready to spring into action if and when dinner was announced.

A bell rang in the hall, a handbell, and like one of Pavlov's dogs, I went bounding out in search of food. Rudi managed to intercept me before I reached the top of the stairs.

"I think we should go down to dinner together. It would look odd if we didn't," he said.

"Sorry, I didn't realize." Then I did realize something. "Hang on, we're not in the same room. Where are you sleeping?"

"At the end of the corridor, with Bunty in the room opposite."

"Which side are you on?"

"Why—so you can sneak into Bunty's room late at night?"

"No—just wondering why we're not in the same room," I said, my lip beginning to quiver.

"I thought that now we'd achieved the desired result, you would want to be free from that."

At the word "that," I nearly lost it, but then Sylvie twittered out onto the landing. I clenched my teeth, thinking, mustn't make a scene, mustn't let go. I will *not* cry. In the event, Augustin distracted everyone by almost plunging head-first over the bannisters. Rudi and Sylvie discreetly helped him down the stairs, and I followed slowly. Bunty clattered down the stairs behind me, just as I reached the bottom, watching Rudi arrange Augustin into an upright position.

"Am I late?" asked Bunty. "Blasted collar stud, you know. I usually need a pretty girl to do them up for me. Does my collar look all right to you?"

"You know perfectly well it does."

My voice had come out unduly harsh, and Bunty raised his eyebrows in mock alarm.

"My dear. Rift in the marital lake?" he murmured, glancing toward Rudi.

"Never even had a ruddy lute to rift," I muttered bitterly, then turned away from him. Rudi came to my side like a homing pigeon.

"Bunty. Suit fit?"

"Impeccably, thank you. Jolly good of you. Your wife looks charming, too."

Rudi's fingers clenched around my upper arm in a crushing grip. "Yes, she does, doesn't she? Shall we lead the way into dinner—darling?"

Numbly I went. The dining room had been laid out in

full splendor, three ornate candelabra on the table, white linen, gold and white plates, silverware shining in the light of a hundred candles. Each candelabrum held at least thirty candles, and the whole table glowed with heat and light, so that even the off-white damask curtains seemed to reflect light back toward the table. A great pastoral scene, an oil-painting of haymaking, took up one wall, and the gold of the painted hay seemed as metallic as the gilding on the plates.

Little place-cards, black Gothic lettering on cream cards, held in place by miniature silver torch-bearers, each torch blazing with a cleft flame into which the card was inserted, demarcated our territory, our range of movement. I was in the center of one side, Bunty to my right and Sylvie to my left. Rudi took one end, and Aunt Adalheid the other, the head of the table. The Bölfingers came in last, Rotraut in a tuxedo or dinner jacket as well, a masculine trouser suit that looked indistinguishable from Heinrich's. Rotraut sat opposite me, but the fierce candlelight made it impossible for me to look at her directly. I noticed, though, that I was the only person not dressed in black. Sylvie was wearing a minuscule tight dress ("Yes, it's an Alaia," she said, when I complimented her on it), more of an elasticated bandage, while Aunt Adalheid had on a high-necked Victorian bombazine dress that reminded me, with a start, of Mathilde.

For one moment I felt homesick for the castle, for "my" ghosts. I felt out of place here, in my bright pink dress, with these cold strangers. Time and place were forgotten, as I thought back to Schloss Drachenfels, my mind searching for the ghosts, to ask how they were.

Bunty broke into the haze, offering a basket of bread rolls.

"If you drop any crumbs down your front, I'd be happy to fish them out for you."

He was brazen, incorrigible. "That's all right, I can

manage. It's terrible, being pregnant, you explode outward in every direction."

"Exciting time, though. I expect your hormones must be racing."

Rudi's voice cut down from the opposite end of the table like a saber stroke.

"My wife's hormones are not racing, she's mostly very tired, and needs a lot of rest."

"If you say so," said Bunty blithely, breaking into his roll. We were too far from Rudi for him to be able to join our conversation without shouting, so Sylvie started talking to Rudi. I was trying to keep one ear on what she said to him, while paying half-hearted attention to Bunty with the other. After the soup, Aunt Adalheid gave up trying to make conversation with Augustin, and started quizzing Bunty on his family, so I decided to try and get to know Sylvie. Her first question was unexpected.

"Did you have a lot of trouble with the paparazzi on your honeymoon?"

"No, no, the Seychelles seemed remarkably free from that kind of thing."

"Oh, the Seychelles. Funny, I thought Rudi always went to the Caribbean for romantic atmosphere. He and Nadine had several hideaways, where the press couldn't find them. They can be so intrusive."

"Yes, well, it's not something I've had to worry about much."

"No, dear, I don't suppose you have." The words themselves were pleasant, but beneath the sweetness was a kind of patronizing venom that made my hair curl faster than a Carmen roller. She continued to plant deadly nightshade in all my hedgerows by saying, "Of course, you haven't met Nadine. Nadine is—used to be—she used to be, isn't that right, Rudi?—his girlfriend. The most wanted woman in Paris, and not by the police." She gave a metallic little laugh, like steel shavings off a mill. "Stunning of course, and a very successful career woman in her own right. Where is Nadine these days, Rudi?"

"Paris, I believe."

Sylvie turned back to me. "I expect Rudi's trying for something quite different this time, I mean, not taking you to the Caribbean."

"I'm not that bothered about tropical islands, really. I've been very busy at Schloss Drachenfels."

"Yes, Rudi has rather kept you hidden away, hasn't he? For a man whose social life—in his position . . . yes—I suppose you're planning on entertaining a great deal then, if you've been there all this time?"

"Ummm—I didn't know. I've been cataloguing some of the library."

"The library?" she said, in the fixed incredulous tones I would have used to say, "So you think you're *Napoleon?*"

"Mm. It's very valuable, and sadly neglected."

Sylvie gave me a pinched smile. I think she thought I was lying. I had no idea what to say to her.

Rudi broke the silence. "Ella used to work at the British Library."

"Oh, you're a *librarian?* I thought they all wore glasses. Not in your usual style, Rudi, hah?"

I couldn't even be bothered to clip her around the ear. I let Rudi explain what I used to do, and she patted his arm soothingly, as if to say, There, there, dear, you've made a terrible mistake but I expect you'll get over it.

At the other end of the table, Augustin's head was nodding slowly toward his plate. Both Rotraut and Aunt Adalheid pretended not to notice, but I could see Bunty giving him the occasional sharp glance. No wonder the poor man drank, with a wife like Sylvie. Or maybe Sylvie was a cow because he drank. I pondered for a while on this chicken-and-egg, which-came-first question, staring into the candles on the table in front of me, the glow imprinting on my retina.

"Penny for them," said Bunty, sticking a surreptitious blunt finger into my lower ribs.

I turned to gaze at him, his image a golden blur, clouded by candle flames. I blinked a few times until my vision cleared, then murmured, "Nothing, nothing. Just—nothing."

"Mm-hmm. Tell me, have you ever been motor-racing? Does your husband let you out much? I mean, what's the p. of a. for the next couple of days?"

I tried to drag myself back into the conversation. "Plan of action? I think that rests with Aunt Adalheid. I believe a spa visit. Aunt?"

Aunt Adalheid had adopted a griffin-like expression, not of a friendly "listening bank" variety, but the old-fashioned, mythological, eat-humans-for-breakfast-they're-very-nutritious sort. She glared at Bunty.

"What *exactly* did you have in mind?"

"Day at the racetrack," said the dauntless Bunty. "If you've never been, it's great fun, bit noisy, and oily in the pits, but great fun all the same. Come along yourself, bring some friends, make a day of it."

She was silenced only momentarily. "I think it sounds just like Frederike's sort of day," she decided. "By all means take my niece with you, but I know Frederike adores cars."

My jaw hung suspended in the air for a long moment, but Bunty noticed nothing, his boyish smile still fixed upon Aunt Adalheid.

"Oh good, that's all settled then. There's time trials on Saturday, the real thing on Sunday. Do ask your friend—Frederike—which she'd prefer."

"Indeed I shall."

Indeed, my thoughts echoed, you're going to have to wait until Frederike's well and truly blitzed before you spring this one on her. She'll never go for it. Aunt Adalheid started to ask Bunty questions about motor sport, while I thought of the pink-and-fluffy Frederike standing behind a pile of tires, watching cars drone around a race-track. *Neeyow, neeyow.* At least fifty times. Once more I gazed into the flames of the table-fire, unseeing, no longer part of the party. The meal seemed interminable. Pudding came and went. Coffee. Black oil in gold cups, golden candles reflected in its black surface.

I stared into the black liquid, and the light on the sur-face seemed to take on a different color, a slightly greenish cast at one edge; the face of Mathilde slowly formed, like a mosaic, on the surface, then settled into an image of pho-tographic clarity. She smiled, winked one eye slowly, then the coffee went black. *What?* I said in my mind. *Watching you,* came back her voice, clear but very distant. Nothing more. I knew she had gone from me. Had she ever been there?

I wasn't sure, but after that, I couldn't drink my coffee.

13

I don't know how long the evening went on, but I do remember Rudi and Aunt Adalheid dragging me upstairs in tandem, leaving Bunty and Heinrich to deal with Augustin. I remember Rotraut, like a Greek marble goddess, unmoving alabaster, eternally fixed hair, standing to one side as Heinrich put both his hands under one of Augustin's elbows, but I didn't see anything else. Rudi had decided it was my bedtime, and I agreed with him. I no longer cared about good impressions. I wanted sleep, cool white linen sheets, darkness and oblivion.

Aunt Adalheid left us at the top of the stairs. Rudi pushed me into my room, shoving the door shut behind him. He turned me around, his fingers on one of my shoulders, and unzipped the back of my dress with one swift hand. I felt the pressure of warm fingertips between my shoulder blades, then he muttered, "Sleep now," and was gone.

I could have cried, but there was nothing in me to cry with. I had been so happy to see him, had even managed

to be with my own husband in my own bedroom, alone—
and then nothing. I let the dress slide off my shoulders,
the shoes fall from my feet, and I dropped into bed, not
even bothering to turn out the light.

I was up late the next morning. It was almost midday
when I went downstairs, and housekeeper, Frau
Hildesheim, told me that everyone had already left for the
Kurhaus, to take the waters and a little exercise. All
except "the French Monsieur," who was still abed. "Now
what can I get you for breakfast?" she asked. "You're eating for two, remember."

"I don't think I can even eat for one. Just some toast,
please."

Frau Hildesheim made mother-hen noises, insisted I
go into the smaller of the two sitting rooms, the morning
room I suppose. I had never been in the room with Aunt
A, she kept the drinks in the other one. I curled up in an
armchair, and with a newly discovered pile of *Paris Match,*
I waited until Frau Hildesheim brought me my breakfast
on a tray. I felt like a very small invalid, especially when
she offered to put a rug over my knees. "No, no," I said
feebly.

"I'll just put the rug here, then, and you can pull it
over yourself later if you want to. It's still only April, you
know. It's still cold outside."

I munched my toast slowly, while enjoying tales of
French political corruption and multiple marriages of the
famous. Not famous to me, and my French wasn't good
enough to translate every word, but the pictures told the
story well enough. "I'm so happy," says famous actress. "I
will prove my innocence," says accused financier. "I'm
stunned it's triplets," says mother of three.

I pushed the breakfast tray to one side, pulled my
knees under my chin, put the rug around myself like an
African refugee, and continued to browse. I slowly

worked my way through the slithery pages of improbably happy people, monumentally breathtaking disasters, graphic close-ups of corpses mixed with advertisements for cosmetic dentistry. A childish diversion, fairy-tales for adults, but a diversion nevertheless. All the same, I was beginning to flag when Augustin prized the door open, put his head around the side of the panels until he saw me, then came in, carefully it seemed, and slumped onto the sofa in front of me.

"How do I get a cup of coffee?" he croaked. "Very strong coffee."

"I'll go and find the housekeeper." I shrugged my covering away. "Do you want any breakfast, something to eat with the coffee?"

"No, no, just coffee."

I had almost reached the door when Frau Hildesheim came in. She had an uncanny sense of where anyone was at any given time. Maybe it's something all good staff have, but there were times when her tracking ability startled me.

"Coffee, Monsieur Courcheval?"

"Yes, please."

"Anything for you, *Gräfin?*"

"I was just going to ask for coffee for Monsieur, but, well . . . another coffee would be lovely."

Frau Hildesheim smiled, nodded and pulled the door silently to.

Augustin looked small and vulnerable against the large blue sofa, his tiny feet in brown suede shoes barely reaching the floor. He had missed a patch while shaving, leaving a dark area on the edge of his jaw, and this sign of incompetence touched me in a way his alcohol-induced clumsiness had not. His drinking concealed his gentler side. Last night he had seemed cold, monosyllabic, uninterested. Now, with aubergine shadows under his eyes, he gave me an impression of openness, a weary acceptance of all that life had to throw in his path. I didn't know what to say to him, so it was fortunate that he spoke first.

"I hope I'm not disturbing you. I believe the rest of the party were going to the Kurhaus."

"Yes, I think so. I was up late myself, and so I'm having a quiet morning with some old magazines."

He raised both eyebrows at the heap in front of me, then smiled indulgently. "As long as you don't believe a single word you read, you'll come to no harm. Please, continue. I shall ask the housekeeper if this morning's newspaper is to hand."

I was reluctant, but realized he meant it. He was beyond the effort of making conversation, or would be until sufficient caffeine had reached his vital parts. I picked up a recent *Paris Match* and started to read again.

Frau Hildesheim came in again with coffee, presciently bringing Augustin that day's *Frankfurter Allgemeine* and the *Luxemburger Wort*.

We sat opposite each other, in comfort, coffee perfuming the air. The morning room was at the back of the house, with large windows in a long sweep along one entire wall, flanked by a broad low windowsill on which rested a few pieces of modern sculpture and a pair of long bromeliads, living sculpted rocks. Outside, the garden was laid to lawn, surrounded by silver birches. There were no other plants, no flowerbeds, so the effect was of a woodland clearing, a grassy open space before the trees closed in again. A pleasing vista, and a relaxing morning companion. I forgot that Augustin was there, forgot where I was, let the armchair enfold me.

The shock, when it came, jolted me forward. There it was, in glorious Technicolor; *Nadine de X shows us her new Parisian apartment. Nadine, former long-term amie of Graf Rudiger von Drachenfels, has banished her heartbreak with the challenges of her eighteenth-century . . .* The words lost focus, but the pictures were of a horrible clarity. A pert redhead, her hand resting on a scrolled Empire-style sofa with gold upholstery, gave a sideways smile to the camera. *Nadine with her four-poster bed. Nadine shows her Picasso drawing.* Nadine. Nadine. With the poodle curls. My little poodle. Don't phone me here, Nadine. I started to chew my left thumbnail nervously, but it splintered with a loud crack.

Augustin looked up from his newspaper. "What is it?"

"Nothing, nothing."

"Something's upset you."

"No, it hasn't, really. It's nothing."

"You were reading something. Come and tell your Uncle Augustin."

"I can't. It's nothing."

"Yes, you keep saying that. Tell me what kind of a nothing."

I hesitated. "Did you ever know—someone called Nadine?"

"Yes." He paused, looked hard at me. "We all knew— still know—

Nadine."

I gestured toward the magazine laid on the armrest of my chair. "There's a long article about her—says she and Rudi . . . He never told me. I mean, he doesn't ever speak about . . ." I took a deep breath. "It's silly, I'm not upset really, I was just surprised."

"Come over here, show me this article. I can't move, I'm too old and fragile."

I did as asked, shuffled myself, rug and magazine over to the sofa, and sat by Augustin. I handed him the *Paris Match,* and he gravely read through the article while I watched him, the fingers of my right hand resting against my lips.

Augustin, finished, shook his head, threw the magazine behind him, over the back of the sofa, with a careless flick. "That's what I think about that article. Nadine is a very clever, ambitious woman. She knows many important people, including of course many magazine editors. Her parties can be stimulating occasions, particularly when she decides to scream at her lover of the moment. And I am surprised Rudi managed to escape from her clutches. Don't tell Sylvie I said that. She and Nadine are old friends." He sighed. "Neither of them have much time for—shall we say—human failings."

I didn't understand him fully. If he meant they were angry when he was paralytic, I could hardly blame them. I patted his sleeve in a reassuring manner. I wanted *him* to reassure me.

"I don't know if Rudi has forgotten Nadine, though?" I questioned him.

"I don't think anyone could. She has this voice, you see, this husky laugh that each man thinks is meant for him alone—but as a man grows older, he no longer needs to be the envy of all his friends. I don't mean that as an insult to you, *ma chérie,* I only wish to say that as a man grows older, he needs comfort. Rudi seems to have found that in you."

I shook my head.

"*Si.* If you had been Nadine, he would never have dared to leave the house without you. He would have been forced to hang around until you woke, growing ever more restless, shown his impatience, there would have been a scene. Nadine would have thrown things, we would all have had to pacify her, and no one would have left the house until afternoon. Yet here you are, alone, curled up like a kitten, content. We are all too old for drama now."

I knew Augustin was trying to comfort me, but the painful sensation, the nagging beneath my skin, refused to go away. "Yes, but . . ." I wanted to ask something, but I didn't even know what it was.

Augustin sighed again. "I'm tired, Ella, more tired

than I can say. Let me lie down, and I'll tell you all about Rudi."

I said nothing, so he took one of the needlepoint cushions from the side of the sofa, dumped it into my lap, and laid himself sideways, head in my lap, little brown suede feet dangling from the edge of the sofa. I rested a tentative hand on his shoulder, the other I kept by my side. "Tell me, then," I said.

"Well, we met at Fountainbleau, and I remember that first day, at our introductory session . . ." Augustin rambled on, explaining how Rudi acted as the brake on some of his group's more exuberant exploits, how his aloofness had led to misunderstandings, how Rudi had saved him from failing his midyear test. Halfway through an involved account of a case-study they had to work on jointly, something to do with the management buy-out of an engineering firm, Augustin slowed down, before crossing the borders of sleep.

I let him rest, enjoying the sensation of warmth, as if I had a large dog beside me, its sides rising and falling gently, warm breath on my knee. I knew Augustin was close to me only through exhaustion, brought on by alcohol, or maybe a lack of it this morning, yet I felt some surrogate intimacy, some borrowed closeness. It was his own lack of energy, or pressure on me, that enabled me to trust him, to sit contentedly in the morning room as the afternoon wore on, waving away lunch, putting one finger to my lips when Frau Hildesheim came in to see if I wanted anything. I thought over the Rudi that Augustin had depicted for me, the same man that I knew, but one capable of strong friendship. There was a warm core there, if I could hack through the rock. If. Small word, big distance.

I settled my arm closer around Augustin. His cream cashmere sweater was soft to the touch. As the spring sunlight fled from the garden, the central heating clicked on, no sounds in the quiet house. I started to doze myself.

✠

The door opened sharply, light pouring in from the hallway.

"There are you," said Rudi harshly. "Ah, Augustin too."

Augustin sat bolt upright. "Rudi. My wife must be back. I'll go and see how she is." He bounded out, puppy-like, restored by his nap. Rudi held the door open for him as he passed, then closed it firmly. He came in, clicked the large Chinese table-lamp on.

"So. I can't leave you alone for a moment, it seems."

"What? What are you on about?"

"Thank God it was I who found the two of you, nestled up together. If it had been Sylvie or Rotraut, this would have been all over town. Several towns."

"Look, Rudi, Augustin was just having a nap. He was sleeping *on* me, it's hardly the same as sleeping *with* me."

"I'm not sure there's much of a difference."

"There is to me. You don't really think I'd sleep with Augustin?"

"I don't know what to think. I hardly know you. I am aware, however, that a woman in your position can't be too careful."

"What position? You mean my position as a lowly peasant wench compared to the noble German aristocracy? You mean I'm embarrassing you in front of your friends?"

"I mean, your position—as *my wife*." The last two words were spoken with venom. "Oh, that." I got up, stalked past him to the door and went out, slamming the door loudly enough to concuss him with the shock-waves.

✠

Dinner that night was a descent into the Underworld, and I don't mean the club in Camden. This was a more muted, slow-motion kind of hell, like one of those films that shows an injection in close-up, the needle approaching the skin as slowly as an ocean liner coming into dock. You wince, you look away, look back; the needle's still there, moving, until it touches the skin, pulls up a tiny pyramid of flesh. Pain anticipated, tension, then more pain.

I don't remember what we ate.

All I do remember is that for some reason all the women were on one side of the table, with me in the middle, Rotraut to my left, Sylvie to my right. Bunty, Augustin and Heinrich on the other side. Rudi and his aunt still at either end, like basilisks. Sylvie and Rotraut began to gossip over my head. The men across the table seemed happy enough. I sat, consumed by my own misery, not daring to raise my eyes in Rudi's direction. If I was embarrassing him that much, then I'd stay silent. I was no longer angry at his comments, but bitter with myself. I'd wanted to get on well with his friends, yet Rudi was so angry that I'd spent the afternoon with Augustin, who'd been sweet, told me about Rudi, and I had been happy listening to Augustin's stories.

Now it was all spoiled. I'd upset Rudi, not behaved with the propriety expected of a Countess. I wanted to make it up to him with my gracious demeanor over dinner, but I was lost when it came to Sylvie and Rotraut. Every comment seemed needle-edged, painful.

"You don't laugh much, do you?" cackled Rotraut. "Nadine had this low, fascinating laugh—one always had to laugh with her."

My only response, a poor worn-out enfeebled OAP of a response, was: "Indeed?" in three languages. *"Wirklich?" "Vraiment?"* That, and the occasional small nod, but my head seemed too loose for my neck, and once I started nodding, little wobbling nods continued long after I wished them to stop. Nothing I wanted happened that evening, not even death. A sudden stroke of lightning, cyanide in the chestnut purée, anything . . . I would have been grateful.

Sunday at the Nurburgring was another apocalyptic vision, an Old Testament idea of a bad time. Everyone had decided to go and watch motor-racing, so I was stuck with all of them all day, plus Frederike. Bunty and I went in her car, and she was charmed by him, and tried to feed him raisins one by one. As it happened, she was no trouble at the track, because she was very fond of men in overalls, and there were plenty of them. Bunty introduced her to all the ones he knew, but she found a few more all by herself. The rest of the party made falsely cheery noises, except for Augustin, who fell asleep in his seat.

There was only one brief bright spot, when Bunty had taken me to one side to explain about metal tolerances at extreme temperatures, and I decided to try to kill the topic of conversation.

"Was Nadine interested in motor-racing then?"

"Nadine was never interested in anything other than Nadine. An absolute killer, though, if she thought there was anything to her advantage. I think Rudi got out just in time." He patted me on the shoulder in an avuncular manner.

I smiled, shakily, but before I could throw myself into Bunty's arms, declaring my undying love for those unkind words, Rudi came over and told me not to get in Bunty's way, he was carrying out technical observations. I drew back.

Sunday night, after dinner at a restaurant on the way to Wiesbaden, they all left. All except Rudi. Obviously he wanted to stay and criticize me some more. I felt as though I'd done nothing right all weekend. I didn't want any more criticism, any more comparisons. As Mrs. Malaprop might have said, "Companions are odorous." I.e.; they stink. I went to bed straight away, and sneered a good night to Rudi and Aunt Adalheid over the banisters, my lip curled just slightly in defiant effort. Go on, then, bitch about me behind my back. See if I care.

Once safe in my bedroom, I sank onto the bed, my hands over my face. I couldn't take this. I wanted to go back to the castle. I was happier alone. Mathilde, I found myself thinking, Mathilde, I want to come back to Drachenfels.

Soft as twilight, a quiet voice came through: "Stay one more day. One more day."

14

It was 7:28 and fourteen seconds as Nadine kicked the revolving door of Banque Globale into a fast spin. She could still be at her desk for 7:30 if she took the stairs. The lifts were worse than useless; sometimes you had to wait for as long as thirty seconds. Her suede Ferragamos barely touched the marble treads as she launched herself upward. She could run six flights in under a minute.

Some people let themselves go by the time they reached their late thirties but she knew, better than anyone, that that was precisely the time to redouble your efforts to stay ahead of the pack. She hadn't got where she was today by relaxing, or waiting for lifts. She burst in through the glass door on the sixth floor, having barely allowed the hand-scanner time to register her palm-print. Already most of her staff were at their desks, or at least their jackets were. She did a quick scan for yesterday's jackets, men who thought they could fool her by leaving their jackets on their chairs overnight, then sneaking in ten minutes late, pretending they'd been in the bog all the time. She was going to have to get a camera installed in the gents, keep an eye on the idle little bastards.

She ignored the subdued morning greetings on her way to her glass-fronted corner office, pausing only at the door to order: "Mimi, coffee—now. And you lot—get your dicks out of your arses and on the phone."

Somewhere, several desks down, she could hear a muttered, "Charming image." If it was that Gilbert again, she'd have him. He had an attitude problem, and no mistake. She ran a tight ship here, and if anyone didn't like it, they could park their bums on someone else's office furniture; they weren't going to clutter up her trading floor for long. Moscow was two hours ahead, the lines were about to hum, but she'd already briefed those boys from home at 6:30. Now she had to brief herself on Poland, Hungary and all the two-bit, one-bank republics. The day's analyses from each of the heads of trading were on her desk, and she glanced through them. Zloty close to its ceiling—get the mid-office boys to re-examine the limits. Within fifteen minutes, she was on top of the situation, then opened her office door to shout: "Mimi! I'm in conference. No calls, no interruptions and no visitors—got that?"

Oui, madame came the lifeless reply. God, that woman was dreary. Still, she'd lasted longer than most. Some of them barely lasted a week. It was a tough life on the trading floor.

Once was she sure no one was looking, Nadine reached into her briefcase for her mobile. The bank taped all calls from its lines, and she wasn't having some geek in compliance listening in to this. If she hurried, she could catch Sylvie between the gym and her salon appointment.

"Sylvie? It's Nadine. How did it go? Tell me *every*-thing." Her voice was warm and persuasive.

A tinkling laugh came through the receiver. "Nadine!

I was just thinking of you. We got back last night. Oh, my dear. Where do I start?"

"Did you meet—*her*?"

"Of course we did. That was the whole point—Rudi's aunt wanted her to meet some people. Why, I have no idea—spread the burden, I suppose. The dullest creature, you have no idea. And, and, and, this is priceless, she's a—go on, guess."

"No, tell me."

"A librarian! Can you imagine anything more dreary? She hardly said a word, she doesn't ski, she doesn't watch polo or go racing, she's not on the committee of anything, I don't know what she does with herself. Rotraut and I tried everything."

"Well, Rotraut's no sparkling conversationalist either."

"No, I know, and who can blame her, married to Heinrich? She couldn't come to Gstadd at New Year because he wanted her to go to Texas with him."

"Texas? The poor girl. I must catch up with Rotraut soon. But you were saying, about. . . . ?"

"Ella? Stupid name. And she's massive. Bigger than Augustin."

"That's hardly difficult."

"Yes, but she's built like a carthorse, absolutely huge. Bosoms bobbing everywhere."

"Oh God, bosoms are so *passé*. It's tragic when people fail to keep up."

"Mind you, I think the reason why she looked so fat might be because she was pregnant. Rudi patted her stomach in a meaningful way."

"Pregnant? Nadine's shriek almost fractured the glass front of her office. "Rudi didn't say anything to me about that."

"Oh, I'm only guessing, calm down. They didn't make a formal announcement or anything. I didn't think you'd care."

Nadine gritted her teeth. She'd had to lie through them for months, telling everyone she'd told Rudi to get lost, and in a fit of pique, he'd gone off and married a total stranger, while nursing a broken heart. It was all part of the plan. No one must ever suspect, when the first wife died, that she or Rudi had any hand in it, that they had expected the death. They would both be hundreds of miles away, and no longer involved with each other. No motive, and no means. It was a business deal, remember, and you don't blow a deal by talking about it before it's signed, sealed, delivered and the press release issued.

And if that woman didn't die in childbirth, she'd make damn sure Rudi filed for divorce before the baby was a week old. It was galling enough to wait a year, a year of facing people's smiles, the knowing nods as they purred, "Back on the market, Nadine? It can't be easy, at your age." She wanted to be a wife, not a mistress any longer, and she had put six years into Rudi, waiting, biding her time. She was not going to let the prize out of her grasp, not once she had come this far.

All she could do now was to act cool, and keep an eye on things from a distance. It wasn't easy. There weren't many people she could trust. Rudi's male friends admired her, but she couldn't grow too close to them, or Rudi would hear. And Rudi didn't have any female friends, she'd made certain of that. She'd seen off the couple of fat old slappers he knew from his college days, once she'd made sure they weren't related to anyone important.

"So who else was there, darling?"

"Oh, me and Augustin, Rotrait and boring old Heinrich, and Bunty, some English lord."

"I know that one. Fatuous and broke, don't waste your time."

"I'm not, my dear, I'm still having some fabulous skiing lessons in Grenoble."

"Jean-Luc? Darling, the skiing season's over. Won't Augustin suspect?"

"I told him glacier skiing, he doesn't know where I go, he just pays the bills."

"How very convenient. And how is dear Jean-Luc?"

"Gloriously firm. What more can I say?"

Nadine smiled sourly at the receiver. "What indeed? Aren't you worried that Augustin might be having his own skiing lessons somewhere?"

"Augustin? Hasn't got it up in years. Mind you, he came pretty close in Wiesbaden, he didn't drink as much as usual. We all went off to the baths for the day, and I sat in the sauna—you wouldn't have enjoyed it, pink doesn't really go with your hair. Mind you, there was this man with pecs like sofa cushions. . . . Anyway, Augustin spent the day at home with the fat librarian, who wore pink herself all the time, quite extraordinary—and he was revved up before dinner. I had to give him double rations of vermouth."

"Yes, they always pick the most inconvenient moments, don't they? Poor old Gus. I had no idea."

"Don't you worry about him." Sylvie's voice was suddenly sharp. "I'm not ready to part with him just yet."

"Oh darling, now would I? Now, would I?" Nadine wheedled.

"Yes, you would, if it suited you. That's why we're such good friends. We understand each other."

"Of course we do, darling," Nadine said. "Speak to you very soon. Bye."

Hah. How little Sylvie knew. The woman hadn't got a clue.

Nadine tucked her mobile back into her briefcase, then bounced upright in her black leather chair. Time to trade.

15

Rudi was there at breakfast the next morning.

"Shouldn't you be at work?" I said.

"No," he said, breaking into a smile. "I've rung in sick."

Aunt Adalheid put down the book she was reading over the table. "You haven't?"

"No, I haven't. I said I was accompanying my wife to antenatal classes."

I was so surprised I laughed. "But I'm not going to antenatal classes."

"No, and I think it's most irresponsible. You'll have to come for a long walk with me instead, for exercise."

"OK, where?"

"I know a place where there are woods and *Wander-stiege*."

"Sounds too. I'll just eat a bit more breakfast then."

He wasn't cross, then; he seemed in a good mood. I began to whistle inside, a little sea shanty, repetitively jaunty.

✠

The woods were wild, but traveled by a tame path. I took Rudi's arm, and together we roamed through springtime glades, pointing out to each other flowers that neither of us knew the names of, a sylvan idyll.

"I'm so happy here," I said, as we wandered. "But Rudi, I want to go back to Drachenfels soon. I know the pines around the castle are bleak compared to this, but I need to see how the castle is doing without me."

"Yes, naturally. Come back with me to Munich tonight, if you want, and we'll call Georg from there. Is everything all right?"

I didn't know how to say no, but clutched his arm more tightly.

"There, you're tired from meeting so many new people at once. I'm sorry. It seemed like a good idea."

"It was a good idea, Rudi, I wanted to meet them. I didn't really get to know Heinrich, but both Bunty and Augustin were sweet."

Rudi's arm stiffened beneath my palm. "Bunty wasn't supposed to be there, I just found him by the roadside. He's an acquaintance more than a friend. And he has a bad reputation."

"What for?" I asked lightly.

Women, of course. I should have thought that was obvious."

The pleasant mood of the day was slipping away from me. "Well, let's not worry about him, then. Which way now?"

We took a right-hand fork. Always the right hand, said Rudi, in these woods. The air was cool in the shadier parts of the forest, but we were warmly dressed, and Rudi led me back out into the sunlight soon enough. We had lunch at a wooden hut, a *Waldhütte*, and stretched out our legs in the primrose-yellow light. Birds sang, leaves rustled. We were at peace together, after the troubles of the weekend.

Afterward, Rudi drove us back to Wiesbaden, and went upstairs to pack.

I sought out Aunt Adalheid, who was reading an obituary notice aloud to Kiki, the ex-parrot.

"Aunt Adalheid, would it offend you if I went back to Munich with Rudi?"

"No," she sighed. "No, I'm not offended. I don't suppose it's much fun for you, with only an old woman like me for entertainment. Rudi's friends aren't much better. They are a sorry shower, aren't they? About as much life in them as a moribund tree-sloth."

"Oh no, that's unfair. It's just that I have things to do back at the castle and, er. . . ."

"And you want to. Yes, do go with Rudi. Your walk seems to have done you some good, you look much brighter than you did yesterday."

"Yes, well, I was tired then. Today, Rudi's shown me the most beautiful places, and it was sunny, and—oh, it was just calm."

She glanced at me sharply, then looked away. "You *have* missed my nephew, haven't you?"

"No, of course not. I'm doing fine without him, and he's very busy anyway. I don't necessarily expect to see much of him, but—"

"But he's never taken a day off work on the spur of the moment before, not ever," she interrupted. "Not the Rudi I know."

"Oh dear, I'm not much of a good influence then, am I?"

"I don't know about that," she said, "but it does him good to think about something other than work. Why not run along and pack?"

"Yes, OK. I'll miss you, you know." My words surprised me.

She rose, took one of my hands in both hers. "You will be all right, my dear. I have a feeling."

All right with what? Tell me, I wanted to beg. Tell me

he'll change his mind, his ways. But she said nothing, only walked me to the door, and closed it softly behind me.

I dragged my feet up the marble staircase, each foot in a sandpapery slide over each step, toes bashing against the risers. I wanted to go, I wanted to stay, I wanted Rudi.

✠

I had Rudi all to myself as he drove down the E12 back to Munich. The noise of the tires on the autobahn formed rhythmic patterns in my head, evoking snippets of long-forgotten rhymes from childhood. Da-dum da-dum. "Betide me well, betide me woe." What next? "Back to the castle I must go." My head nodded against the window. Betide me well. I'd been woe betided already. If a diety exists, then go on, betide me well.

Rudi, in a pale gray shirt and black jeans, pale hands gripping at the wheel, black leather beneath beige hands, the golden hairs on his wrist glinting where the light caught them. I could see the sinews at the side of his thumbs, their tautness the only indication that Rudi was exerting any effort to keep the car on the road. The speedometer showed 150 kph. It was a lot in miles, but I couldn't remember what you multiplied it by. Rudi just looked straight ahead, flicking the car past other vehicles. A car, a rush of air, a small picture in the rear view mirror. The same sequence, again and again. I surrendered to the speed and the road. Dark gray tarmac to infinity.

Munich was unwelcome, lights in the dark. Rudi's sparse modernistic flat. He dumped our bags in the hall, then put coffee on. "You might as well stay the night. No point in calling Georg out for a long drive in the dark."

I agreed mutely. The last few miles could wait till morning. I wanted to seize a few extra hours with Rudi, too, even if I wasn't wanted. I didn't like this flat, but if it had Rudi, then it would do.

Rudi clicked cupboards open and closed in his stainless-steel kitchen.

"No milk, damn it. I'm just going out to the station."

"The station?"

"It's the only place I can buy milk after six. Won't be long."

"I'll go, if you like."

"No, I know where it is, it'll be quicker if I go. Make yourself comfortable, I'll be back soon."

I sat down, carefully, on the wrought-iron sofa, avoiding its finger-slicingly sharp edges. The black cushions were soft, yielding back to the point where I could feel the metal skeleton that sustained them, and I was aware of the uncushioned arms, the bony legs with knobbly knees, the sharp little scroll at the back of the cushions were only an illusion, like flesh over bones, giving an impression of warmth and softness, while underneath cold minerals lay.

Like Goldilocks, I leaped up to try another seat, a chair this time, burnished steel with raffia-like strips of fabric between the metal sides. Nope. I didn't think any of this furniture was going to be "just right."

The phone rang. I looked round, trying to locate the source of the ringing. One ring, two, three. Then the clicks of an answering machine. I still couldn't see the phone, but I could hear Rudi's voice, speaking in German. Then a long tone.

"*Chéri, c'est moi, Nadine. T'as été où Ça fait quatre jours maintenant que tu ne m'as pas appelé. C'est méchant, chéri. Appelle-moi.*" Click.

Nadine. He hadn't spoken to her in four days. Four bleeping bleeping every-expletive-known-to-mankind days. While I'd been in Wiesbaden, and almost happy—stupid pathetic misguided deluded cretin that I was. *Call me, darling.* That pouty, testing tone. Where was that answering machine? I was going to rip its innards out, I

was going to tear it limb from whining little limb. There
was nothing visible, yet there had to be a cupboard somewhere. I started to tap the sides of the walls. No curtains,
only white blinds, so the telephone wasn't there. Like a
fox in a trap, I whirled around, despairing.

Rudi came back in.

"There was a call for you," I burst out. "Only I couldn't
find the phone to answer it."

"Oh, I keep it hidden. Ruins the aesthetic." He went
over to the steel cube next to the window, which I had
assumed was some kind of a pedestal for a sculpture yet
to be bought, pressed the top, and a lid flew up. Rudi
reached down and pressed a button.

"Who was it?"

"Nadine."

He didn't turn to face me, just said, "Really?" I could
detect nothing from his voice. The message played. He
turned.

"Don't worry about that, it can wait till tomorrow."

I was determined to say nothing, not to let my jealousy betray me. I knew the score when I married him.
Marriage of convenience. His affairs were none of my
business. I had no rights, it would be ludicrous for me to
expect otherwise. He had never pretended to me that I
was, or would be, the only woman in his life, or even *a*
woman in his life. I was the mother of his heir, a surrogate
mother if anything. His friends probably all knew he was
still seeing Nadine, and Sylvie's comments were just to let
me know how matters stood. Trying to keep me au fait
with what was going on. Not trying to attack me, but trying to inform me. My perspectives shifted. I hadn't seen
anything clearly, was seeing nothing as it really was. This
phone call made it visible. Rudi and Nadine were still an
item, while I was some kind of inconvenient necessity.
One woman, descent-perpetuating, for the purposes of. I
was something you'd leave a distant relative in your will,

because it might come in handy one day, but no one really
wanted it.

The silence spread, until I managed to say, "Coffee,
then?"

"Oh, yes."

I didn't want coffee, I wanted to rush to the loo and be
sick. Physically, actively, nauseously sick. I could feel my
innards bubbling. Oh Rudi, pouty pouty, that voice on the
phone. A plague on both your houses.

It might have been the uncomfortable silence after the
phone call; nothing was quite the same. Rudi put in the
spare room to sleep, a white monastic cell. Marriage, this
time, seemed to have a great deal in common with monas-
ticism: chastity and obedience, at least; poverty seemed
less of an issue. I sat on the bed in the dark, the blinds not
drawn, looking at the lights of the city. As the clock struck
the passing hours, the darkness increased. The lights were
going out one by one all over Munich. I felt I was in Rudi's
flat under false pretenses, the mistress snatching an illicit
night in the marital home while the wife was away. I
wanted to go back to the castle badly; I didn't belong anywhere else.

I almost fell into Georg's arms when he arrived the next
day with the castle BMW. Rudi had gone to work early,
having woken me briefly at 7 a.m. to tell me what to do
with the keys. Then he was gone, leaving me to prowl his
barren flat.

Georg laughed at my effusive greeting.

"City life not suiting you? Never did me, neither.
Come on with you. Let's head for the hills." He said the
last phrase with a mock cowboy voice, eyes squinting into
the distance, tipping up the brim of an imaginary hat.

"Foot to the door, Georg. Pedal to the metal."

He clicked the boot shut over my bags, and I hopped
into the front seat, slamming the heavy door behind me.

Georg slid in beside me in one smooth long-limbed movement. Then we were on the move, out through the sub-
urbs of Munich and onto the fast road to the foothills. We
said nothing, but once or twice I caught Georg's eyes
scanning my face carefully in the mirror.

At one point he said, "I trust Graf von Drachenfels is
well?"

"I expect so." I shrugged.

Georg raised the fingers of his right hand off the steer-
ing wheel, as if to acknowledge defeat, a wordless "OK,
Oh, I won't ask."

We said little until we reached the gatehouse at
Drachenfels, where I started to breathe freely again. We
were far from Munich or Wiesbaden. This was my
domain.

Georg unloaded me at the inner courtyard. "You will
be all right, won't you?" he said. "Elsa and I are always . . .
I think you—you must speak to Frau Feldstein. I'll come
in with you. I believe there was something she wanted to
say to you."

"Frau Feldstein?" I'd forgotten about my evil-visaged
housekeeper.

Georg would say nothing more, but came with me,
carrying my bags down the Stygian corridors, checking
the kitchens as we passed. No sign of her.

"We should try the wing," he suggested.

"No, hang on, George, I'll phone her. Come up to the
Master's Apartments, where the phone is."

Georg followed, to the haven of my own sitting room.
Spotless, no dust. Frau Feldstein hadn't given up the
ghost, she'd still been arranging the cleaning. Trivial
point, but if things are very bad, the cleaning generally
goes to hell. Whatever Frau F. wanted to say or do, she'd
maintained domestic order, which was above rubies. I
began to realize how much I'd depended on her.

Reluctantly, I dialed her number.

"Countess, I must speak with you most urgently," came the forbidding tones. "Please ask Georg to stay, I would like him to drive me to the station. And Countess, I beg of you, do not unpack. You cannot stay in this house. You must not." She cut the connection.

16

Georg and I sat on the sofa, awaiting the approaching footsteps. I'd left the door open, and could hear Frau Feldstein before I saw her. I stifled a gasp as she came in. She looked terrible, her previously sallow skin now gray, more strictly stretched across her large-boned face, her eyes bloodshot, whether from lack of sleep or tears, I could not tell. She wrung the hem of her black apron between febrile fingers.

"Oh, Countess, Countess," was all she said.

"Frau Feldstein? Sit down, please. Now, whatever is wrong?"

I felt agitated. I had never been kind to her, had been alarmed by her presence, had found her physical appearance offputting, but I had never intended her to have a nervous breakdown or to suffer grievous ill-health through living with me.

"What is wrong?" I repeated.

"Countess, I hardly know how to say this. You will think I am insane. I have wondered myself. I have prayed.

I can only say that I can stay here no longer—this castle is haunted!"

I almost laughed. I could have told her that. No, no, pay attention. "What makes you say that? Have you seen anything?"

"No, not seen, but the voices! And the tricks! Pulling my hair, cold fingers on my hand, my face, the cold mist. . . ." She buried her face in her hands. "They never leave me alone. I cannot bear it, I cannot stay."

The ghosts had never done me any harm. Why torment the innocent Frau Feldstein? I wanted to ask her more, but she was weeping now, silently, fat tears trickling over the tips of her fingers. I went over to her, patted her awkwardly on the shoulder. Georg said nothing.

"Of course you cannot stay, it must have been terrible for you."

"But my notice—the Count asked that I give a month's notice. I had a year's contract."

"No, no, that won't be necessary. I will insure that the *Graf* pays you to the end of your contract. I don't know what I would have done without you, such a big house. . . ." I let myself run on, platitudes billowing from my mouth like sails in a strong wind.

"Where will you go, Frau Feldstein?" I asked, as her tears began to slow.

"I—have—a sister—in Hamburg."

"Hamburg." Marvelous." You should have a holiday, go to the seaside, that sort of thing," Rudi had given me a checkbook, and I'd considered it useless up till now. I rummaged until I'd found it, wrote a satisfyingly large check out to Frau F., then said, "Perhaps we could let Georg have some lunch, while we discuss what is to be done about the house. Then he will take you to the station."

Georg rose hurriedly and gave me a sharp warning glance, but said nothing as he left.

"I've never liked the mountains," Frau Feldstein admitted, drying her eyes on a large white cotton handkerchief. "I feel trapped—enclosed."

"Yes, yes, ummm . . . I'm sorry I was away for so long. I hadn't realized . . ." I became inarticulate in the face of Frau Feldstein's emotions. It was the first time we had ever talked freely, and I didn't know what to make of her. We had spent months as the two people in a vast building, yet I had never even asked her, for example, if she had a sister.

"Yes, well, perhaps the open vistas of the sea would, you know, cheer you up a bit." I moved my hands helplessly.

She straightened herself. "Countess, you cannot stay here. It is terrible. It is dangerous."

"I think I'll be all right, at least for the time being. I'll see how it goes. Tell you what, have you packed? Do you want me to come with you to your wing? I could give you a hand."

"Thank you, Countess, I have already packed," she said with dignity. "And I have prepared a light luncheon, which is in the kitchen. Perhaps you would be ready for lunch now?"

"Yes, yes, of course."

Back down into the darkness at the foot of the castle. Despite all the electric lights, the kitchens and the servants' halls were gloomy. No wonder the poor woman was going barmy—except I knew she wasn't. Suddenly I couldn't wait to get rid of her, because I wanted to speak to Mathilde. We ate lunch with indigestive haste, then I telephoned Georg. I assured Frau F. I would give her an impeccable reference, insisted once again that a couple of weeks at the seaside would do her the world of good, then bundled her and her baggage out into the car.

✠

As soon as she'd gone I rushed back upstairs to the Master's Apartments, my footsteps echoing. I whirled around, once inside the sitting room, and called out, "Mathilde! Mathilde!"

Only silence.

I turned around again. "Mathilde!"

Turn three times for a ghost. Once more, then: "*Mathilde!*"

Still silence. Damn, but it was cold in here. There had been no fire in this room for weeks. I bent over the hearth, which was neatly swept, and began to arrange the kindling. The matches were on the mantel, and as I reached up, my fingers searching for the little cardboard box, I felt something cold. Cold fingers, reaching for mine. I screamed, and stood up hurriedly.

"Ssh!" came a faint sibilant noise.

"Mathilde? I can't see you."

"Can't. Light. Later." The voice was faint, unutterably tired, immeasurably distant. Not recognizably Mathilde's, not recognizably anything. There was a faint chill pressure on my wrist, then an absence, a sensation that something unnoticed was now missing from the room.

I sank back onto the sofa, depressed by my failure to speak to the house ghost. How *did* one summon spirits from the vast deep? It had been an old childhood superstition that ghosts came if you turned around three times on the spot. Yet it had worked. What else would work?

I could think of nothing. All my other childhood fears had revolved around paving cracks and bears. I now had no other human being near me, no support, no one to cook—the cleaning had been done by someone from Oberkirchen, someone I had never seen. They came when I was in the library. How would I manage now, how would I deal with people? I had been sheltered, and too ungrateful to realize it. Self-reproach crackled like the logs in the grate by which I crouched, poker in hand, turning the wood from side to side, trying to build up the fire, to gain some heat from its inner glow. I played with the fire for a long time, watching the poker tip grow red with heat, white ash forming on the red-black surface where I touched a log. Little gray curls of ash, like permed pensioner hair-clippings, drifted onto the hearth. The flames pulled upward in the chimney, trying to bear the wood beneath them aloft, but always anchored by their source. Ever-striving flames. A little pop, as the fire found a knot in a log, and a few sparks, igneous tracer-fire across the black sky of the chimney-breast. Man is born to trouble as the sparks fly upward. Heedless of my stiffening knees, the cold gray hearthstone beneath me, I sat by the fire like a medieval child until the blushing warmth in my face told me that I was too close, the fire was hot now.

I drew back a little, and sat on a footstool close to the hearth, putting the poker back on its stand. Alone again. The silence seemed to press in, the sounds of the fire tiny in the vast confines of the castle. I had only ever lived in three or four rooms of this building, had ignored the surrounding spaces, the endless empty rooms. They had always been there, but I had paid them no heed. Once all these rooms had served a purpose, there had been teams of footmen and under-footmen and upstairs maids and scullery-maids, extended families, half a dozen resident aunts, or poor relations, widows and orphans, to say nothing of the house-guests. Riding-parties, hunting expeditions, Christmas balls, summer picnics. The space to wear crinolines, and stairs to come down with the train of one's riding habit looped casually over one wrist. A busier, closer, bygone era. Bloodier, perhaps; one in which the battle-axes and halberds, now ornaments in the hall, were ready to hand, kept polished for use.

What would I have done, on a late-spring afternoon, with an unexpected few hours of free time? Embroidered, or practiced the spinet, learning a new piece for playing after dinner. I smiled sadly as I thought of the worm-eaten harpsichord downstairs. None of those instruments would ever play again; the days of music at Drachenfels were long since gone. This century had seen no laughter here, no games of charades or sardines, giggling as people hid among fur coats in deep wardrobes, dancing in the ballroom, whispered assignations to meet on the terrace. The castle had been empty for Rudi as a child, and for his father before him. Rudi had described to me how his father had treated the suits of armor as toy soldiers on a large scale, and had talked to them as if they were real people. Even Mathilde's diary, written before the young Queen Victoria had taken the throne, gave no sign of bustling life; the castle was bleak and empty of life then.

Some old houses give the impression of only just having been vacated, of indentations still on seat cushions, the newspaper flung aside this morning (even though the headlines say *Tsar Inspects Troops*), of laughter in the next room, and that if only you could run fast enough, like *Alice Through the Looking Glass,* you would catch up with the occupants, enter the breakfast room to find them all still seated around the table, toying with half-eaten kippers, and one of them would look up and say, "Ah! There you are!" And you would sigh with relief that you had at last caught up with the members of the house, with the day's activities.

Here there was nothing to catch up with, a castle so repeatedly abandoned that it no longer made any attempt to hold your attention. It would go to hell in its own way, and you could too. *The lion and the lizard keep/The courts where Jamshyd gloried and drank deep,* is the melancholy lament from *Omar Khayyám.* It was too cold for lions and lizards here, bats and wolves were as close as you could find, and I hadn't seen either. All I had seen were dusty rooms, one live housekeeper and one dead-in-law. Georg's cheer and vitality had seemed out of place inside the castle, and he himself had been visibly anxious to return to the gatehouse.

It started to grow dark. Television, I thought. That was the one other source of life I had seen here, those brightly colored images of "real" people, living carefully scripted "real" lives. Reality only happened in installments, weekly, bi-weekly episodes of normality. Whenever the camera followed people with no script, showed what actually happened in their lives, it was so ludicrously improbable that the people *had* to be real. No scriptwriter would ever dare ask an audience to believe such stories. Only scripted people are sensible, and think things through, and discuss everything with the neighbors: "I was thinking of going to Australia to see my Cousin Frank, the one who ran off with the lady wrestler from the betting shop after her husband tried to shoot them both."

"Oh, is that the Frank who works as a fireman, and rescued his neighbor's mother from a sheep-dip inferno, only to come home and find his youngest child had been taken to hospital with leukemia?"

"Yes, that's the one, and his sister's just been released."

Oh, heady reality. Remote-controlled, of course. Click. The gray-green screen sparked, a rising high-pitched whine came through the ether, and the screen decomposed into multicolored chaos. Oompah music from a tulip festival, where this year's winner is . . . I point the little red eye—to call up a new page. Color, sound, light, from different worlds. The fire and I watched new people lead old lives.

I sat, almost cross-legged, on my bun-footed footstool by the fire, until it was quite dark. Slowly, creepingly, millimeter by measured millimeter, I felt a chill seep into the air. I had not closed the curtains, and in that faint glow of light that comes from outside on even the bleakest night, I could see the dark air beside me take on a new quality, a faint luminosity. Mathilde was trying to return. I made no

comment, but waited, hugging my arms around my chest
to counteract the intensifying cold, feeling the prickle of
goose pimples despite my heavy woolen sweater. Cold
and fear are allies, but I kept repeating to myself, "It's only
cold, nothing to fear, only cold." I watched the television,
remembering that the first time I had seen Mathilde, I had
seen her sideways, through the corners of my eyes, and
how it had taken ages before she was fully visible.

This time I was aware of the process going on beside
me, and was gratified when I looked to find Mathilde, in
her green dress, sitting beside me.

"I have my own footstool," she said, patting the side
of her dress. "Caroline made the one you're sitting on, but
don't get up. She's brought another one."

I looked again. Beyond Mathilde was a pair of figures,
still very indistinct, leaving me with only the vaguest
impressions of shape and color. One white, one gray.

"Who—?"

"We are many. We are all the Drachenfels women that
ever died." The voice came from behind Mathilde.

"All right, spare the ceremony," said Mathilde over her
shoulder. "Listen, Ella, we come as a representation. We
have a request to make."

"If I *can* grant it, I will, but I don't know that there's
anything much I can do to help you."

Mathilde allowed a smile to flicker across her mouth.
"Oh, I think you can. I don't believe you'll find this too
difficult."

"Well, what is it?"

"We want to watch Frau Feldstein's television, but we
can't turn it on by ourselves. We need you to come and do
it for us."

I began to understand why Frau Feldstein was so keen
to leave. "Did you try to ask Frau Feldstein?" I inquired.

"Yes," said Mathilde, "but she is not of the blood; she
cannot see us, and shout as we might, she could not hear

us. We pulled her hair to get her attention, tried to lead
her back to the television, tried jamming doors so she
would have to stay in her room, but she almost never put
the television on, and then it was only to watch dull religious programs." One of the other ghosts, the gray one,
shook her head reproachfully.

"But if you can jam doors, why can't you turn on the
television?"

"Something to do with electricity," said Mathilde.
"Our animal magnetism interferes with it."

"Yes, but you're dead, so you shouldn't . . ." I gave up.
Physics never was my strong point.

"So if you could come with us, we won't trouble you
any further."

"Yes, you will, you're bound to," I grumbled. "OK,
allons-y. Where is Frau Feldstein's room, anyway?"

"The east tower. Come."

All three ghosts rose from their imaginary footstools,
which faded immediately. Then the three of them vanished from the room. I opened the door out to the hallway, and there they were. Grimacing to myself, I followed
them. I was reluctant to leave my warm fireside, but they
seemed determined, and the sooner I had dealt with
them, the sooner I could return.

Through the dust and dark we went to the furthest
tower. There, at the same level I guessed as the Master's
Apartments, was a well-furnished suite of rooms, in a
style that was brand new in 1950, comfortably old-
fashioned now. In the first of the rooms was a three-piece
suite in a hideous shake of khaki, and an enormous television set on four black legs, a little button at the bottom of
each leg.

"There it is," said Mathilde. "Can you put it on?"

I could, but nearly broke my finger in the process.
The spring mechanism behind the on/off button was stiff,
and required the strength and persistence of a Rottweiler

to make it yield, the sudden plunge of the serrated knob deep into the interior of the television took me by surprise. There was a crackle, then the electronic whine. The picture would come soon.

The three ghosts drifted into place on the sofa. Mathilde looked up at me. "You can go now."

"No, I can't, I'll never find my way back."

She sighed, and rose again. "I will take you then, but mark the way well. You will always find us here."

I went back down the corridor with her. "Why don't you watch television with me?" I asked, rather hurt.

"You would never stand the cold, my dear—see how you're shivering already. Even when I alone was there, you felt it. Imagine if ten of us turned up. You are not with us yet, you must keep to your own place."

There was something in what she said, I had to grant her that. The temperature in Frau F.'s room had been arctic; I could see the breath cloud in front of my face. Strange how the ghosts lowered the temperature.

"We are thankful, you know," Mathilde continued in an amicable tone of voice. "If you had not come, we should have been so bored. Now we can see so many other spirits, in far-off places, without ever moving. It has been a great blessing, particularly to the older ladies, who cannot move so easily now."

"Right. Hardly my doing, though. There must have been a television in the castle before?"

None of us remembers seeing one. We did not know the word until you came."

"So how do you know the word now? Did I mention it?"

"You thought it to us."

"Oh—what else do I think to you? Do you read all my thoughts?"

"Oh no," she said blithely. "Who would want to?"

Thank you very much, I thought bitterly.

At which *Bitte sehr'*, she replied immediately. Thank *you!*

"Oh shut up. Look, I can find my own way from here." I recognized the picture gallery.

"No, no, I will see you safely to your rooms. Who knows what might be hiding in the shadows?" she mocked.

"Can't be anything worse than you lot," I muttered.

She stopped and glared at me, serious again. "Yes, it could. It could be very much worse. That's why I'm here."

I didn't know what she meant, but for some reason I wasn't too keen to ask.

It was only the next evening, while rummaging for my supper, that I remembered to scold Mathilde for frightening away my housekeeper.

"Oh, you never liked her anyway," said Mathilde airily.

"Yes, but beneath that forbidding exterior I am sure there beat a heart of gold. And she was a brilliant cook."

"It's a bit late now. And she never turned her television on when asked."

"But what will become of her, cast aside like a worn-out glove."

"She's having a very nice holiday on the Baltic coast. She bathes daily."

"I should hope so too.

"In the sea," said Mathilde firmly.

"How do you know?"

"Because I can see, when I want to. Ask me something different."

"What's it like, being a ghost?"

"It isn't like being anything else. You won't know until you are one."

"I don't want to be one just yet."

"That's something you have no control over." She began to fade.

"Don't go."

She clarified in front of me. "I have to, now. But any time you need me, stand in the east tower and call. If I don't hear, one of the others will answer." She blinked out this time, like a light being turned off.

17

High summer, deep depression. Despite the sunshine, the warm breezes that played around the castle, the doves that cooed from the woods below, the birdsong, the bright light.

I was lower than an ant's ankle, and there was nothing I could do about it. Unrequited love, that was my problem. Unrequited love for my husband, the father of my baby, a man to whom I was bound in every way except the one that mattered—he didn't love me, and there was nothing I could do about it. In the eyes of the law, he was mine, but I knew, as did Nadine and probably a few hundred of her closest friends, that Rudi had no intention of standing by me. I felt like an employee, and it hurt.

He came nowhere near Drachenfels, and all I had to go on were a few hoarded memories from those days in Wiesbaden. One memory, in particular, of Rudi in a gray shirt, with a five o'clock shadow around his jaw, haunted me; it was almost a monochrome image, a faded black and white photograph of a man I had known and loved. And loved still. It was all impossible, he wasn't mine, would never be mine; he belonged to some other woman who would never let him go. Well, they always said, "Never mess with another woman's man"—oh, that's *so* country music. I didn't give a bugger for the social niceties; I wanted Rudi, I wanted him bad, and I wanted him now.

What hurt most of all was my own powerlessness, my inability to influence the situation. Here I was, a whale with a melon shoved up the front of her dress, a good couple of hours from Munich, where Rudi was probably cavorting with the most sexually desirable and experienced woman since Mata Hari or Nell Gwyn. It did not feel good. Waves of teeth-grinding jealousy alternated with a smooth wash of memory—of a blond brow wrinkling in puzzlement when I teased him, of smooth thick forearms laid against a white linen tablecloth, a red and black shirt crumpled around his narrow waist, a low laugh on the telephone. No, I would not telephone—that was *her* territory. I didn't want to be greeted with: "I told you not to call me here." I had my pride.

Since I couldn't call him, and I couldn't see him, I decided to do something. I wanted to spend time out of doors, and do what my parents had always done in the summer, sit in the garden and smell the roses. I had spotted, earlier in the year, a level patch below the west tower, with a tangled thorn thicket, an embryo version of Sleeping Beauty's briar-wall, and I realized now that despite the years of neglect, pink single flowers, with fluffy yellow centers, were struggling out from the confining hedges. I trotted down there with a pair of shears and some rubber gloves, and cut myself to ribbons trying to force a way into the garden. A cold presence at my elbow reminded me I should have asked for advice from the residents' association. Mathilde was unable to make herself visible in sunlight, she couldn't lower the temperature enough, but she did guide me around to an overgrown archway on the far side, where the hedge still allowed an entry, and where peonies, no longer in flower, proved less formidable guardians of the gate.

I'd always been a bit scathing about gardening, looking on it as something of a sex substitute, and therefore perfectly suited to middle age but not to me. Now that I was alone, and unregarded, I came to see how healing plants can be—not that they give back affection, how can they? Particularly not these roses, after I had decimated them, hacked some of them down to stumps. It was the act of tending them, of providing nurture (yes, all right, and the odd act of random savagery) that saved my soul from endless brooding, interspersed with bouts of daydreaming, fantasy and make-believe. I kept hoping that Rudi would be involved in some terrible accident and wind up in a coma that only I could bring him out of, and then he would realize how much he loved me. I would always stop myself—how could I wish anything so horrible on the man I loved? It was too much to hope that he would ride *ventre-à-terre* to my deathbed. Maybe I could rescue him from something terrible, or maybe my sweetness and patience would win him over. Yes, I know, I know, but I was desperate and pregnant.

The rose garden saved me, a little—that and the ghosts' interest in it. Rosa-Margareta, who had had it established in honor of her name, told me, as best she could, how the plot had originally been set out, and though many of the roses she named were now lost to rose-growers, substitutes were available, and with the help of a few rose catalogues, I established a list of romantic-sounding replacements. I grew tired of endlessly turning over pages in catalogues, with my fingers growing colder and colder as ghosts clustered around my elbow. "What's that one?" they would whisper. "Oh, *Köningin von Däne-mark*. Do you remember?"

"The night of my wedding, I had roses that color."

"Blue roses—*häßlich*!" "Look at that red—deep as blood."

Their nostalgia for life overwhelmed me in the end, and I had Georg drive me to a garden center, where I unromantically bought a dozen Iceberg roses in full flower. Georg kindly planted them around the crumbling stone fountain, silent now, and I sent off a long wish-list to David Austin Roses, for the start of the planting season.

I spent long afternoons near that fountain; its fluted pillars were a form of landmark for me. The ghosts came out to join me at twilight, though it was chilly to sit down for long, so I would wander down the entangled paths, pausing only to admire my own handiwork or to formulate a new plan for a flowerbed, a bush, a vista. Mathilde often accompanied me, and I would tell her what was on my mind.

"Mathilde, I love him, I want him."

"You're not the first woman to love a Drachenfels," she said drily.

"I know, and it's so stupid. You know, when he asked me what I wanted for a wedding present, I laughed and said a lemon-squeezer, joking. But what I should have said, didn't know how to say, was—a husband."

Mathilde's lip curled. "Lemon-squeezers last longer."

I tutted. "For a young ghost, you're very cynical."

"Anyone who's been altered for as long as I have becomes cynical. You start to see the patterns. And the pattern here is Drachenfels one—women nil."

I stared at her. "Where did that phrase come from?"

"I've been watching the football results—they seem very much like real life."

Ghosts aren't dead, they're just "altered," apparently. *Verwandelt*. They hate the "dead" word, since it implies "gone," and they're not. Some of them took more interest than others in current life, but here at the castle, the television seemed to have given several of them a new lease on—something. Radio was of little interest, except that

Leopoldine had picked up the phrase "Get with the groove, Ian," which had kept her amused for many days; she had taken to hiding in doorways and whispering it to me as I passed.

"It's not real life, it's gladiatorial fantasy," I retorted.

"So? Don't you understand anything at all about men?"

"Yes, actually I do. I was married before, you know. We talked about football. Once, I think. He was called Mark . . ." My voice trailed away. Poor Mark. I had thought about him so little in the last few weeks. What had happened, that he should seem so distant?

"Yes, I know. He came, one time. We talked. Not about football."

"You—you've seen him? How is he, what did he say?"

"I can't tell you any of it. We have laws about the future, even if you think you don't."

"Oh, Mathilde, please—"

She vanished before I could beg.

✠

It was on one of our crepuscular preambulations that I first had the idea about the dog. Mathilde and I had been talking about affection versus love, and come to no conclusions, but had argued long and hard as to which one it was you felt for pets.

"My mother had a dog," she told me, "a little pug called—oh, I don't remember—Mina, I think."

"I'd want something a bit bigger than that, I don't want anything that yaps. Something with a deep woof."

"What color?"

"I don't know that it matters. It doesn't have to match the furniture, it just has to be here with me."

"Oh, aren't we enough?" said Mathilde, pouting with mock reproach.

"It's nice to have you to talk to, but I can't touch you, and you won't bark when strangers come."

An amused smile spread across her face. "You don't think we'd let strangers near you?"

"Wouldn't you?"

"Ah, you'll never know."

"Well, I will if you tell me."

Like the Cheshire Cat, she started to fade, leaving behind only the ghost of a grin. She enjoyed teasing me.

✠

It was at twilight the next day that I heard the barking. A subdued *rowf* came from behind a boxwood hedge, now fat at the top and bald at the bottom. I pushed my way through the long grass, the dew trailing across the top of my feet, soaking my ankles. A thin sliver of moon hung just above the trees, and for the first time there was a breath of true summer in the air. A lone cricket chirped somewhere beyond the rose garden, but apart from the insect and the barking, all was silent, no fleeting presences or ghostly whispers. The world was darkening to deep blue and cypress green as I followed the sound. As I grew closer, I could hear scrabbling, then a clicking sound, as dog-claws reached paving-stone. I came around the corner of the now-trimmed laurel hedge, to find, standing on the path, a large brown deerhound.

We both stopped and looked at each other.

"Nice doggy," I said uncertainly.

The dog quivered for a moment, then stepped forward, nose held aloft. He sniffed the air in front of me, then took another few steps forward, until his muzzle was inches from my waist. I patted the top of his head with one hand, cautiously. Slowly, his tail began to wag.

"Aren't you a magnificent animal? Where did *you* come from?"

He rubbed his head against my side, and I began to caress his floppy ears with both hands. He let me for a few moments, then frisked away, and gave a couple of gamboling leaps.

"Are you lost? Have you been out in the woods with someone, and can't find your way home?"

The dog made no reply. I didn't know why I was speaking to him. I'd lived with the ghosts for too long; voicing my thoughts had begun to seem normal to me.

"Come with me. We'll see what we can find in the kitchen. I don't have any dog food, but we'll see what else there is."

The dog looked at me, then started to trot off in the direction of the castle. He seemed to know the way, and led me surefootedly along the wet paths and shining cobbles. Well-briefed for a stranger to these parts. At the door, he paused, then sat down with a thump, his tail wagging.

"*Good* dog," I said, ruffling the fur at the base of his neck. His thick gray-brown fur was damp at the edges, but soft and warm further in, where my fingers sank through. He was a solid dog, not fat, but with big long bones. A heavy dog who was light on his feet, with none of the lumbering qualities I associated with St. Bernards or Pyrenean mountain dogs. I opened the door and he rose off his haunches and followed me into the house. He was no stray; he had been trained to walk to heel. In what language I had no idea. There was no sign of a collar.

I took the dog into the main kitchen, filled a bowl full of water and placed it on the floor in front of him. He took a few laps, then sat back and looked at me expectantly. His faith in me to come up with the goods was touching.

Fortunately for both me and the dog, Frau Feldstein had left several tins of ham in one of the cupboards, I opened a tin, chopped the entire contents into cubes, then put the little pink lumps onto a plate for the dog. I waited until he had licked the plate clean, then said, "OK, upstairs now. Come."

He stayed at my side all the way. I had to sigh. There was no point in naming him, I would only have to give him back. He obviously belonged to someone. He was no stray. Though thin, his eyes gleamed. His coat looked healthy and unmatted. I decided to ring Georg for advice.

"Ah, Countess, good evening," he said.

"Georg, I seem to have found a dog. A large brown deerhound. He was in the garden as it was growing dark, so I've taken him in for the night. I've given him some food, but I don't really know what to do with him."

"If it can wait till the morning, Countess, I will ring the vet in Oberkirchen. Many dogs have microchips or tattoos now, and he will know how to trace the owners. Or I could ask the police to come and take the dog away."

"Oh no, don't do that," I said hastily. "No, the vet in Oberkirchen tomorrow, I think. We could take the dog down there."

"Will you be safe with the animal overnight? Does it appear tame?"

"Oh yes, perfectly, Georg. I'm sure he's someone's pet."

"Very well, Countess. I will telephone you tomorrow after I've spoken to the vet."

"Thank you Georg."

"Not at all, Countess. Good night."

"My regards to Elsa. Good night."

I clicked the phone off. The dog sat up, and put a paw in my lap.

"Yes, what is it now?" I asked.

The dog shuffled forward, put his head in my lap, then closed his eyes with a long sigh. I stroked the top of his skull, and we sat like that together, while the mantel clock ticked away the evening. I refused to allow him into the bedroom when I went to bed, though, and left him by the sitting-room fire. A hearth dog. On medieval tombstones, I recalled again, knights who lay with a dog under their feet were the ones who had died at home, not on a crusade. I could see that this dog would make a good footrest, if I were to die at home. I did not want to give him back.

When I rose the next morning, Dog was sleeping across the threshold to my door. As I opened the door, he half-lifted his head, gave his tail a desultory wag, then subsided to the floor. I stepped over him and went off to the bathroom; by the time I was ready for breakfast, so was Dog. We raided the kitchens downstairs for Dog-food, then pottered back upstairs. I was on my second cup of tea when Georg phoned.

"*Gutten Morgen, Gräfin.* I have arranged with the vet, Herr Riemschneider, that we will take the dog to see him this morning. Shall I bring the car up in half an hour?"

Reluctantly, I said, "Yes, Georg. Meet you in the court-yard."

I put the phone down, then gazed longingly at Dog.

"Oh Dog, I don't even know your name, and now you're leaving. Oh well. Another one-night stand."

Dog let his jaw drop open in a large grin, and wagged his tail. Then he leaped up next to the sofa, put both paws on the armrest, and licked my ear.

"Down! Stop it!" I said, but I could summon up no anger. I wasn't going to see Dog again, so there was no point in trying to train him. Or take him for a walk, or anything. But maybe just a little walk. Until Georg came.

Dog and I wandered down the drive toward the gate-house, and met Georg in his own driveway as he was preparing to take the car out.

Georg smiled when he saw the dog, and whistled to him. Dog stopped in his tracks and looked at me. I nod-ded to him, and he ran away from me, to Georg; he ran twice around Georg, then sat down at his side. Georg pat-ted Dog, and greeted me as I came up to join him.

"He's enormous," he laughed. "I know you said he was a deerhound, but I had forgotten how large they are. I must show Elsa—do you mind?"

"Please."

He called for Elsa, who came out of the house in a pair of wooden clogs that tapped along the drive. She laughed too, when she saw Dog.

"I don't know how anyone managed to lose a creature of that size. There can't be many like him in these parts."

"I know I'll have to give him back. Already I don't want to."

The two of them looked at me sympathetically for a moment.

"We'll see what the vet says," Georg decided briskly. "Since you're here, let's go, shall we?"

He walked over to the garage doors, and opened them. I held Dog by the shoulder close to my side as Georg drove the car out. As soon as he had parked, Dog barked, then ran around to the passenger side, and sat by the door, panting.

I followed him. "Nope," I said, "back seat for you." He lowered his head, and whined softly, but I opened the rear door for him and he slunk in. I decided to sit in the front next to Georg. It was a silent drive to the vet's, but a quick one.

When we reached the surgery, the vet was seeing his final patient of the morning, so we sat in the empty waiting room, crowded, it seemed, by the vast bulk of Dog.

Soon a woman bustled out clutching a cat basket to her chest. Then the vet came through.

"Good morning, *Gräfin*—dear Christ!" He laughed.

Everyone seemed to laugh when they first saw Dog. Dog didn't mind, he laughed back, and wagged his tail.

"I'm sorry, *Gräfin*, allow me to introduce myself—Jürgen Riemschneider, your local vet. I don't have much experience with elephants, though," he joked, gesturing at Dog, whose tail still thumped against the floor. He was a young man in his early thirties, with brown hair and wire-rimmed spectacles, and a pink open face. The face of a man who got up early every day and lived a healthy life. "No one around here has a dog like this, or I would have known about it. May I check him for tattoos and the like? Does he bite?"

"He hasn't bitten me yet, but I only found him last night."

There was no need to worry. Dog let the vet inspect his ears, and then take him into his surgery to run the microchip scanner across his neck. I followed anxiously, awaiting the worst.

"So, does he have an owner, Mr. Riemschneider?" I asked, unable to contain myself.

"If he does, and he must have, as he's well-trained and in good condition, they have not bothered to mark him. We will notify the police, of course, and they can arrange to take him for you. Though where they'll keep a dog of this size, God only knows," he grinned. "The police pound is tiny, and doesn't see much business. People take good care of their dogs up here."

The thought of Dog in a tiny cage was more than I could bear.

"The dog can stay with me for the time being," I volunteered immediately. "I just need to know what to feed him on."

Mr. Riemschneider looked at me, then said, "You know, the longer you keep the dog. . . . No, it would be a shame to put the animal in the pound, he seems happy with you." He paused. "They take a lot of feeding, *Gräfin*. If it was anyone else, I'd say give the dog up, but I know you have a large house."

"And how," I said, relieved. "He'll get plenty of exercise."

"Be sure he does. Dogs this size can be very destructive if they're bored, and he's a young dog, not more than three. Now, about feeding. . . ." We talked dog food for several minutes, and he sold me several sacks of dog

meal, and recommended which injections I should bring
Dog back for if no one claimed him. Then I thanked him,
and said, "Do come up to the Schloss and visit us—bring
Mrs. Riemschneider, too."

"I'm afraid there isn't one. My mother died a couple of
years ago." He smiled at me; he knew what I meant.

"Well, anyway, do drop around if you're in the neighborhood. Dog and I will be happy to see you."

"Dog?"

"Yes, I'm working on that. Say goodbye to Herr Riemschneider, Dog."

Dog lowered his head and whined once, then turned
and trotted toward the door. I shook Mr. Riemschneider's
hand, then followed Dog.

What a nice man, I thought, as we drove back to the
castle. Georg said the same, aloud. "*Ein netter Mann,*" he
remarked. "*Ja,*" I agreed. Our conversations may not have
been riveting, but we always agreed. Elsa was a lucky
woman. So was any future Mrs. Riemschneider.

✠

The ghosts had been suspiciously absent and silent ever
since Dog came. When I arrived back at the castle, I went
to summon them, leaving Dog shut up in the Master's
Apartments, since I had no idea how he would react to
spectral presences. Around in the east tower, still chilly
despite the blazing sunshine outside, I called Mathilde's
name three times.

There was a phosphorescent flicker, then her voice.

"Yes? What is it now?"

"Mathilde, I have to ask you about the dog."

"Well, you said you wanted one."

"Yes, I did. Did you bring him? Where did you get
him? Won't someone miss him? I'll have to give him
back."

Her voice was weary. "We took him from a very long

time away. Even if they do miss him, he can't go back now."

"You took him? How?"

She sighed. "It's very tiring, you know, I'm quite worn out. You have to stand by one of the passageways, and try to lure the animal in. Once it's in, you can then take it back to your usual time. There are passageways in time, short-cuts, but you have to know where they are and how to use them."

What do they look like?"

"They never look like anything in particular. They're hard to walk through accidentally, though, unless you're very curious. Cats wander through all the time; they're so inquisitive, they investigate anything, and before they know where they are, they're two hundred years ago. Mice and rats are bad, too. Rabbits aren't—they're cautious little creatures."

"So, rabbits don't time-travel. What about Dog? How did you get him?" I had a mental picture of a group of ghosts sitting in a tunnel shouting, "Coo-ee!"

"I don't know. I just tried several passageways until I found one that looked promising—out in the woods. The dog was hunting. Well, you said you wanted a *big* dog," she added defensively.

"I did, I did. Thank you."

"You like him then?"

"I think he's wonderful, he's a beautiful dog. Thank you."

"Good. Enjoy him then. I must go."

"Wait! Can he see you? Will he be disturbed by you?"

"He wasn't when he came through the passageway with us. He can see us, but he'll be used to it."

I let Mathilde fade, and went back to Dog.

✠

Dog settled into the castle routine like clockwork, and I stopped calling him Dog. He became Prince Igor, because we'd Borodin (borrowed him). Feeble pun, I know, but he seemed noble to me, and if you have a castle, you have to be able to shout *"Igor!"* when the doorbell goes. I don't think the castle *had* a doorbell, but then my Igor wasn't a hunchback either, so things never work out like they do in films.

I know it was the right name because Igor responded when I called him; whenever I said his name, he would bark and jump up. Nothing else made him react in that way. Nothing, at least, until I received the first phone call.

18

Rudi picked up the phone several times a day, each time putting the receiver back down before the number had finished dialing. He would press the memory button, call up the castle number, let the high-pitched bleeps start, then cut them off again. Why was he doing this? He had to stop. He allowed himself one phone call to her every ten days, no more, no less. That way it would never be on the same day each week, never an expected routine that she could then avoid; he always caught her by surprise, and she would pick up the phone, a little breathless and confused, and say, "Oh Rudi, it's you." She never said much else, but he could remember every word. He'd stored them away in his memory, and on other days, between telephone calls, he would pull the words out and play them again.

They weren't conversations that would have mattered to anyone else. "I've had to let the housekeeper go, she wasn't happy," and, "I've been doing a bit of gardening." She'd adopted a stray dog, she'd been on a picnic on the

Drachenfels rocks with Georg and Elsa, she was thinking
of ordering some roses. The weather was nice, she'd been
to the doctor in Oberkirchen. No, she still didn't want to
see an obstetrician in Munich.

Rudi wheeled his chair over to the window of his air-
conditioned office. Munich was packed with tourists from
the end of May onward, and the crowded streets were
stuffy and close, exhaust fumes hanging over the city in a
yellow haze. Normally, at this time of year, he would
spend much of his time out of town; he'd go to Cannes, or
a friend's *quinta* in northern Portugal, or at the very least,
visit the lakes at weekends. Somewhere, though, he had
lost the urge to travel. France was out of bounds, except
for the briefest of business trips. Nadine or her spies
would be out in force; she kept on telephoning him on the
flimsiest of pretexts, despite him telling her not to, and a
couple of her magazine friends had "just popped in" on
him in Munich with no excuse at all.

He hadn't seen Nadine for six months, and strangely
enough, hadn't missed her much. He had thrown himself
into his work, cut back on his socializing, much of which
had been Nadine-prompted, and spent more time with
friends and colleagues in Munich. As long as he stayed
here, he reasoned, Ella would always know where to
reach him. She had his home and office numbers, not that
she ever used them much.

He liked hearing her soft voice telling him what she had
found in the library, what she had done that morning, the
little details of her life that mattered, because he couldn't be
there to share them. He wanted to go back to Drachenfels,
but he had told her, "This is your domain," and had
promised not to interfere in her life. He could not turn up
without her express invitation, or rather, his pride would
not allow him to do so. He had made an agreement with her,
and while the terms of that agreement had not been closely
defined, he wanted her to know he was the kind of man

who kept his side of the bargain. Besides, he had no wish to hear her say, "No, you can't come this weekend, it's not very convenient. Some other time, perhaps."

He leaned his forehead against the double glazing, feeling his skin stick to the cool glass. The sunlight bounced in, but the air-conditioning resisted it fiercely. Should he phone, should he go, should he stay?

His phone rang, three rings, the private line. He wheeled himself back to the desk. "Yes?"

"Heinrich here, I'm in Munich and it stinks. I've finished with my lawyers for today, but I have to see them again first thing tomorrow. Can I stay the night at your place? And how about us renacting some of the scenes from the *Oktoberfest*?"

"Yes, and yes." A reluctant smile slid its way across Rudi's face. "Beer and plenty of it?"

"I need to wash the dust out of my lungs tonight. God, I don't know how you live here. I can't wait to get back to Heidelberg. See you later, then."

Rudi met Heinrich in the rear courtyard of an eighteenth-century Kneipe, an old-fashioned drinking den, off a quiet back street. Geraniums in baskets and window-boxes surrounded the wooden tables, and as Rudi picked his way around the tubs on the cobbles, jacket over his arm and tie already loosened, he could see Heinrich with two one-liter steins lined up on the table in front of him, two more on the opposite side.

"Those are yours, lad," he said to Rudi. "Get those down your neck."

Rudi slung himself onto the wooden bench, and took his first swig. He never went to these places normally, but Heinrich had working-class tastes, had come up the hard way, and was respected in the oil business for that reason. Since his marriage to Rotraut, he had learned to spend time in more refined surroundings, but underneath it all, he was a beer and Bratwurst man.

Rudi continued to drink the first tankard almost to the bottom before asking, "So how's business?"

"Rubbish, as usual. Who gives a toss? You mustn't let things get to you. You're looking peaky. Bank in trouble?"

Rudi shook his head. "No, better than it's ever been. I've been working like a dog, though."

"You need some time off. You spending weekends at Drachenfels?"

"No—er, no. Wife's doing it up. And she's pregnant. I don't want to interfere."

"Say no more." Heinrich tapped the side of his nose. "You don't want to pay attention to what they say, though, when they're in that state. Rotraut was impossible with both kinds. I didn't know whether to call out a psychiatrist for her or for me. One minute she'd be telling me to go on, get out of the house, she never wanted to see me again, so I'd go off for a round of golf, and I'd come back, and she'd be clinging around my neck saying, "Darling, where have you been, I missed you so much," and bursting into tears. "Drove me mad. You don't want to listen to a word they say."

Rudi looked at him with interest. "Do you think she—I mean, did your wife want to see a lot of you when she was pregnant?"

"Course she did. She never said so, mind you, but whenever I was home, she wouldn't let me out of her sight. Now she comes everywhere with me. She'd be here tonight if I'd known I was staying over, but I thought I'd be back on the six o'clock."

Rudi picked up his second glass. "So you're saying that women like to have their husbands around when they're expecting."

"Of course they do, and don't let them tell you otherwise. She a solemn little thing, your Ella, isn't she? Self-contained. But you turn up there, offer to massage her back—Rotraut had trouble with our second, he was lying low, and she . . . you don't need to hear all this."

"Yes, I do. I don't hear it from anyone else."

"You will if you ask them." Heinrich wagged a meaty finger at Rudi. "You ask any of the blokes at the bank what they went through when their wives were expecting. Women!" He drank deeply.

Rudi smiled back at him, his first real smile in weeks. "Yeah, women!"

Filled with hope, Rudi made discreet inquiries amongst his colleagues. They were all in agreement, and words such as "impossible," "hormones" and "temperamental" were bandied about, along with the oft-repeated advice. "You want to keep a close eye on them." They had all been unexpectedly sympathetic, warm even, and his secretary, a stout woman in her fifties, had inquired cautiously, "Boy or girl, Count?"

"Oh, boy," he said unthinkingly. "I mean—we can't be sure. You know, tests."

She had beamed at him and said, "Whatever the child turns out to be, I'm sure you'll be happy. Pass on my regards to the Countess."

"Of course I will. I'm going up there this weekend."

As soon as he had said the words, he knew it was the right thing to do. It was his duty as a husband, to keep a close eye.

He set off at dawn on Saturday, humming his way down the motorway and up into the mountains, windows wide open to embrace the cool fresh morning air. The sun was high over the pine trees by the time he guided his BMW into the courtyard of Schloss Drachenfels.

He climbed out and stretched both arms over his head, feeling his spine uncoil and the loose old T-shirt fall away from his back. His jeans were already beginning to feel too hot; he would change into shorts once he was upstairs. As he stood in the courtyard, reveling in the peace, the clean air and the distant sound of birdsong, he heard a dog barking somewhere in the castle, close at hand.

That must be—what did she call the dog? Something operatic. Prince Igor, that was it. There was a rattle at the door, the clunk of an iron latch, and Ella's voice, "Down, Igor! Down. Stop that."

He smiled to himself, and turned toward the door, waiting to see her face. It was all he could have hoped for.

"It *is* you!" she said, surprise and pleasure in her expression as she took several rapid steps toward him. She was flushed, her hair down over her shoulders, her loose pink cotton dress no longer able to hide her barrelled abdomen. "I saw the car, and I thought it couldn't be, but it is!" She looked welcoming and happy, and Rudi thought, I was right to come here.

Then she seemed to collect herself, and remarked, in an indifferent tone: "You needn't have bothered. Everything's fine here."

"I'm sure it is," he said, and dropped an arm across her shoulder. "I just wanted to see for myself."

She leaned toward him for a moment, pressing her cheek against his collarbone for the briefest instant before pulling away again to say, "There's nothing much going on here. You'll be horribly bored."

But he wasn't. The thought had never crossed his mind as he drove to see her, that he would be short of things to do, and in the event, he wasn't. There was the garden to inspect, the dog to take for walks, and then the cooking. He'd offered to cook dinner, and she had laughed, and said, "You can't cook."

"Yes, I can," he protested.

"What, more than two things?"

"I can cook hundreds of different things. I'll prove it to you. How many meals can you eat between now and tomorrow evening?"

"Lots. I'm hungry all the time."

The two of them had adjourned to one of the dungeon-like kitchens, and while he sautéed mushrooms and stirred white wine into a sauce, Ella sat on the edge of the kitchen table, long legs swinging, and the two of them discussed where, in the Master's Apartments, they could fit in a modern kitchen. At Ella's insistence, they took their food upstairs rather than out into the garden. At twilight, she wanted to go out and walk the dog alone.

"I must go down to the garden with him."

"I'll come," he offered.

"No, you stay here. I'll be fine."

"Really, I'll come."

"I'd rather have some time alone. I won't be long."

What had he done? Why did she need to get away from him? He walked around the gallery until he found the windows overlooking the garden, unwilling to let her out of his sight for long. She appeared to be talking to herself, an animated conversation, though he couldn't make out the words. She must be talking to the dog; she was spending too much time on her own. He wanted her to spend more time with him.

As they lay side by side in bed that night, all his old fears returned, bringing with them a new one: he was going to lose Ella. He had only just found her, and would not be allowed to keep her long. She would vanish, as his mother had vanished, without him ever knowing her, and these fleeting moments of happiness stolen within the castle walls would be the only moments they ever shared. This weekend might mean nothing to her, she might still want to die, but when he thought back to her flushed face, the easy banter in the kitchen, their two heads bowed over an auricula in a pot by the castle wall (he'd never known what an auricula was until that afternoon), he thought: She can't die now.

He turned to her, aware that she was still awake, and

said, "Ella? I'm worried. The family curse I mentioned—I can't stop thinking about it."

She didn't move. "I'll deal with that when I get to it."

"Seriously, I think we need to try and do something, but I don't know what."

"I've had all my injections, and the doctor in Oberkirchen says I'm in good nick. People don't die of the things they used to." She turned over, her back to him. "Anyway, what did they all die of?"

"Nothing in particular. They just stopped breathing. There weren't detailed accounts for all of them. They all seem to have slipped away. All except one."

"What happened to her?"

"She committed suicide. Went off to the woods the day after the birth and hung herself from a tree. Post-partum psychosis they call it now, but there was no name for it in the 1700s. He leaned over and put an arm around her, feeling her shoulders hunch as he did so. "She left a note, saying 'They can't get me' x paranoid delusions, clearly. Although we don't have the note in the archives, the local magistrate of the time kept it."

He pulled her resisting body close, putting his face next to her fine, tangled hair, stroking it back from her ear. "I'm sorry, darling, so sorry. Don't listen to me, lie still." He held her for a long time, listening to her breathing as it slowed, until he was sure she slept.

✠

On Monday, he had walked to the office with a spring in his step, and when, as before, he reached for his phone to call the castle, he was able to put it down without even dialing. He looked up to find his secretary standing in the doorway, and he gave an almost bashful nod toward the phone.

"I was about to ring my wife, but there's no point in phoning her ten times a day."

"Yes, I noticed you doing that before. I'm sure she'll be fine," and the gray-haired woman gave him an indulgent smile.

✠

When he came back from lunch, and the lift doors pinged open on the top floor, he could see his secretary in her sensible suit learning into a nearby office, her back to him as she said, "Yes, the Count's expecting his first. He's ever so nervous about it, poor man."

"They say it's made him much more approachable, though," her unseen co-gossiper replied.

What was this? What did she mean, "more approachable?" He'd always been approachable! With a guttural, "Harumph!" Rudi straightened his tie and strode toward his office.

19

Maybe it wasn't the first phone call she'd ever made to me, but it was the first one I knew about. I never took the mobile phone with me, now that Frau Feldstein was gone. I knew that if Rudi rang, it would be in the evening, when I was back in the Apartments, and I didn't expect anyone else to phone.

It was by chance that I happened to be in the sitting room that morning, after a long ramble with Igor. I had picked some wild grasses which had pleased me so much, I wanted to put them in a vase on the windowsill. When the phone shrilled, I was surprised, but answered all the same. Igor started barking wildly, to the point where at first I could barely hear anything.

"You know who this is," a female voice said, managing to snarl and hiss at the same time. "Rudi will always be mine. Leave him alone or I will kill you."

"No." A voice answered the phone, but it wasn't mine. It was a female voice, icy as a vault unopened for centuries. "You leave him alone, or—I—will—kill—you."

The connection was broken. I stared at the phone.

"Who was that?" I asked aloud.

There was no reply, only a kind of whisper and the sound of a garment, the hem of a dress perhaps, dragging across the floor.

The phone rang again, and without thinking, I answered it. There was a forced burst of laughter from the other end. "You think you can frighten me with your threats, you know nothing. I will tell you—"

The cold voice interrupted. "You are dead already." Again the connection broke.

"What?" I said. "Who *are* you? I don't know you."

There was the sound of a footstep, and a swishing, dragging noise. "Come."

The voice unintermediated by the telephone, was scarcely audible, but I could feel its chill weight. I followed the dragging sound, down long galleries and up and down stairs, until we came to the ancestral portraits. The faint smell of mold I had noticed grew stronger, and I felt myself forced toward one of the first pictures in the darkest part of the gallery, to a small black-framed painting on wood, the panel beginning to crack and the paint to blister. Even on a bright summer's day, no light reached this part of the room, and I could hardly make out the picture, or read the tiny gilt writing on the frame.

"Wait," I said. "I need a candle. I can't see."

The pressure at the base of my neck lifted, the smell fell back a few feet. I knew that I had stored a candle and some matches on a nearby window ledge; during the winter I had left caches of candles at strategic points around the castle, so greatly had I feared being left helpless in the dark if ever my torch failed. The brass-based candlestick was where I remembered, the box of matches a little soft, but dry enough to light. I came back to the dark embrasure, the candle flickering, to examine the portrait. It showed a hard-featured fair young woman with a very pronounced chin and flinty blue-black eyes, against a dark background. Behind her was a table on which a dead hare bled into a large platter. The lettering was still indecipherable, until I placed my nose a couple of inches from the wood. In words only a brush-hair thick, it stated that this was Johanna, daughter of Graf Joachim von Echterengen. There had been more, a date perhaps, but the little gilt flakes were too far apart for me to make sense of them.

"Johanna?" I said tentatively.

I heard a peal, as of a church bell, the deepest sort, one slow toll of the bell, that seemed to fill my whole body, then I remember nothing.

✠

When I came around, I was on the floor of the portrait gallery, the white candle sitting in its stand beside me, now only an inch or so above the brass holder. If I had dropped it, it had had the fortune to fall on its foot. I sat up, wiping the hair from my face. That candle had been new when I lit it.

It was still light outside, just. I blew the candle out, then scrambled to my feet. I felt drained, and clutched the wall for a moment, until the giddiness left me. I made my way back with cautious steps to the Master's Apartments.

Igor met me halfway and sniffed at me, snuffled all around me until, with a gruff sigh, he decided to escort me back to the sitting room I had left however many hours ago. Once I collapsed onto the sofa, I felt terrible but not ill, clear-headed yet indescribably weak and wraithlike. My nose started running, with a clear fluid that would not stop but gushed for several minutes while I went to hold my head over the bathroom sink. I thought it was a nosebleed at first, but this was less worrying, yet stranger.

I ate early that night, frozen pizza I think, and went to bed without taking Igor for a walk. He refused to leave me for an instant, and I slept with him laid out along the side of the bed, so that I could not step out of it without treading on him. We both felt safer that way.

✠

I awoke the next morning to the telephone ringing. It was late, the sun was high already. I hurried across the hall.

"Hello?"

"You think I'll give up. Never. He belongs to—"

A voice broke in. "Get with the groove, Ian." Then the dial tone.

"Leopoldine?" I asked. "What are you doing?"

A little chuckle in my ear. "Answering the phone for you. No need for you to."

"Yes, but that was Nadine, wasn't it?"

"Whoever."

"Why is she ringing me like this?" I despaired. "What is she up to? I've never even met this woman."

"Ask Mathilde. I don't know."

"OK, OK."

I shuffled back across the hall, found my elastic-waisted jeans and a clean white T-shirt. Then breakfast. For Igor first, then me. Where was Mathilde?

She came to my summoning, a little huffily, I thought.

"What is it now?"

"Mathilde, I have to ask you about someone. Someone I haven't met before. She hardly spoke, but I think she's called Johanna."

"Johanna? You spoke to Johanna?" She seemed to flicker around the edges, in agitation I thought.

"Yes. She spoke on the phone to Nadine—I'm sure it was Nadine—who rang and threatened me, and this cold voice threatened back. I never had the chance to say a word. I asked who she was, and she led me to a portrait that had the name Johanna under it, but then I blacked out. It was strange: I don't know what I want to ask you, but—"

"If you are still alive after experiencing Johanna, that's all you need to know. *Johanna* came? The need must have been great. Why didn't I see that? Now listen to me," and here her tone took on a great urgency, "never, *never* summon Johanna. There are powers in time and space that few can withstand. Johanna has some of that power. You must have felt that—you *are* still unaltered?"

Goose pimples rose on my bare arms as she stretched out a hand toward me.

"Yes, as far as I know. But I blacked out for a long time."

"She can have meant you no harm, if she was blocking phone calls for you. But there are others, far younger, who were supposed to do that. I wonder . . . no never mind," she said, pressing her transparent fingertips together to a point near her lips.

"You've been answering my phone?"

"Why not? We don't want you disturbed. Nothing unpleasant need happen while you are here with us. The spirit voices are easily reached by us, much easier than becoming visible. I had no idea such things existed, until you came."

"There's been a lot of technological change in the last thirty years," I explained, "and you're a little out of the way here. But I can answer the telephone myself, you know."

"No—it will upset you."

"It upsets me to know I'm missing phone calls."

"You wouldn't miss these."

"Wouldn't I? I can't tell, I haven't heard much. The only times I've heard Nadine, I've had no chance to answer."

"Good. I'm glad we're doing something right."

"Well, could I at least listen? How do I know you're not putting off everyone? Rudi, for example."

Mathilde sighed. "We might let you listen."

"Yeah, do that." We glared at each other, but it's hard to glare at someone whose image is so unstable. Her glare back was much more convincing.

"You should go back now," she said. "Your phone's going to ring in a couple of minutes." I took that as a concession, and went back to where I had left the phone.

I hadn't expected it to be Jennifer.

"Hello, Sis," she said.

"I hate being called Sis," I replied.

"Is that why you never phone?"

"No, I never phone because I'm antisocial, and don't have anything to tell you. How are you, anyway?"

"Fine, but that's not what I rang to tell you. Kevin's parents want to take the boys to Disneyland in the autumn, and Kevin's going to go with them. I'm happy to pass up on men in mouse costumes, and thought, if we could get the dates right, I could come over when the baby's due, spend a fortnight with you."

"Would you?" I tried to keep the gratitude out of my voice. Never let your sister think you're grateful in any way. In case they think you owe them one. Might give them the upper hand.

"Don't sound so bloody pleased."

"I am, I am." I gave way. "Oh please, Jens, it would be great to have you here, and the castle's huge, stay forever."

"I'm keen to see your shack, I must admit. Is it still as much of a hovel as when you first moved in?"

"Yeah, actually, it is."

"Bloody tidy up then. There'll be no time for that once you've sprogged. Anyway, I thought you had a house-keeper and stuff."

"No, got rid of her. It's not all a dump, the bit I live in is fine, and the two women from the village flit in and out. It's just the rest of it."

"You'll have to wait till Bob-a-Job week then. Michael's

just joined the Cubs, and you should see his pack. They're frightening. Twenty Boy Scouts would soon sort you out."

"Take more than that, dear. State I'm in."

"How's that husband of yours?"

"Umm—he's in Munich. I don't see that much of him."

"Doesn't sound that good a deal to me."

"Maybe not, Jennifer, but it is the deal we made when we married."

"Keep your hair on, no need to sound so sniffy. So he's a callous rat, and you're worried he's shagging his secretary, and you want him with you."

"No—I mean yes. Look, everything's OK."

"You mean, shut up Jennifer. I'm sorry, I'm making things worse. Look, mid-October—two weeks—due date?"

"Thirteenth. Possibly."

"Right. I'll be there. And Ella—don't worry. I'm your sister."

I didn't see the logic connecting the last two sentences. Still, I believed her.

✠

Speaking to Jenny reminded me that I had a family, and a past life, a life before Drachenfels. I must have been trying to blot it all out, because I realized, with a rush of horror, that I had not thought of Mark in a long time.

"Forgive me, love," I whispered, as I searched through still-unpacked boxes for our wedding photograph in its Art Deco silver frame with stylized lilies at each corner. It was in the second box I opened, and I clutched it to my chest as soon as I had found it. I used to speak to that photo every night, even before Mark died, while he was still in that hospice in Surrey, so awkward to get to; I had prayed, in its ugly little chapel, begged, pleaded for Mark to be spared, and my prayers had not been answered. I was sure, then, that prayer was useless, and I was on my own.

I ran my fingers over the glass, touching Mark's springy hair once again in my memory, knowing that the dead do live on. I had spent months with another family's dead, and was forgetting my own, had wanted to forget the pain of losing them. I had felt, when Mark first died, that he was there with me, but only for a few days, and then he was gone, and I wanted to follow him, anything to regain that feeling of togetherness.

Now, things were different. I had the baby on its way, and I was not alone. Rudi had turned up unexpectedly the previous weekend, and we'd had one of those blissful times that were like the old days, *my* old days, one of those happy evenings in with just the two of us.

I was the most callous woman alive. All I'd been missing was Mark's role as husband, not Mark himself—slot another man into the chitchat over cooking, and bingo, instant happiness. I was a treacherous, faithless, forgetful. . . . Tears began to roll down my cheeks as I held the photo away from myself. I was that shallow.

Then, and I can't explain how I knew it was him, there was a little puff of air at the back of my neck, and a clicking sound, *Tch-tch-tch.* I know what you're thinking, it's a drafty old castle and all the timbers are probably infested, but Mark often used to come up behind me while I was washing up, and blow the hair away from the back of my collar so he could kiss my neck and, whenever he disagreed with me about something, he used to click his tongue disapprovingly, as if to say, "How could anyone possibly think that?"

"Mark?" I said out loud. "It's not that I don't still love you. You'll always be my first husband. Remember we used to joke about that? I still love you, but—life goes on." It was an old cliché, but it was the simplest way of reminding him that he was—altered, the way Mathilde was altered. We moved in different circles. Mathilde had once said that those who die happy have no need to stay.

I felt the photo-frame grow cold beneath my fingers. As I looked at the picture, a fascination linked to fear took hold of me: all the color was leaching out of the photo, second by second, until I was left holding a black and white snap of the two of us, Mark suddenly black-haired and white-faced. The photograph seemed thirty years older, more like my parents' wedding photo from the 1960s. There was a puff of air at the base of my neck, and I knew he was gone again. Later, I told Mathilde that Mark had been to see me.

"Nah. That was me," she laughed.

I was appalled. "But—that back of the neck stuff. How could you know?"

"He told me, *Dummkopf.* He even asked me to kiss the back of your neck, and I was going to, but then I got the giggles, and I couldn't, but I thought you'd work out who it was meant to be."

"Why? Why did you do it? All that photo business and everything."

"That bit was my idea. Nice touch, no? Listen, Mark is further away than you could ever imagine. He knows that, and he wanted you to know that too." She spoke slowly, emphasizing each word. "He left because he'd finished what he came to do, and now he can't return to tell you. He asked one of us to do it, but I had to wait until you were ready to listen."

"So you came and—oh, great. Is there anything you wouldn't do."

"Not much." She smiled modestly.

✠

Mathilde kept her word, and let me hear a few calls from Nadine. But every time I tried to answer her, to counter the hysterical threats, the connection was cut. I stopped wanting to answer the phone. I felt under siege. Nadine's poisonous tide of calls had had a toxic effect, of pollution in a river slowly coating the surface in scum, stifling the life beneath. In letting her words glide over me, they had formed a slick of non-biodegradable slime above my head. I was depressed. She hated me for having a husband I didn't really have. Why was she doing this?

"Mathilde," I asked, "why is this woman doing this? What's wrong with her?"

"She's worried that her plans won't come off. She's trying to frighten you."

"She's succeeding, I can tell you. What plans, anyway?"

"I didn't want to tell you this, not now . . . but I think you ought to know. She and Rudi are expecting you to die."

"Rudi?" I rubbed my fingers under my eyes. "You mean, Rudi wants me *dead*?"

That's when Mathilde told me the story, or at least some of it—the very beginning in Paris, when the lovers concocted the scheme—just as I told it to you. Later, she passed on some of the other scenes she'd tuned into, but this she wound up by saying, "Nadine always intended to marry Rudi, but was ready for someone else to produce an heir. Don't cry."

"I'm not crying. Rudi always said . . ." I gulped, "He never pretended to love me, but I always knew that he just wanted an heir. I didn't know that about Nadine, though. I didn't realize they were waiting, just counting the days. Did he put her up to making the calls? Do you think he's laughing?"

"No, no. You didn't marry him for love, though, did you?"

"I've done that one already, and look where it got me. No, Rudi was for no very good reason. So he just wants me dead?"

"Nadine certainly does. Why don't you ask him what he thinks?"

"All right then, I will. Pass me that phone."

Mathilde couldn't, of course, and I shooed her away. I didn't want to see her mocking smile as Rudi told me the truth. I poked my fingers hard at the telephone buttons, dialing Rudi's number with an intensity to make my fingers bleed.

"Rudi. Are you alone?"

"Yes, at the moment. What's the matter?"

"Someone's just told me a very interesting story, about you and a woman called Nadine, who is apparently the one true love of your life. You were so keen not to lose her that you chose someone to marry to draw off the family curse. Someone expendable." I bit back the tears that threatened to flood into my voice.

"No—well, yes, some of that is true. But it wasn't quite like that. You don't understand."

"Damn right I don't. I understood, when I married you, that you wanted an heir. I didn't realize you had Countess No. 2 waiting in the wings. How long were you going to wait after I'd popped my clogs?"

"Popped what?"

"Died, deceased, *kaput*—stop quibbling about details! You're just waiting for me to go. Taken out a hefty life insurance policy?"

"No, Ella, that's not how it is. Nadine wanted to be married, and I—she was all I had. I didn't want to lose her then, and she was going to go. I explained about the family curse, and she pointed out a way around it. She didn't want stretch marks, never wanted to be a mother, but she wanted me. Do you know how that feels?"

"You arrogant little shit! You'd have done anything to keep that woman panting for you, right up to sending me to my death."

"We had a business arrangement, you and I. Ella, I

know you're angry, but listen to me, please. Everything has changed since then. Yes, I planned with Nadine to marry someone unknown, and yes, when Dr. Schuber told me that the only young woman he knew was a depressive with suicidal tendencies, I admit you seemed ideal. . . ."

"Wow, you know the right things to say to a girl. I hate you, you are loathsome, you are scum. . . ." I gasped for breath, the pain was crushing my ribs.

"Yes, I am," he said quietly. "But I'm scum that cares about his wife."

"Hah!"

"I made a mistake, back then. You had to have been there. Listen to me. Stop hating me for a moment. Let me describe it to you. Calm down. Are you listening?"

I jammed one fist into my left eye-socket, but the other fist relaxed its grasp on the telephone a little. "Yes." I let Rudi's voice lull me as he told me how it was. . . .

I was in Nadine's apartment in Paris, after an engagement party for one of her cousins. She was in a temper as she paced across the Aubusson. "I want to marry you, I *want* to!"

I sighed. "It would be most unwise, *mein Pudelchen*. We both know what would happen."

. . . "And the next day, I came to London. You know the rest."

I put down the phone without saying a word to him. Mathilde was waiting for me, her face pitying. I think I would have preferred open derision.

"Bastards," was all I could say. "Why did you have to tell me all this? I want to be dead all over again, but that would be giving Nadine what she wants, and I'd die rather than do that."

Mathilde's mouth stretched into a grim approximation

of a smile. "So you want to be dead, or would you rather die?"

"Shut up, shut up! You're all in this together. Leave me alone."

"As you wish."

✠

I dragged myself around in misery, too dispirited to eat or speak. What was wrong with me? Rudi had never pretended to love me, but he had never told me much about Nadine either. Never told me that he'd cold-bloodedly planned my murder, in a way that let him off the hook. Wasn't me, m'lord, must have been a family ghost. I haven't been anywhere near my wife in months, ask anyone. Oh yes, he would have his alibi all sewn up. The perfect crime. Death by misadventure, or by person or persons unknown. And what could I do about it? Nothing. Absolutely nothing. I'd agreed. Might as well have dipped a quill pen into my veins when I signed the marriage register at Camden Town Hall. I'd signed a pact with something infernal, a pact there was no way of retrieving. Even with a quickie divorce, I'd still be the mother of Rudi's heir. What if I gave birth to a girl?

I knew it wouldn't be. I don't know how, but I knew my luck wouldn't stretch to producing the first girl in five hundred years. Or if I did, there would be some loophole, some diabolical technicality that insured I ended up dead.

And I had known. I had been told. I remembered Rudi telling me. I had agreed to everything. I had believed nothing, or been asleep, or away with the fairies, but I had agreed. Stupid or what?

20

Nothing budged me from my self-reproach until Bunty called me.

"Hello," I said dully.

"Bunty here. Turn your personality on, dear."

"Can't. Haven't got one."

"How can I sparkle if you won't respond to my rapier-like wit?"

"Must you sparkle?"

"Indeed I must. Although your husband threatened to remove my sparkle if I went anywhere near you. He then insulted my manhood and implied I was a raving poofter. Stay away from my wife, you nancy."

I laughed. "He didn't say that, did he?"

"Yes, he damn well did. But I forgive him. I am a simple soul, whose object in life is only to bring happiness."

"On your bike."

"For you, my sweet, anything. But first, I must beg for a teensy weensy favor. I need some information that only you can give. How long is Rudi in New York for?"

"I have absolutely no idea. Have you asked his office?"

"Yes, and they're remarkably mute on the subject. I wondered if his going to New York was in any way connected with the lovely Nadine resurfacing in Munich. She may be up to no good, but it seems Rudi has left town rather than face her."

"You're just ringing to wind me up, aren't you?"

His voice took on a placating tone. "No, not this time, my little peach-blossom. I'm trying to do Rudi a favor."

"Oh yeah, what for?"

"So that he'll lend me some money. My agenda's not very well hidden, is it? Look, we both know Nadine's a nightmare, and that Rudi's avoiding her. If, therefore, he doesn't know she's in Munich, he might be glad of the tip-off, decide it's time to check his investments in Hawaii, or the Pitcairn Islands or somewhere. With me so far?"

"How do you know he's avoiding Nadine?"

"Everyone knows that. It does you great credit that he's turned into a faithful husband."

"Rubbish," I said miserably. "I've no idea what's with him and Nadine. I'm the last person he'd tell."

"Don't be silly. He spent an inordinate amount of time telling me he needed to beg your forgiveness over something or other, I was half cut at the time. You're doing a marvelous job on him. I still haven't got over him introducing me to his aunt's friend Frederike. I'd been searching for a sponsor for ages, and she's been—well, I won't bore you. How's the castle going, by the by?"

"Still a tip. Ripe for modernization, only I can't be bothered."

"I'll ship my mother over, if you like. Ever since she finished restoring the Dower House, she's been like a fiend who's lost his pitchfork. You've only to say the word."

"I think the word is no. I mean, I'm sure she's lovely . . . "

"I may have mentioned to you that she isn't. You're moping, aren't you? I can spot a mope at a thousand paces. Come to Monte with me at the weekend and get slammed."

"You're too kind. I'm staying here to grump."

"Have it your own way. But remember, Lord Buntingford is at your service. I'll give you my number in Munich, the one in Monte, and at the widgetry back in England. And do tell me when Rudi's back."

"Yeah, right."

✠

Everyone was having a go at me to clean the place up. It was the Augean Stables all over again. Where did I start? I trailed through the downstairs rooms, sunlight forcing its way through the grimy panes. Blackened gilding, fraying curtains, the fabric rotting into nothingness. Everything needed restoration. It could keep a school of restorers busy for years. A whole school. If ever anyone needed practice. . . . Suddenly, I had a Cunning Plan.

Long ago, someone had mentioned the Augsburg School of Art and Antiquities, and how their students were considered, after a seven-year-apprenticeship, the master craftsmen in their field. I rang Aunt Adalheid.

"If I wanted to invite an entire school to come and stay for the summer to practice, how would I go about it?" I explained my plan.

"I would ring the principal—with whom I used to go to school, incidentally."

"Ah. You know him, then?"

"Yes. Are you sure you want him under the same roof? Only joking, Ella. He's very dull, but an expert on Renaissance marquetry."

"Umm. Don't know if there is any of that in the castle."

"Doesn't matter. You want a bunch of students who

can turn their hands to anything. Can they stay in the castle?"

"That was the idea. There are several kitchens, lots of bedrooms, or they can camp in the woods if they don't want to sleep indoors. I've probably got fifty rooms or so."

"I'm sure it will be possible to fill them. Let us make a few phone calls."

I agreed, and left it to Aunt Adalheid to reorganize the universe. She had the ability to sort out solar systems. One little castle was nothing.

Even with almost a hundred students, most of them living inside the castle walls, Schloss von Drachenfels seemed to have room to spare. Downstairs, the largest rooms hummed with life; the extra kitchens were filled with shifts of youthful cooks; the courtyards outside were covered with sacking and turned into open-air workshops. Smells of varnish, sounds of sandpaper, earnest voices, twanging as a harpsichord was disassembled.

I spent much of those weeks in the garden, Igor and I patrolling the borders of our domain. The heartlands were full of strangers; even the Master's Apartments contained a pair of lecturers. I had offered them the space, they were intelligent and interesting company, and reminded me both of Mark and my former colleagues at the British Library. That part of my life seemed distant now. I had once been a student, keen to learn. Now the students and their tutors seemed aliens. They came in peace, from a galaxy I could no longer recognize.

I has asked them not to use the east tower, and hinted that it was structurally unsound. I wanted the students to stay, not to be scared off or to spread strange tales in Oberkirchen that the castle was haunted. Perhaps it was a little late to worry; strange tales had probably been circulating in the nearest village for the last five hundred years. I didn't want to add to them, though. The public face of the castle was not a frightening one. It was to be an electoplasm-free zone. I had told the ghosts this, and we had negotiated for some time.

We agreed that they could observe, but not participate in, the renovation works. In return, I would visit them nightly to talk about the day's events, to keep them informed as to where work was taking place, and where they could safely walk. They seemed to relish the increased activity, the tramp of feet down the corridors, the noise that started soon after dawn, and subsided into sleepy laughter only after midnight.

I had feared that they might resent the intrusion, but the only thing that seemed to shock them was the sight of so many people in shorts.

"Oh, don't be so old-fashioned," I said to Mathilde.

"Some of the elder ladies—in fact I myself—do not feel it is quite seemly," she insisted.

"It's what people wear in the summer," I replied firmly. "It's a custom. People are used to it, just as you are used to your clothes. Why do you dress the way you do?"

"It was the custom," she said sadly. "I do not like to think of customs changing so much."

"Why the green dress?"

"It was my favorite. I wore it before. . . . It doesn't matter."

It must have mattered a great deal, to judge from her face. I decided to leave her to her thoughts, and left the east tower, quietly closing the door behind me. I was so intent on closing the door properly, I failed to notice a pair of students looking at me curiously.

"Excuse me, *Gräfin*," said one of them hesitantly, "but I think you have left your television on. I can hear it."

Oh blast. "Yes, I leave it on deliberately."

"Is that ecologically sound? And besides, you warned us that the tower was not safe."

"Umm—yes. It's the death-watch beetle," I said. "It's

silence, particularly at night, that brings them out. By leaving your TV on, the beetles stay dormant. Noise, you see. They can't stand it. Once I find exactly where they are, we can treat just that area. Much more ecologically sound than coating the whole tower in highly poisonous chemicals. I was just checking to see that the television was still on."

"Ah. I had not heard of this solution."

"An old folk-remedy," I said as convincingly as I could. "Well, must be getting on. I won't keep you from your work." I hurried back down the corridor, pink with the effort of lying. I was going to have to keep a low profile for a while.

The ghosts and I grew closer during July. I started to feel like a spirit myself, an invisible being on the fringes of normal human doings, who ebbed and flowed in a tide that I was powerless to swim in, much less control. Even the two tutors sharing my apartment were never there, and I seemed still to be living on my own. When the castle was empty, or empty of live people, I never noticed my solitude, but now, surrounded by a throng of people who all knew each other, I was the odd one out, and a transparent veil seemed to separate me from the current inhabitants of Schloss Drachenfels. If this was my future, I didn't want it.

Igor and I would wander around the edges of the castle, no longer cutting through rooms we had once boldly possessed. I was pleased that the building was slowly returning to life, but it was a life in which I had no place. Like a street-urchin with her nose pressed up against the shop-window, I watched the main rooms of Drachenfels take on an order and an elegance they had not possessed in living memory.

Rudi arrived unexpectedly, the night before the students were due to leave.

"Aunt Adalheid rang," he explained. "I wanted to see how the old place looked. And to thank the school for its work, of course."

I gave him a sour smile. You slimeball, I thought. You and that malevolent Bonnie Langford look-alike. Mathilde knew all along. I didn't. I missed you. I may even have loved you. While all along. . . . Bitter thoughts twisted my mouth.

"Nice of you to drop in," I murmured.

"And to see you, of course. I mean, of course I wanted to see you, too."

"Sure you did. Well, I'm not dead yet."

"You seem to be in very good health. How is your pregnancy progressing?"

"At the usual speed. Were you hoping for something quicker?"

"No, no," he said placatingly. "It must be difficult for you, though, with so many people around. I'm sure you're tired, being pregnant."

Hah! He thought I was being sarcastic out of sheer exhaustion. Think again, sugarpie.

"I'm not in the slightest bit tired. Just surprised to see *you* here, that's all."

"I should have phoned." He ran a hand over his face, started to turn away, then looked back at me. "I am glad to see you again."

"How nice." Come to take your farewells, hmm? He looked guilty as hell. Expecting me not to dicker on for much longer? Better go look at the bird one last time, check she hasn't mucked up the family home too much. Only another couple of months to go. Oh yes. I know your game, Mr. Clever-Count. You wolf in sheep's clothing.

I gave him no quarter all evening. I would have made him cook his own dinner, but the students had organized a final farewell meal, and invited both of us to join them. We found ourselves in the old banqueting hall, the

wooden table now gleaming blackly. Long benches
stretched down each side. Spare tables from all over the
castle, chairs, camp-stools, had all been put in along the
walls. We were in one of the lowest reaches of the castle,
the stone flags chill beneath our feet, the only windows
high up. There were no pictures on the beige-plastered
walls, but in a festive mood the students had moved
several suits of armor from the entrance-hall to deck out
the corners of the room. Someone had trailed lobelia
around one of them, and put crêpe-paper streamers around
another.

Happy jousting. Happy Tournament. Pass me a lance,
page. There's someone I must just run through before dinner.

There was no time, though, before we were swept up
in a jubilant throng of celebrating students. We were
asked to admire handiwork, and shake the hands of
enthusiastic young men and women, who all wanted to
tell us what jolly super hols they'd just had. Shut up, I
wanted to snarl, but their good cheer brought out the
Lady of the Manor in me. I nodded graciously, and said,
"How interesting!" fighting back the frowns. This must be
how the Queen feels much of the time, I thought. Nod
and smile. While wondering where you left your trusty
elephant-gun.

Bloodshed and mayhem had to be postponed until
after dinner. Fortunately, Rudi and I were at opposite ends
of a forty-foot table. My Paddington stare was less effec-
tive at that range. The students took it in turns to wait at
table, in organized batches, and the meal flowed with an
easy grace. My immediate neighbors were happy, and
exerted themselves to be charming. I was able to talk a little of book restoration, and I realized we had much in
common. Had I grown up in Germany, I might have been
one of these shiny-faced young things. When had I
become so hard and cynical?

After the meal, there was a move to the main eighteenth-century rooms next to the entrance-hall. I had not been here in over a week; there had been a transformation. My dusty Cinderella of a castle had been visited by a hundred fairy godparents, and was having a ball. I had been consulted on a hundred minor decisions, had even driven down the valley with Georg and a girl student to pick up fabric from the main post office, fabric I had agreed with the girl for which I had written a check. It had not occurred to me that some of the fabric would turn into curtains, almost overnight, or that worn-out gray moldering silk-covered chairs could become pale blue and gleaming.

I was no longer in a lumber-room, I was at Versailles. The summer twilight was dazzled by the candlelight, reflecting off the newly silvered mirrors in the Salon des Mirrors. One of the tutors, a Herr Weigel, gave me the best gift of all: a series of before and after photos.

He was a keen photographer, and had taken copious pictures, but had selected only a dozen "before" photos which he had stuck onto a card, with the after photo on the reverse side. I sat in a corner, turning the cards over and over like an idiot child, scarcely able to take in the rooms around me while drinking in every detail of the pictures. I kept thanking him as he sat beside me. He wanted to see if I was pleased, I could tell, and I hope he saw that I was.

"It has been an incredible month for us," he said. "We have achieved so much, so quickly—as if we stood outside time. I still find it hard to believe, without these pictures, that we have done what we have done. Do you know the story of the elves and the shoemaker?"

"Yes, the one where little elves come and help him in the night?" Normally I'd run a mile from men who wanted to talk about elves. But Herr Weigel was serious.

"Exactly. It seems absurd, I know, yet it is as though we had supernatural assistance. Others have shared this feeling. There is one photo I took—late at night, with the flash—I could swear there is an impression of a hand against a curtain. Yet I know I was the only person in the room."

You little minxes, I thought. No wonder they'd all looked so good and well-behaved. They hadn't been at all, they were pretending. They'll been out running up curtains. Or something. At least they hadn't hindered matters.

I responded to Herr Weigel as seriously as he had spoken to me. "Old castles contain more than is apparent at first sight. I don't think you—or your camera—were supposed to see that hand."

He nodded. "You're not saying. . . . No, I don't think I want to know."

"I think the photo is enough," I smiled. "No point in stirring up trouble."

He shook my hand heartily and we parted with smiles and understanding, I was still clutching the photos to my chest.

Music started up in another room; the harpsichord was still waiting to be restrung, but around its now-gleaming form, three students with guitars and one with a flute had taken up position and played a mixed collection of tunes. I recognized some early Simon and Garfunkel, and even, but I may be wrong here, a version of Dolly Parton's *Jolene*. It seemed to fit the rooms, and people drifted in and out in time to the music. I could have stayed all night, admiring the rooms, now filled with happy laughing people. This was how castle life should be. Why have the space and the echo, without the people and the music? I wanted to freeze these moments, so that I could take them out in bleaker times and enjoy them all over again.

Rudi put paid to that, though. He came up and took my left arm.

"I think we should retire for the night. I need to speak

to you."

"Do you really?" I said, snatching my arm back.

"Yes. Please come upstairs now."

I saw the plea in his face and relented, I didn't know why. We slipped away quietly, and retreated behind the areas to our own bedroom.

He sat down heavily on the bed, and looked up at me.

"Ella, I know when we agreed to marry, I said I wouldn't interfere. . . ."

"Well, don't then."

"There is something I want to say, though."

"Go on." I turned my back on him and started to undress in a desultory manner, not caring where my clothes fell.

"It's about—look, I know it's too late to stop this pregnancy. It would be too dangerous. Otherwise, I would say, let's stop this. I don't know if I can change anything if we divorce, but I want you to know, if you wish to divorce, there's just time to arrange it before the birth. You can end this marriage if you want to."

There was silence while I pulled on the baggy pink T-shirt I slept in.

"What are you going to divorce me for—adultery?" I sneered. "Fat chance."

"No. And you wouldn't be able to divorce me on those grounds either. I mean that. I want you to know that."

"Oh, you do surprise me."

"I don't know what you think, but I've led a quiet life in Munich since I met you. No one could say otherwise."

"I'm sure you've been terrible discreet, I'll give you credit for that. So discreet that everyone's been ringing me up to ask where the hell you are. Even Nadine's taken to checking in with me regularly."

He paled. "Nadine phoned here?"

"I could barely get her off the phone at one point. Admittedly she's been quieter the last month. While you weren't in Munich."

"No, I was in New York, then London, seeing lawyers. Divorce lawyers." He spread his hands in a second-rate cabaret-singer fashion. "I'm trying to offer you a way out. I worry about the effect living in this castle may have. You've changed."

Yeah, I got wise to you. Stop looking appealing, I can't bear it. I'm not going to crack, though.

"Keep your worries to yourself," I said unpleasantly. "And your guilty conscience. If you want to get rid of me, piss off back to London and do your worst with the lawyers. I'm staying right here."

I flounced into bed and pulled the covers over my head. He moved up the bed and sat by me, trying to prize the sheet from my fist. I kept my grip tight until he gave up. He put his head close to mine and said, "I don't want a divorce, Ella. I want what is best for you."

"Like hell. Go away."

He went.

21

What the hell was she doing here? Nadine threw the yellow ostrich-leather Hermès holdall onto the white lace bedspread. She was sure this wasn't the best guest-room, and she'd had to work bloody hard for the invitation. Left to himself, Laurie would never have invited her to the Douro Valley, she knew that, and equally she would never have wished to come—had she not wanted so badly to track Rudi down.

She hadn't seen Rudi since New Year, and hadn't been able to reach him by phone in over two months. Anyone would think he was going off her! She'd have to put a stop to that. She knew all his hide-outs. The trouble was, if he was staying at the Marques's *quinta,* they would never invite her to stay at the same time; no one was so gauche as to put wife and former mistress around the same dinner table. So she'd had to wangle an invite further down the valley, and listen to Laurie blather on about his vine-yards—why did anyone want to spend their day looking at little green pustules?—And even worse, he'd invited that bitchy little queen Aziz and his latest toyboy. To cap it all, Laurie had then announced that the obligatory single man they'd invited to make up numbers was that towering cretin Buntingford.

That wasn't exactly how Laurie had put it. He'd said, "Dragged old Bunters down, hope you don't mind."

She'd smiled, barely showing her teeth, and murmured. "I can hardly wait."

Laurie had given her a sharp look, but he was only some poxy little grape-grower, his sherry didn't even have his family name on it. He hadn't seen Rudi, either, although he'd had drinks at the Marques's earlier in the week. Someone would know where Rudi was, though. Otherwise she'd have had a wasted trip, and Nadine hated to waste time.

She didn't waste much time on social niceties with Bunty over a pre-dinner gin.

"Ah, Bunty. Seen much of Rudi recently?"

"Not a sausage. Holed himself up in Munich."

"I phoned his office, they said he'd gone to New York."

"They should know. Top-secret mish, I expect."

"So he hasn't been racing then?"

"Not seen him at the track." Bunty swirled the ice around in his glass and pondered, before saying, "Newlyweds, eh? He won't be away from Munich long, far from his blushing bride."

Nadine's mouth fell open, but she hastily covered it with her hand, pretending to yawn. "Oh come on. Rudi's hardly the type."

"Ah, you might think that, but I saw the two of them at Easter, and he was frightfully possessive. I made some completely harmless comment about brushing crumbs out of her cleavage, and he was absolutely livid. Nice girl, too. Adores the castle."

By this point, she could barely force the gin into her

mouth, she was so tight-lipped. "Rudi's so good at hiding his true feelings," she drawled. "I know he'll have kept up a good front."

"Front, back and both sides, old girl. That's an unusual dress you're wearing, black and yellow. Reminds me of something. Ah yes—a hornet. Can't think what the word is in French. I'll go and ask Aziz—I expect he'll know."

And Bunty had the bad manners to leave her standing on her own, her half-finished drink in one hand.

✠

Dinner had been vile, seated between Aziz and some Portuguese sherry-shipper with an incomprehensible lisp. Aziz had leaned confidingly toward her and said, "I'm so lucky to have found my new boy—you should do the same. It takes years off you."

"Frankly, Aziz, I have better things to do. Other people can use up so much time and give so little in return."

"They look like quite *large* diamonds to me. Shame Rudi's gone off to play Happy Families with that English girl."

"Oh, is she English? I wouldn't know, I haven't really stayed in touch."

"I haven't met her myself, but Augustin says she's a sweetie. Bit quiet, but then after Sylvie, who isn't? And it's nice to see Rudi settle down at long last. Everyone says he's a different man."

"Oh dear, I don't think I can bear to hear that Rudi's become boring. He used to lead *such* an exciting life." She gave a little pout of regret, and turned to her Portuguese neighbor.

Back in her room, long after midnight, Nadine flung her earrings onto the dresser with a resounding crash.

This was serious. Things were looking worse than she'd thought. Rudi seemed to be using his own initiative,

which was always fatal. Never let a man do things by himself, he's bound to get it wrong. Fortunately, you can generally see when they're thinking; little cog-wheels start
whirring, and that's when it's time to head them off at the
pass.

Women are harder, they've been trained to hide the
fact they're thinking, but at least she knew how to set
them off thinking in a direction she had chosen. It was
high time to set to work on that dumb woman Rudi had
picked up. He was bound to have told her about the curse
by now, and she'd be stupid enough to believe it, too. No
harm in emphasizing it a little bit. Nadine had watched
boxers in training for a big match, announcing to the
world, "The bear will fall in five," repeating the message
over and over, until lo and behold, in the fifth round, the
opponent was on the floor with the referee counting over
him. The Power of Negative Thinking, she called it. Tell
your opponent they are going to lose, and often they quit,
even without wanting to, because the message has gone
so deep. Yes, it was time to get rid of that English tart.

Christ, if you wanted a job done properly, you had to
do it yourself.

22

It was the end of August, and the students were long gone. The whole of July had been chaotic, but August had lulled me into dozing tranquillity. The castle was a different place in its new clothes, and I reveled in the new light that seemed to flow through it.

Much of my time was spent in the garden, where I would lie on the lawn idly twisting blades of grass around a finger, looking out at the surrounding mountains. Even in strong sunshine, the air was never heavy, but the clear oxygen-laden breezes seemed to make me sleepier, not more alert. Even the insects buzzed more slowly, and Igor would lie guard beside me for hours, his usual explorations suspended.

I had been upset after Rudi left. How dare he claim he wanted what was best for me, when it was obvious he simply wanted rid of me even faster than he'd planned, so Nadine would stop hassling him? And pretending it was my choice. I replayed his words over and over. "You can end this marriage if you want to." I didn't want to. Ever since Mathilde had shown me the scene in Paris, where he and Nadine had plotted my death—even if they didn't know me personally—I had no reason to trust any of Rudi's motives.

That's the funny thing about life, that you have no idea what's happening while it's happening. You only find out much later what really happened, and it changes everything you thought. Your past ends up no more fixed than your future, because everything you thought happened to you wasn't like that at all.

Niggling doubts about Rudi remained. Had he been trying to say something I hadn't understood? He had suggested a divorce, as if he thought it would change anything. Did he think he could stop Fate in its tracks?

I wasn't facing up to mine, that was the problem. I had been told repeatedly that the Drachenfels women died in childbirth. All of them. Without exception. I had no reason to believe I was exempt, yet I acted as if I were going to live forever. I remembered once thinking, What would I do if I only had a couple of months to live? See all my friends, travel the world, write my will, go bungee-jumping, all the usual last rites. So why was I lying on a patch of grass, day after day, at the back end of beyond?

All the evidence pointed to my imminent demise. That was why Rudi wanted a divorce, surely. His conscience had woken up. Yeah, sure. What a lamebrain, to think the ghosts could be bargained with. Or foiled by shuffling the paperwork. They weren't that stupid.

They had been very quiet since the students had left. The east tower still whispered and froze in their collective presence, and the television was always on, but none of them walked in the garden at twilight, or came to look over my shoulder after dark.

I began to feel a need for human company. Against my own inclination, I had gone to see the doctor in Oberkirchen, been for ante-natal check-ups, and in doing so had run into the vet, Jürgen Riemschneider. He had invited me and Georg to join him for a drink on that occasion. I met some of the "neighbors," who were obviously curious to find out about the castle. I had invited them to "come up and see me sometime," and a couple of them did so.

Georg and Elsa had strolled over to see the renovations, and now started to drop in regularly. I welcomed visitors, finding comfort in the local gossip. Other than Georg, Elsa and Jürgen, the visitors were nervous at first, and looked anxiously over their shoulders as I led them down the dark corridors, but once in the lighter reaches of the house, they always seemed charmed by the relaxed elegance they found there.

My sister Jennifer had agreed to come for October, to be there for the birth. I was looking forward to seeing her again. Apart from her visit, I had little to think about, and the days floated by until the first chill dew of autumn.

There is a morning every year when you wake up, and know that summer has gone for good. There is a bite in the air, the first hint of cold; the icy fang of winter is bared just a little for all to see. I loved this time of year, when leaves turn golden and the summer haze vanishes. Everything takes on a sharper outline; the horizon becomes clear again.

I woke up, that first morning of true autumn, and saw my own horizon with a horrifying new clarity. I was going to die.

It had seemed a joke all along, something that had no effect on me and could never have any effect. Like selling your soul to the devil, Mr. B. L. Zebub to collect in seven years' time. And you're fine for six and three-quarter years, and then you think: Oops.

Rudi hadn't been so far off the mark, trying to find legal loopholes. He didn't know the ghosts the way I knew them, or he wouldn't even have tried. I knew what I was up against; I had lived with these women for the last few months, and had begun to appreciate the laws under which they operated. Nothing a live lawyer would understand.

There's a Bergman film, *The Seventh Seal*, in which a knight plays chess with Death. There wasn't one thing I felt I could challenge Death to, and stand any chance of winning. It was a typically male solution, anyway: the challenge, followed by the battle to the death. What did women do? Negotiate. (Called yakking, by the unsympathetic. They have no idea.) I was going to have to talk my way out of this one, all right, although I didn't even know who to talk *to*. I would have to start with Mathilde, and work my way up through the ranks, or back through time.

Time that I didn't have very much of. I was a jerky Victorian black-and-white heroine, tied to the railway tracks. Cut to steam train puffing in the distance. Cut back to frantic white face, tousled curls, black-ringed eyes wide in mute appeal. The plinking piano music speeds up, the chords crash more widely. Cut back to train, larger now. Will the hero reach me in time?

No, because no mustachioed villain had tied me to the tracks in an excess of hand-rubbing skulduggery. I'd superglued myself to the sleepers for no apparent reason, and laid around idly all day, not even looking a little way down the track. Stupid stupid stupid. I got myself into this mess, and guess what, no one else was going to help me now. I was negotiating for my life.

I approached Mathilde for the opening round.

"Mathilde, you know this curse thing? It's a bit counterproductive, don't you think?"

"I don't make the rules," she said.

"No, but do you *want* to stay in the castle for all eternity? Wouldn't it be more interesting if you could drift off, move to another plane, be more free?"

"We can never be free. We are bound to this one spot by the line of blood."

"Yes, but it's not very exciting being bound to the one spot. And it must be crowded by now."

"Granted. There is that." She looked thoughtful for a few moments. "Still, it has become more interesting. This television and telephone invention has given us all new avenues to explore."

"You do seem surprisingly keen."

"We are bound to this place, as I said. We can see other places, but it is hard for us. If we use up too much energy in entertainment, we lose much of our presence in this world. Most of the older ghosts have scattered their substance over the centuries to the point where they only appear every few years. With television we can see new things with no loss of substance."

"You don't draw energy from each other? I mean, you don't need there to be any more of you?"

"It makes no difference. We are here already."

"It makes a big difference to me. I'm not one of you yet, and it doesn't make sense to me that I have to join you."

"The principle of the curse remains."

"What *is* that principle, though? To upset the male line of Drachenfels? We both know Rudi doesn't want me, that I was a convenient means of producing an heir. He would be much more upset if I survived."

She gave me a sharp glance. "Men change, you know. Don't be so sure he hasn't changed."

"I'll believe that when I see it. And if ever a Drachenfels reforms, then surely the curse could be lifted?" Then I saw I was digging myself into a deep hole. If my fate depended on Rudi not being a rat-fink, I might as well cut my wrists on the spot. "I mean, why do we always have to do the same thing? If the curse hasn't achieved anything in five hundred years, then perhaps it's time for a rethink?"

"I know what you want rethinking," she said. "All right, what do you wish me to do?"

"I'd like you to speak to the others, or let me speak to them. I'll speak to any of them you think. Even to Johanna." I felt a cold sweat break out as I said the last name.

"You have to be very sure if you speak to her," warned Mathilde. "I wouldn't. You might be altered too early."

"It's worth the risk." I didn't believe the words as I said them, but they lingered in the air until I realized they were true.

"I'll have to ask up the line." She faded from the corner of the library where she had come to my summoning.

✠

Caroline came the next time, a dim gray ghost whom I had seen once before. She was older than Mathilde, and fainter, her voice less easy to hear. "There is already a problem with finding you here," she said without preamble. "Your former husband has lodged an official complaint."

"Mark? But I'm not even—you know."

"He is thinking ahead. It is causing certain difficulties. Though not insoluble."

"I want to speak to someone else. I've met Johanna before. I want to speak to her, but I don't know that I can summon her."

"I do not know that you could, either. I will ask her."

✠

Perhaps it was a premonition of my own death, but at that point I stopped being able to sleep well. As twilight fell each night, the castle no longer seemed a haven or my own domain. I had been allowed to occupy a small corner, on license, but soon I would be free to move on. I was on my own in the evenings, and though in the day Igor and I would go visiting together, at night there was only me, the castle, and a horrible sense of nameless dread.

I blamed everything: the phase of the moon, my hormones, the mountains, the room I slept in. For some reason I took a dislike to the wardrobe. It seemed more and more coffin-like, and I feared even opening it, in case I was swallowed in its depths and buried alive, suffocating in a tangle of my own shirts. To all outward appearances, it was a normal, heavy oak wardrobe with brass handles, but to me it was something immeasurably more sinister, a maw-like open grave yearning to be filled.

It was this that led me to spend a night in the Green Room. I had bedrooms to spare. Why then sleep in the same room as the hated piece of furniture? I had lain in bed one evening, watching the brass handles glint evilly in the light that came under the door from the hallway, and I made a spur-of-the-moment decision to sleep next door. Gathering up my pillow and duvet, I padded down the hall to the next bedroom, the one with the lush painting that took up a whole wall. I threw my bedding down on the bare mattress, then closed the door. The room was cold, but I was tired, and fell asleep instantly.

At some point during the night, I woke, or thought that I woke. The room was lit with a light that seemed to come from within the painting. The painted forest was alive, leaves rustling, branches creaking. Something was stirring in the depths, a slow tread was approaching. The shadows intensified, the room seemed to darken to a dim green half-light. I could see a shape, half-hidden by the trees. I heard a snap, as a twig broke, then I saw an arm, through the greenery, beckon to me. A black-clad arm, visibly female, the end of the long black sleeve ragged, trailing into the foliage.

Scarcely knowing what I was about, I rose and walked toward the painting. I could feel the breeze rustling the branches, could smell the damp odor of leaf-mold, of wet soil and toadstool-sprouting earth. I drew closer and closer, until the ivy climbing around the nearest tree seemed to quiver, and then, as I was almost close enough to the tree to touch it, the ivy launched itself at me and lassoed itself around my throat and started to draw me in, into the picture. I clawed at the tendrils wrapped around my neck, but I could hardly breathe. Tearing at the rubbery, unbreakable strings, I gasped, "Mathilde! Help me!" But it was not Mathilde who came.

The owner of the black-clad arm looked down on me with an implacable white face. I had fallen to my knees, the ivy pulling me down as I fought its labyrinthine tentacles. She opened her mouth to speak, but my vision was clouded, the blood pounding in my temples, the world turned to dark green and black, and everywhere pointed jagged attacking leaves. There was a glimpse of something white in her hand this time, a rope, tied in a hangman's noose. Croaking for help once more, I turned my face from the woman, and fell to the forest floor, sobbing . . . then the scene melted away.

I was on the floor of the Green Room, freezing, a dull ache in my throat. I clumsily picked up the bedding once more, and retreated, to the sitting room this time, where a gray dawn was breaking over the mountainside. As I pulled back one crimson curtain, my gaze fell on my hand. All the nails were stained a dark, bitter green, the color of Night Nurse, and under one thumbnail was a fragment of leaf. I couldn't be sure, but it looked like ivy.

✠

All my helpers had deserted me. Mathilde didn't appear that day, no matter how much I called. My sense of unease grew. When Nadine telephoned, I didn't even have the energy to listen to her. My spectral friends were friends no longer, and had stopped shielding me from the calls, so I was determined to put a stop to them myself.

Before she had drawn breath to utter more than one obscenity, I started in on her.

"You're wasting your time, sweetie. I'm not about to die, not now, not any time in the next forty years. I will outlive you, and your stupid plots, and you will have what you have now. Nothing. Nothing at all. Because I belong here and you don't. You belong in hell, so why don't you hurry along there right now."

I broke a fingernail on the Off button.

✠

I was bluffing. It was a very bad habit, committing myself to things I had no control over. I needed to speak to Johanna as a matter of urgency. I had no idea what to say to her. This was the ghost who had left me unconscious for the best part of twelve hours after minor contact. She hadn't even spoken to me, though she had spoken to Nadine. She must be able to speak, then.

Caroline came, with Mathilde, after dark a few nights later.

"Come to the east tower. We need you to telephone yourself. Then return here. Johanna will speak to you."

"I don't understand."

"We have Frau Feldstein's mobile phone. You have yours. We're not sure about making the right connections. It is hard to push the buttons. Come and do it for us. Open the line," said Caroline.

"But don't stay," added Mathilde. "Johanna thinks you should be further away than you were last time. Come back here and wait."

It made a strange kind of sense. I went over to the east tower, the chill palpable as soon as I opened the tower door. My teeth chattering, I dialed the number of my own phone, then, feeling foolish, answered my own ringing handset. Clutching the mobile in my stiffening fingers, I hurried away to the library, trying to breathe warmer air back into my lungs. The east tower had become as cold as a polar ice-cap. Even trying to breathe in there set me coughing with shock.

I sat upright in a red leather armchair, the open line crackling with static. I waited, blowing on my blue fingers, holding the phone until that chill voice grated, "Ella."

"Johanna. I'm sorry to disturb you, but I am most grateful you can spare the time." I still had no idea how I could persuade her that I needed to survive. "It's about the curse. I think it's time to act differently. I don't know how to neutralize the curse, and I need your help."

"I am the only one who can still reach Anna-Maria."

"Not to cast aspersions on all her hard work, but it's not exactly logical, is it? If I've understood this properly, her husband was unfaithful while she gave birth. He takes up with a gypsy girl, and the wife, dying, curses him. He dies, fine, but then the curse falls on all Drachenfels women in childbirth. Now I'm in the same situation. If I die, my husband takes up with a gypsy-girl equivalent. But he doesn't have to die, only me. I don't think it's fair, and it doesn't solve anything."

"You want the current head of the family to die?"

"No, that's not what I want. I think it's time to stop punishing everyone. Stop the cycle of death and betrayal. Nothing will ever be solved, otherwise. The same story will repeat for a hundred generations. Why?"

"Why?"

"Yes, why?" I repeated.

I knew she was still there; there was silence rather than static.

"I will have to return," she said after many minutes.

✠

I knew the negotiations were continuing when Mathilde returned unsummoned to the library most evenings.

I asked her about the picture in the Green Room, and told her a little of what I had experienced.

"I know who you mean, but few of us have any influence over her. She chose to take up residence in that wood, and not to join us. Perhaps she is hungrier for company than most. I have to tell you, the net is closing in on you. I know you want to avoid the fate we have all met, but the pull toward the spirit world is stronger than you realize."

"Yes, but who's doing the pulling? I'm not. Isn't it a bit selfish of you to want me with you—in altered form?"

"What happens to us?" she asked me. "If our ranks do not increase, what happens? We rely on new company— for company."

"Weren't you all a little bored, though? You had far more entertainment out of the television, and the students, than you'll ever get out of me."

"That's true," she said slowly.

"Can't you ever get away? Exorcism? Surely something must release you?"

"No, for us there is nothing. All we can do is wait, until we lose the ability to speak in a language that can still be understood. There will come a point when the language of the day will have changed so much, we can no longer communicate with the living. Even the images we use will cease to have currency. We will fade. Eventually."

I felt a wave of compassion for the sad green ghost beside me. "I'm sorry you have to wait so long."

She shook her head. "You're the first ever to ask why. That alone was worth waiting for."

✠

If the ghosts could reach me in thoughts and dreams, then perhaps I could reach them in the same way. I had read of "guided mediations," in which one followed an imaginary journey in order to gain insight into present-life problems. I needed to think of a way to reach Anna-Maria, the author of the original curse, and Mathilde's words about images had given me pause for thought. It was no good calling on a woman who spoke Old High German or Middle High German, or some other archaic form of language. By pictures I could communicate, a form of mental sign language, where words were useless. There were no pictures of Anna-Maria, though, and for some time I despaired, until I remembered the woodcut in Dr. Schuber's possession.

Summoning up a mental image of the scene, I imagined myself there, standing outside the walls of the castle. Nearby, the nameless gypsy fell to her death, an expression of grim triumph and despair on her face, while the heedless Count clutched unwittingly at his lost hat, the horse's hooves scrabbling for purchase on the rocky slope. They were unaware of my presence, and it was too late for me to cry out, to warn them. There was a clatter of stone, a boulder dislodged somewhere higher up the mountain, and the Count was gone, fallen into nothingness.

I looked up at the castle, and the white face I thought I had seen, in London, the previous year, was there, staring out of the first floor of the east tower. I had to speak to her. The castle gates were open, gates that no longer existed in my time. The courtyard was full of people, all going about their business, oblivious to the tragedy that had just taken place beyond the castle walls. I followed the corridors around to the east tower. Though the castle was different, I seemed to know my way, and no one challenged me, or even noticed my presence.

There, where I had seen her, in the east tower, was a slim, drooping blonde ghost, her long blonde plait trailing over her white shift. She turned to me, an expression of abject misery in her watery blue eyes. In contrast to her wilting body, every feature of her face was tense, her mouth half open in a sob, the muscles in her cheek drawn so tight I could see the veins.

"Happy now?" I said.

She shook her head.

"Well then," I said, and walked away. Whatever I had planned to say to her, to try and argue my own case, was irrelevant. Faced with her deep unhappiness, I knew I could not reach her. Johanna sent messages at regular intervals, all to say: No Answer Yet. I tried to master my rising anxiety and impatience, but bombarded Mathilde with new questions whenever I had the opportunity. Why is it always the woman who suffers? Does suffering change anything for the better? Would happiness bring about change rather than suffering? What's wrong with happiness anyway?

I received my answer one morning, with a hard frost, the cold waking me early. There was a lump under my pillow, a soft scroll of copper sheet, a twin to the one over the fireplace in the hall, but not an oxidized green. This was still copper-colored and shining, words etched into the pliant metal with a sharp nib in an antique shift. It was a contract.

One of its terms was that I must reveal the conditions to no living soul, and the penalties and proviso clauses gave me nightmares for days afterward. There was one phrase that I am not afraid to repeat, however: *twenty television sets.*

23

I was glad my sister was going to be with me for the birth. It was the beginning of October, and there had already been several falls of snow. Some of the highest mountain passes were cut off from September to April; Schloss Drachenfels was lower than that, no more than 2,000 meters, and Rudi had arranged for the snowplow to come up as far as the castle once a week during the winter. The snow, as yet, had not been heavy, and the road showed black down the white mountainside. Jenny had been trying to persuade me to move, at least down as far as Unterkirchen, to be near the hospital, but I wanted to show her the castle, to explore its furthest reaches, play hide and seek around the courtyards, wanted her to admire my work in the library.

That particular afternoon, though, I was not in a good mood. My back ached horribly, from all the extra weight I was carrying, and my head hurt, and every time I tried to go up and down stairs, I overheated. I was only wearing leggings, a T-shirt and an outsize sweater; I couldn't fit into anything else. I felt like a hippo, huge and fat and rolling, and very sorry for myself.

Even the news of Igor's accident failed to shake me out of my self-pity.

"Ella, Igor's done something terrible to his foot, and he won't let me near it. He's hopping around on three legs and whining, and I can see a whole strip of raw flesh. God knows what he's done. Get on the phone to the vet."

"Can't it wait? I don't feel well."

"No, it can't. If you won't, I will, even if I can't speak German. Give me that phone."

"No, I'll do it," I grumbled. I had the mobile phone within reach of the sofa, and called Jürgen, ready to explain that I was too pregnant to lift an injured deer-hound into the car and bring it down to his surgery. Jürgen took this in his stride, and said, "I'll be straight up. If I do it now, I can be back in time for my evening surgery. See you soon."

I sank back onto the sofa, worn out by the monumental effort of making a phone call. I grizzled and grinched a bit, until Jenny lost all patience with me, and told me that if there was any more of that nonsense, she would drive me straight down to Unerkirchen and abandon me on the first street corner.

When we heard the vet's car come up the driveway, Jenny went down to meet him. She was gone a long time, and I was beginning to fret by the time she reappeared with Jürgen.

"Good afternoon, Countess," he said cheerfully. "That dog of yours puts up a good fight. I had to knock him to get at his leg. I've stitched it, and given him a shot of antibiotics. He'll be a bit groggy for the rest of the day, but no lasting damage has been done. How are you, anyway?"

I managed a feeble smile. "Too pregnant to move. Thank you so much for coming up. Would you like some tea, or a drink?"

"Sorry, can't stay," he said, rubbing his hands together briskly. "Now that the clocks have gone back, it gets dark so early. I don't want to drive that road in the dark, if I can avoid it. I'll be back in a couple of days to look at the stitches. I'll call you, yes?"

Jenny and I agreed, and she showed him out. The light was already dimming, although it was barely four o'clock, but I did not want to turn the lamps on, not yet. I heaved myself over to the window, and watched Jürgen's car snake away down to the invisible village; I always watched cars from this window, for no good reason. They were lost to view so quickly. Then, as I stood, wondering what to do next, what would fill the long evening hours, I heard a rumble which grew in intensity until the sound, magnified by the walls of mountain, filled the horizon, the whole valley. As the sound died away, I said, "Great! A thunderstorm. Maybe that's why I've been feeling so terrible all day. A good storm will clear the air, and if that rumble was anything to go by, this'll be the mother of all storms. Looks like Jürgen went just in time."

I looked down, and realized I was standing in a puddle of water, and that my leggings were soaking. I was puzzled it had not yet started raining, and anyway, I was inside.

Jenny came back into the room. "My God! Your waters have broken."

I was still bemused, and shook my head, but then the worst cramp I had ever had pulled my head toward my knees. I'd had dysentery once, on a low-budget student trip to India, and had felt just the same—as though all my guts were trying to leave by the nearest available exit. After a moment, the feeling left me, and I was able to stand upright again.

"How far apart are the contractions?" asked Jenny urgently.

"What contractions? I'm not having contractions."

"Yes, you are. You're in labor, you stupid cow."

"Don't call me *a cow!*" I doubled over again.

"Oh shit. Come on, into the bedroom."

There was enough time between the spasms for me to hobble into the bedroom and keel over on top of the bed. Jenny pulled off my shoes, and then eased the sodden leggings from my doubled-up body. She pulled the bed covers from one side of the bed, and rolled me under the covers.

"I'll go and get the phone," she said. "There's no time to drive you to the hospital, you're too far gone. We'll have to try and get the doctor up here."

"Number's—on—the—pantry—wall," I managed to gasp, my breathing under no kind of control at all. Jenny disappeared.

She came back to find me with the sheet plaited through my knuckles.

"Hope the doctor understood. I just kept saying 'Schloss Drachenfels—baby—quick!' Look, Ell, I think I heard a car. I'll be right back. Don't go anywhere, will you?"

"This—is—no—time—for—jokes," I panted, but she ignored me and dashed out of the door. I lost any ability to keep track of time, trapped in my own world of breath and pain and blood pounding in my head, but it seemed only moments before she reappeared, with a worried face and Jürgen the vet.

"Wrong—number," I tried to reproach her.

"Countess, there has been an avalanche, just below the gatehouse." Jürgen looked green as an Amazon parrot. "I could go no further, so have returned to ask if I might stay."

Jenny interrupted. "Look, we'll have to deliver this baby ourselves. The doctor can't get through now, and I did three months in Obstetrics once. I expect you've delivered calves, or lambs, or something. Please—go and get your bag from the car."

"Yes, but I cannot be responsible. . . ." I could hear the protests as Jenny hustled Jürgen out of the room again. Personally, I was past caring, and Jenny and Jürgen came and went around me, with towels and hissed instructions, and metallic clinks as Jürgen sorted through his bag. I'm going to die, I thought. I'll be given horse tranquilizers, they'll pull the baby out with a rope, I'll bleed to death, I'm going to die here. Where was Rudi? I wanted Rudi. I whimpered his name a few times in between the screaming and crying and struggling for breath.

"Come on," my sister urged. "The baby's well on his way. Come on, push."

"I *am* pushing," I wanted to scream, but I couldn't say anything; none of my body worked. All I was conscious of was the huge wall of pain below my chest, that prevented me even from raising my head, my head that throbbed like distant machine-gun fire, a persistent thump, thump, thump. The noise grew and the pain grew, and I could hear faraway words from my sister and Jürgen, then a surge, of resistance overcome, a drain unblocked, and I could breathe freely again.

✠

"It's a boy," I heard Jenny say, somewhere on another continent.

"I'll clean him up—Jürgen, will you go? Take a towel, you're covered in blood."

I lay there, sticky, wet, exhausted, my stomach still giving strange little lurches, as my sight and hearing slowly returned to normal, except that I could hear a strange high-pitched whine, slowing down, but audible still.

Jenny was handing me a damp, still glutinous baby, when I heard scuffling in the corridor outside. "What have you done with my wife? If you've harmed her, I swear you will die."

The door slammed open, and Jürgen, bent half-backward, tottered into the room, held in place by Rudi, who had his left arm around the vet's throat and in his right hand, a pistol pressed into his ear.

I clutched the baby to my sweat-soaked T-shirt. "Rudi! What are you doing? Let him go!"

Rudi lowered the pistol, but kept his choking grasp around Jürgen's neck. "Are you all right? Where's Nadine?"

My sister cut across our babbled questions with a loud, but very careful, voice. "OK, let's all stay calm. Nobody move. Rudi—put down the gun. Please—put—down—the—gun."

Rudi looked at her, then at me. "I thought—he was covered in your blood."

"He is," I sighed. "It happens when you have a baby."

I could see Rudi do a double-take as he realized the towel clutched to my bosom actually contained something. He let go of Jürgen abruptly, and glared at him.

"Why are you here? This is not the doctor."

"No, Jürgen's the vet. He came to look at Prince Igor's paw, and then the landslide cut him off. How did *you* get here? The road is impassable, or so Jürgen said." I looked suspiciously at the vet.

"I came by helicopter. I've left the pilot in one of the kitchens, where the range is still warm. It was my only hope of reaching you before Nadine did. When did the landslide happen?"

I had lost all sense of time, and could only shrug, but my sister said, "About two hours ago?"

"It's been less than three since Bunty rang to warn me. Nadine apparently left the von Reinharts with a rifle and two pistols, heading this way. According to Bunty, she rushed out of the room while von Reinhart was showing around his baby photos. It seemed an extreme reaction, but no one expected her to raid the gun room. Bunty said he was in pursuit, and would try to stop her if he could

catch her up. If the rockfall prevented her from driving
further, she might try to climb over and keep going. We
haven't much time, and the armory's at the other end of
the castle—we need more weapons. Jenny, can you
shoot?" He held the pistol out to her.

"No, I bloody well can't," she snapped. "And what's
more, I don't want to."

He turned to Jürgen. "A vet should be able to handle a
pistol. Here, take this, and stay by the door. If a small redhead tries to come in, shoot to kill. She will."

Jürgen took the pistol doubtfully. "The safety catch
isn't on."

"Damn right it's not! Don't you understand? There are
lives at stake here. Nadine will stop at nothing once her
mind's made up."

"Rudi, don't go," I called.

"I have to. I'm the only one of you she won't shoot."
He ran out of the door, and I could hear his footsteps
recede down the corridor.

Jürgen, Jenny and I looked at each other. "Do you
think he's flipped?" I asked.

"I have to say—no," Jenny answered. "We get loonies
brought into Casualty all the time, and he seemed quite
rational."

Jürgen rubbed his neck carefully. "Didn't seem rational to me," he muttered.

Both Jenny and I felt sorry for him, but a sudden
somberness came over us. It was now dark, and growing
colder, an oppressive silence on all sides. We waited, long
silent minutes, Jürgen nervously fingering the matt black
pistol. I became aware of my knickerless, rubber-legged
state, and pulled the bedcovers tightly around myself.
Jenny removed the soaked towels. The bed was in a terrible state, as though I'd already survived one murder
attempt.

A slow tread approached, and we froze. Too heavy for

Nadine, surely. A man's tread. But too slow to be Rudi's—
too hesitant. We heard a tap at the door of one room, then
the next, then closer. I stuffed my fingers in my mouth,
trying to prevent a scream. The steps stopped outside the
bedroom door. Jürgen raised the pistol slowly.

"*Gräfin? George hier. Sind Sie d'rein?*"

I waved Jürgen away from the door. "*Ja, Georg? Sind
Sie allein?*"

"*Ja.*" I could hear the confusion in his voice.

"*Bitte, hereinkommen.*" The door opened slowly, and
Georg entered. Jürgen sprang behind him and closed the
door.

Georg shuffled in, peering at me, propped up in bed,
and let the puzzlement show in his face. He opened his
eyes wide when he saw the baby in my arms, and said in
German, "You had the baby here? Just now?"

"I had to—the landslide. We can't get out."

"Yes, it is about that I wished to speak to you. We
found an English gentleman, half-crushed; he is going to
hospital, but he insisted that I come up to speak to you. A
Herr Bunty—his legs are broken, I think."

"Did he want you to tell me he was going to hospital?"

"No. I was coming to that. He wanted me to tell you
that a lady in her car went under the rocks. He saw her
car being pushed down the mountain. He was very lucky,
he was not under the main fall, and by chance the doctor
from Oberkirchen arrived just a few minutes later."

"That wasn't chance," I said. "I called the doctor up
here, but I didn't know there'd been a rockfall, and that he
couldn't get through."

Georg nodded. "The mountain rescue people are still
searching, but it is dark now. No one could have survived
that weight of rock."

In the corridor outside, another, lighter footstep. A
wooden thud, then Rudi pushed the door open with an

eight-foot-long pike, two blunderbusses over his shoulder.

"Most of the stuff's useless," he said. "Haven't got the bullets. These are the only things I could find that I could put lead shot into. Hello, Georg. What brings you here?"

Georg explained all over again about Bunty, and the car pushed over the edge.

"I don't think it's wise to be lulled into a sense of safety," said Rudi harshly. "Nadine's always had the devil's own luck. Georg, I'm glad you're here. You know how to handle one of these things, don't you?"

Georg took the blunderbuss in a bemused manner. I could not believe this was happening.

"Rudi, I'm tired, and I need a bath. Don't you want to see your son?"

"You're not going anywhere," said Rudi, trying to barricade the door with the pike. "I'm trying to keep you in one piece a little while longer."

"I just want you to know, she did not die in childbirth," said Jürgen defensively. "I know I'm the vet, but I did everything I could, and whatever they say about family curses, she is healthy now."

"Oh, shut up, Jürgen," Jenny and I said almost simultaneously. I added, "I'm not going anywhere—I made a deal with your family."

At that precise moment, the electric light started to dim, and Mathilde slowly materialized in front of us. I was used to it, but I don't think the others were.

"You." Rudi gave a strangulated gasp, and seized the pistol from Jürgen.

Mathilde said nothing, but moved from the foot of my bed to stand by the head. The room grew colder and dimmer as more ghosts entered, all women, as misty vapor at first, then ever more solid, more and more of them, until I felt I could scarcely breathe.

"We have come to see the newest Drachenfels of

Drachenfels," Mathilde said in a clear, penetrating voice. Holding the baby tightly to me, I pulled the towel away from his head a little

"NO! You shall not have her. Take me. For once, after all these centuries, take the one who deserves to go with you. Take me in her stead." Then, raising his right hand, Rudi took careful aim, and fired directly at Mathilde. The bullet passed through her and thudded into the wall behind me, showering me with plaster dust and flakes of paint. The baby yelped, then gave an ear-splitting scream. Poor little mite. His life was not getting off to a good start.

The assembled ghosts quivered; a frisson of anger went through them as they gave out a low hissing noise.

Mathilde drew herself up to the ceiling, and Rudi took aim again.

"No, Rudi!" I shouted. "I had a deal with her."

"You still have a deal with me," boomed Mathilde. "Spare your powder, Drachenfels."

Rudi looked at me questioningly, then slowly lowered his arm.

"The ricochet could kill us all," I told him shakily. "Mathilde, you haven't come to fetch me?"

"No. We have come to take our leave of you, and to see the last Drachenfels who will see us. Our bargain stands. We move to the east tower and the televisions you agreed. As our attachment to the castle fades, we may be able to leave, but while we wait . . . and waiting may be long. For many of us, the desire for revenge is the common cause that binds us, and once released from that desire, we are free to go. There are two things, however, that I would ask."

"Yes?"

"One—please leave the televisions on at the wall switch. Many of us are unable to move physical objects, though we can interrupt electricity to turn things on and off. Second—Albertine saw a man in the seeing-box, as she calls it, talking about a satellite. This satellite brings more, different things into the seeing-box. Is this true?"

"Mathilde, if it is at all possible to get satellite TV into the east tower, I will arrange it, and then come and tell you about it."

"Thank you." Mathilde smiled graciously, and floated down by the bed again.

I could see Rudi shake his head, as if he had water in his ears, Jenny, Jürgen and Georg looked frozen into ice. I would worry about them in a moment. I pulled the towel back from the baby's head, and smiled at him.

"Say goodbye to your ancestors, Alexander."

His little navy-blue eyes opened, and swiveled around. I knew he couldn't focus, or see anything, but I could feel him trying to move his head. Mathilde brought a transparent hand down to touch his cheek, and he made a small noise, deep in the back of his throat.

"Bring him to see us when he's older," said Mathilde. "If we're still there."

"Sure," I said. "Er—one last thing?"

"Ye-es?"

"Where is Nadine? Is she going to come bursting through that door at any minute? I need to know. We can't wait here, barricaded in, all night."

"Oh, I think she's gone now. Emilia, you were in charge of that. What did you do with her again?"

There was silence.

"Emilia?" Mathilde's voice was sharp.

Emilia, a small pale ghost who had been on the verge of fading into the wardrobe, reclarified herself and came back into focus. Her off-the-shoulder mauve gown revealed a pair of shining shoulders that shrugged defiantly.

"You know how we fetched the dog? I sent her back the same way." A sulky adolescent voice. The girl was barely out of her teens. It struck me how young all the ghosts were. All married to a Drachenfels before they had had any experience of life. I thought of them as being hundreds of years old, as all ghosts should be, with a maturity accumulated over centuries. In fact, I was at least ten years older than any of them.

I felt like a parent as I asked, "Where exactly did you send her?"

Another shrug. "Do I look like a woman who gives a shit?" she said, in perfect American-accented English. Too much television already.

The other ghosts murmured amongst themselves. "How on earth did you manage it?" asked Mathilde.

"She wasn't much bigger than the dog. It was a tight squeeze, but she's gone now."

"Where?" I asked again. "Or should that be, when?"

"Ask the dog," said Emilia. Around about then."

"Anyway," interrupted Mathilde, "I thought you wanted to confine the bad to the past. I think we have. We must go now."

"Yes, but—we can't just leave her. Can you get her back?"

There was a collective ethereal shrug.

"No," said Mathilde firmly. "You can't bring people out of the past if you don't know exactly where they are. Nadine must stay where she is now."

The ghosts all began to fade out simultaneously, and as they did so, the other people in the room began to move again. Only Rudi maintained a semblance of calm.

"Do you see these women regularly?" he asked.

It took me a couple of moments to be heard, over Georg's repeated, "*Gott in Himmel*," and my sister's muttered collection of swear words. Rudi came and sat down on the bed next to me, draping his arm around the headboard, and bent down so that he could hear me.

"No, only Mathilde. She died in 1860. She came to me while I was watching TV. The ghosts do like television."

"So I gathered. Were they—*are* they—the authors of the Drachenfels curse?"

"Yes, but Anna-Maria herself doesn't appear. The younger, more recent ghosts are stronger."

"What about—my mother?" There was a little break in his voice that brought tears to my eyes.

"I never saw her," I said gently. "I don't think a mother would curse her own son."

Rudi patted me roughly on the shoulder. "Speaking of sons," he said, "may I look at mine?"

I carefully transferred the warm heavy bundle into Rudi's arms, and he held Alexander a little awkwardly, and looked into the small face.

"He's like an unripe poppy—all pink and crinkled."

"That all right," I said. "The petals unfold. He'll be smoother in a day or two."

This domestic interchange was enough to bring Jürgen out of his catatonia. "Herr Graf," he said, "if you have a helicopter, might I recommend sending for a doctor? This is the first child I have ever delivered, I have no experience, and I would strongly urge immediate medical attention."

"Oh God," said Rudi, "the pilot. What do you think, Jenny?"

"I'm sure he's lovely. But can he fly in the dark?"

I propped myself further up on my pillows. "I want a cup of tea, and a bath, and some clean bedding, and a cheese sandwich. Then you can get the doctor if you like."

"Yes, dear," said Rudi.

✠

EPILOGUE

IT TOOK TWO DAYS AND THE JUDICIOUS USE OF gelignite to unearth Nadine's car. The rescue services never found a body, but we held a funeral all the same, to account for her disappearance. No one would ever have believed the alternative. It was strange: this woman, whom I had never met, changed the course of my entire life. In many ways, I had her life now—the life she had planned for herself until the Drachenfels women intervened. Bunty stayed stumm about the whole affair, and it was generally believed that Nadine was paying a social visit when the tragic accident occurred. Bunty himself came to convalesce at the castle, and he and Rudi began to get on quite well. We hired more servants, invited some of Rudi's friends to stay, and now we have several merry house parties a year. For a long time, I hesitated to drive down to the village, in case shades of Nadine lingered by the road, still set on revenge, but nothing ever happened. She was gone, as if she had never existed.

☩

The electricity bill for the east tower is enormous.